A Few Drops of Blood

ALSO BY JAN MERETE WEISS

These Dark Things

A FEW DROPS OF BLOOD

JAN MERETE WEISS

Copyright © 2014 by Jan Merete Weiss

Published by

Soho Press, Inc.

853 Broadway

New York, NY 10003

"In the Museum of Old Lovers" from *Begging for It* © 2013 by Alex Dimitrov.
Reprinted with permission of Four Way Books. All rights reserved.

Library of Congress Cataloging-in-Publication Data

Weiss, Jan Merete.

A few drops of blood / Jan Merete Weiss.

p. cm

ISBN 978-1-61695-353-9

eISBN 978-1-61695-354-6

1. Women detectives—Fiction. 2. Art museums—Italy—Naples—Fiction. 3.
Camorra—Fiction. 4. Organized crime—Italy—Naples—Fiction. I. Title.

PS3623.E4553F49 2014 813'.6—dc23

2013045382

Printed in the United States of America

10 9 8 7 6 5 4 3 2 1

For Dave, and in memory of Tara.

"In bed a man once asked
to be blindfolded while another choked me.
But in the end our ghosts find us three ways.
Through the familiar fist a body will bleed for—
heaving under the sheets—
and by every mouth we open for in the dark."

"In the Museum of Old Lovers"

ALEX DIMITROV

A Few Drops of Blood

Chapter 1

The moon was a ghost when the call came in. The caller said she wished to notify Captain Natalia Monte about two bodies. Routed from another Carabinieri station to hers on Via Casanova, the voice announced herself a countess and said that she didn't trust ordinary police.

Moments later Natalia Monte raced through the pre-dawn gray, siren blaring, flashing lights throwing blue and white bolts across buildings and intersections. She drove along Via Carducci, turned onto the Riviera di Chiaia, past its expensive shops and the aquarium, still run down since the Second World War when the hungry raided its tanks.

The Alfa Romeo zipped along the boulevard, palm trees arched overhead, the plazas dark, the Bay of Naples a blur to her left. On Via Petrarca she shot past a fountain she'd loved as a girl, with marble cherubs blowing trumpets. Finally she slowed and searched for the turn.

Natalia spotted the driveway of Palazzo Carraciulo and

passed through its open gates, up a long curved drive lush with royal palms. So different from the cramped alleys of old Naples where she lived and worked. A hundred yards in, she pulled alongside a new police Ferrari parked in front of a grey stone mansion, its pristine façade incorporating sleek pediments discreetly illuminated. An ancient butler directed her to the garden. Natalia followed a stone path around the side of the building and flashed her identification at the Carabiniere guarding the scene.

The lush garden was beautifully wild with grasses and flowers. Several cats dozed on the edge of a patio. Honeysuckle and jasmine perfumed the air. A yellow butterfly on an orange lily slowly opened and folded its wings.

Natalia stepped onto the grass and walked toward the rose bushes that surrounded a life-sized horse cast in metal, the centerpiece of a dry fountain half filled with potted blooms—white roses. The sculpture was enormous. Two male figures sat astride the unbridled steed—one man pitched forward, his arms draped along the animal's neck. The second man leaned into him from behind. Neither was clothed.

Natalia stepped closer. Dark splotches marred the creamy petals of flowers encircling the fountain. Already there were flies. She circled the statue slowly, shining a light up at the two, just barely making out dark punctures that riddled their chests. Young men—shotgunned from the look of them. Blood dripped down their torsos and loins, along their legs and the flanks of the horse into the fountain's basin. Its iron scent mixed with the lush bouquet of the roses.

Suddenly she noticed the woman by the rhododendrons, motionless as the men. Silver hair framed her face and flowed past her slim shoulders. She wore a white silk kimono printed with orange and purple cranes. Cranes symbolized long life, Pino, Natalia's ex, had told her once in an intimate moment. The woman's eyes were a startling shade of lavender.

Natalia held up her Carabinieri identification. "Captain Monte. As you requested."

"Contessa Antonella Maria Cavazza," she said and extended her hand, the tiny fingers like a child's. "Thank you for coming."

Natalia took the delicate, age-splotched hand.

"You found them?"

"Yes, I made the unhappy discovery."

"Do you know the victims?"

"The second man in back. Vincente Lattaruzzo. He's a senior curator at the Museo Archeologico."

"When did you find them?"

"Just before seven. I'm an early riser. Unless it's raining, I take my coffee here in the garden."

"Did you see or hear anything during the night or early this morning?"

"Hear? No. My bedroom is in the wing over there." Antonella Cavazza pointed to the far end of the building. "When I have trouble sleeping—which is often these days—I wander the house. But the windows are all double glazed and sealed for the air-conditioning. So, no. I didn't hear a disturbance."

"How do you know the victim?"

"I'm on the board of the museum. Once a year I host a dinner party. Senior staff are invited. I first met him there—last Christmas, I believe. And he had occasion to address the board at times. Terribly likeable."

The medical examiner, Dr. Francesca Agari, arrived, followed by the forensic photographer draped with equipment.

He proceeded immediately to the dead men and began taking still pictures and videotaping the crime scene. A groundskeeper brought a ladder, and the photographer mounted it to get closer to the dead equestrians.

"Captain Monte," Dr. Agari said, acknowledging Natalia as she came forward, then, "Nell." She kissed the countess on each cheek. "How terrible for you!"

As usual, Natalia's colleague was perfectly groomed, blond highlights symmetrical. She wore a filmy gray blouse, tasteful yet sexy under a black suit jacket, and slacks.

"Yes," the countess said. "How are you my dear? How's Mama?"

"Difficult as always," Dr. Agari replied warmly.

The countess moved away to let the detective and the doctor confer.

"Mama?" Natalia said, as she pulled on rubber gloves.

Two mortuary men entered near the hedges.

"Over here!" Dr. Agari called. "She and my grandmother were great friends. I had my tenth birthday party here in this garden."

Mortuary staff earned a good living in their coveted jobs. Nepotism abounded: The husky men looked to be brothers.

"They'll need another ladder." Natalia returned to the countess.

"There's one in the tool shed," she said and escorted the men toward the far end of the garden.

Natalia searched the perimeter. Fancy topiary abounded: bushes shaped like turrets, azalea trimmed to a perfect circle around the base of an olive tree. Something interrupted the perfect symmetry. She stepped closer. It took her a moment to understand what she was seeing: a cotton work shirt. This one appeared old, the kind once worn by laborers in the fields, patched and mended many times, laid out across a bush as if to dry. It may have been white when new, but this morning—except for the rust-colored sleeves—the shirt lay dark and stiff, heavily stained, its fabric torn.

Natalia called for an evidence bag, slipped it in, and returned to the corpses. Dr. Agari was peering in and around the bodies, looking for signs of sexual union between the two. Soon, Natalia thought, she would peel away, remove, examine and weigh their secrets, as Dr. Agari would their flesh and organs.

There were no discernible tracks in the hard earth along the walks. They'd kept to the grass.

A dove regarded Natalia from its patch of dirt beneath a flaming bougainvillea. Checking for footprints, she followed the pebble walkways radiating from the fountain. A profusion of flowers—giant lilies, amber and rose—enveloped her path, their sweet scent thick. A bee anchored the velvet petal of a petunia.

Such a strange place for a gruesome murder. Out of the way, certainly. The countess's paradise seemed light years removed from the rest of the city. Someone had gone to a lot of trouble to stage it here, someone familiar with the garden.

The countess had taken refuge under a large awning that shaded a stone patio and the table where she took her coffee. Lilies, thistles and wild flowers surrounded her. The mortuary men had taken down the bodies and laid them on gurneys. Dr. Agari stood over the corpses, securing her swabs and evidence envelopes.

Natalia approached the countess. "Would you mind taking a look?" She indicated the dead men. Francesca approached across the lawn.

"She's going to try to identify the other victim," Natalia said.

"Nella, are you sure?" Dr. Agari came and put her arm around the countess.

"My dear, you know me better than that."

The mortuary men stepped away. The countess bent from the waist and studied the unidentified corpse. He was short and stocky. Not as young as the other victim, but no more than forty. Prematurely bald, cheeks ashen.

"Carlo Bagnatti," the countess said, standing.

"The gossip columnist?" Natalia asked. "Are you sure?"

"He writes for *Rivelare* and is carried in *La Stella*. I've seen his photo and once or twice on the chat shows." She looked exhausted.

"Perhaps you should lie down inside," Dr. Agari suggested. "Here." She held out an arm to escort her.

"No, I'm fine. Really. I can sit on the terrace." The countess and her friend made for the house.

"Excuse me," Natalia called.

The countess looked back. "Yes? What?"

"I'll need to ask you a few more questions. Would you mind?"

"Of course not."

Francesca touched the countess's shoulder. "Are you sure?"

"I'm fine. Don't let me interrupt your work, *cara*. We'll talk later, yes?"

"*Certo*," Francesca said. She joined the photographer, and they spoke quietly.

The countess led Natalia to a bench obscured by a large magnolia.

"So, you knew Carlo Bagnatti as well?" Natalia said.

"Only from his column," she said. "Vile trash. Stories that might shock even you, Captain. Really salacious stuff and, more often than not, he was accurate, unlike the usual tabloid nonsense."

"So, you knew Vincente Lattaruzzo from the museum and had encountered him at their functions?"

"A number of times, yes."

"And Bagnatti? You never ran into him at social affairs?"

"No. Though he did contact me once—he was looking for dirt about someone I was acquainted with. Naturally, I was of no help."

"The way the murdered men were posed," Natalia asked, "do you have any idea if the victims were involved? Romantically, I mean?"

"I don't know about that. I do know Vincente lived with a significant other. I believe that's the correct term. A male. About Bagnatti's personal life, I have no idea."

"Would you have Mr. Lattaruzzo's address?"

"Certainly. I'll get it for you."

Natalia closed her notebook. "I will have more questions later today or tomorrow."

"Of course. Just call ahead. My calendar isn't full."

Natalia returned to the victims.

"She okay?" Dr. Agari said.

"Seems so. What do we have?"

"Shotgun blast," Dr. Agari said, indicating Lattaruzzo. "Small gauge. The other victim the same."

A small gauge shotgun—the traditional execution weapon of the rural mafia, a stubby weapon for hunting small game and two-legged mammals.

"Victim One," Francesca said, "also has ligature marks around his throat."

"He was strangled?"

"More likely hung."

"The other victim too?"

"No. Both also show signs of having been tortured."

Natalia squatted to look at the wounds more closely and

played her flashlight on Lattaruzzo's face. Vincente, he was lightly made up.

"Is Bagnatti wearing makeup, too?" she asked.

"Both are, yes. Cheeks rouged, a faint white dot at the outside corner of each eye, lashes thick with mascara, eyebrows penciled. Across the lips, the slightest suggestion of color."

"Were they killed here?" Natalia said.

"I don't think so. Not enough blood present."

"Any clues as to where?"

"You might look for wherever Mr. Lattaruzzo left his privates."

Chapter 2

Vincente Lattaruzzo shared an apartment with a Stefano Grappi on Vico Santa Maria a Cancello. A small *latte* van painted with cheerful images of cheeses and milk bottles cut Natalia off as she turned onto the quiet block. It wasn't far from his job at the museum: easy walking distance.

"Watch where you're going!" she yelled and blasted her horn.

The curly-haired driver opened his door and threw her a kiss and a wink.

Right, she sighed. God's gift to women. Thinks he's cute. Which he was, she had to admit. Luckily there was a parking spot in front of number 5, a gray *palazzo*, its tall windows ornamented by carved pediments and green shutters. Nice digs. Natalia wondered what Lattaruzzo's partner did for a living.

The names LATTARUZZO / GRAPPI appeared in a fancy font next to a lighted button set in a sleek brass plaque just outside the iron gates that barred the courtyard. Natalia pressed and waited. No response. It was after ten. Lattaruzzo's partner was most probably at work. She tried again. Nothing.

It was a relief in a way. She dreaded informing loved ones of such losses.

Natalia drove back to her station on Casanova. In the lobby, a postal worker was distributing mail in the green mailboxes that belonged to the residents two flights above. Casanova was the only station in the city that shared space with civilians. Odd, but no one ever suggested they move. Space was at a premium, and Casanova was not in a fancy neighborhood, so any request would remain a low to zero priority.

The lobby was plain, institutional green walls and brown terrazzo floors. The only flourish: the dark green mosaic tiles that stopped halfway up the walls. When she'd been there a year, Natalia had lobbied for new light fixtures for the hall stairs, as the fluorescents seemed unnecessarily depressing. But there they were, several years later.

She climbed the one flight. Whoever was on desk watch saw her on the monitor and the lock clicked, and Natalia pushed open the heavy reinforced door. Bypassing her own office, she proceeded up an inner stairway and went to see her boss.

She hovered in the doorway. A black fan rotated, gently ruffling the papers on Colonel Fabio Donati's desk as he sat, phone cradled against his ear, facing the window.

"*Si, si,* of course." He swiveled and waved Natalia in. "We understand. Correct. Terrible, yes. Yes. *Ciao.*" He hung up the receiver and raised an eyebrow at Natalia.

"That was the director of the museum. A friend of my Elisabetta. He's shaken, naturally. What do we have?"

"Double murder, two men."

"Two dead males riding naked on a horse statue, found in some kind of erotic repose? Neapolitan killers are so . . ." His hand circled the air.

"Elaborate, yes," she said.

"Clues? Evidence? Conjectures?"

"Judging from the low-gauge shotgun pattern, the murder weapon may have been a *lupara*."

"Quaint," the colonel said. "The traditional instrument of vengeance."

"The murders seemed smoothly done—unnecessarily elaborate, yes, but professional."

"Camorra, without question," her boss said.

"That's what I thought at first. But why do in an art curator?"

"Perhaps he wouldn't cooperate with a counterfeit," the colonel said. "If he's gay, maybe he came on to the wrong man. Camorra aren't known for their tolerance of gays. You reach his boyfriend yet?"

"No."

"Anyway, I want you to handle it. The countess is insisting, and who am I to refuse her?"

"Yes, sir."

"Also, I have a new partner for you to break in."

"That was fast. Who?"

"Angelina Cavatelli. She requested a female partner."

"Why do I know the name?"

"She's from Palermo."

"Their first Sicilian female officer."

"Correct."

"She's a rookie, no? Why transfer so early? There aren't enough thugs down there?"

"Confidentially?"

"Someone didn't appreciate a female colleague, or she stepped on someone's toes."

"Something like that."

"I like her already."

"Good. She's reporting for duty later today."

"What if I had said no?"

"I didn't think you could resist the idea of a female partner. Besides, Captain, it's an order." The colonel's gaze grew benevolent. "By the way, I'm sorry about you and Pino."

Natalia nodded. "As am I, sir."

"I didn't have a choice once you two got involved. I had to transfer one of you. You had seniority and outranked him. And, frankly, fond as I am of Pino, I could not afford to lose you."

"Yes, sir."

"You know, as you're no longer partnered at work, headquarters might be persuaded to look the other way concerning your domestic arrangements."

"Thank you, but no, Colonel. I knew the chance we were taking. I should have known better. Matters of the heart . . . they don't belong here."

"All right, Captain." Colonel Donati leaned on his desk with both hands. "Find those responsible."

Natalia rang the doorbell. A dog barked.

"*Momento!*" As Lola Nuovaletta opened it, a fierce ball of fur charged past her, jumped up Natalia's legs and scratched. It was a small designer dog, all the rage: gray and white, shampooed and clipped with a bow in its hair.

"Since when do you have a watch dog?" Natalia asked.

"Down, Micu! Isn't she cute? Come to mama!" She snatched her into her arms and nuzzled her. "Present from the boyfriend. In case I get lonely when he's not here."

"Sounds like Dominick's getting serious."

"Maybe." She kissed Natalia. "Come with me into the kitchen. I gotta feed the princess."

Natalia followed her back. They were two sides of a coin, she and Lola. They had grown up together, pampered by each other's grandmothers. As teens, they'd practiced staying upright in high heels, discussed the finer points of kissing and confided their dreams and ambitions. Lola wanted a man. Natalia wanted an academic life but wound up a Carabiniere. Lola had grown up in the Camorra—her family and her husband's family both went back for generations. She'd never thought to be anything else but a *camorrista*.

Lola took a plastic container from the refrigerator.

"I'm heating her some meatballs. She only eats people food, cooked. You want something to eat? Some lunch?"

"Thanks, Lola. I only have a few minutes."

"These fucking containers are hell to open. Down, Micu! Want me to break a nail?"

"Can we be serious here a minute?"

"Aye, aye, *Capitano!* What is it?"

"We found two bodies this morning."

"The faggots on the horse?"

"How the hell could you have heard already?"

"Bianca Strozzi didn't have anything to do with it, if that's what you're asking."

"Relax. Your boss isn't a suspect—yet."

"All I've heard is gossip," Lola said.

"God's truth?"

"Aren't we suspicious today," she baby-talked, as she cuddled her new dog. The dog mewled. Lola looked up. "What about the museum guy's boss?"

"Director Garducci?"

"Word is he and the deceased Vincente were an item."

"For real? How do you know this?"

"Frankie's cousin, Beatrice—Bibi, remember her? She was their maid for a while. According to Bibi, Director Garducci is a very particular guy. Everything aligned and in its proper place, exact—or you'd hear about it. You know the type: pencil up his ass. Screamed at her a couple of times. He and the wife had separate bedrooms. Must have fucked once, though. Their daughter's thirteen. Bibi says she's shy, nose always in a book. Like our Mariel. Anyway, her father had male 'friends' stay over sometimes. The wife tolerated it. She's from Milan. No tits, if you know what I mean. So Bibi walks into the bedroom one morning, and one of Garducci's 'friends' is bleeding like crazy all over the Milanese sheets. Bibi and the wife rush him over to Cardelli Hospital. The happy couple paid Bibi a lot of money to keep her mouth shut. Imagine what they paid to keep it out of the papers."

"When was this?"

"Six, seven months ago. The wife took the kid and left. Went back to Milan. According to Bibi, Vincente Lattaruzzo was a regular guest of Director Garducci's. There's your killer. You think?"

"Could be, I suppose."

"Who's the other dead guy?" Lola asked.

"Carlo Bagnatti." Natalia picked up a gold and turquoise cushion. "Nice."

"A cousin of Frankie's opened a new shop on Duomo. Everything's one-of-a-kind. Bagnatti? You're talking about the dirt diva?"

"One and the same."

"I wonder who did him," Lola mused.

Natalia stood and started toward the door. "Are we on for Saturday?"

"Of course." Lola picked up the dog, and they slobbered over each other for a moment. Then she pointed the creature toward Natalia.

"That's okay." Natalia said. "I appreciate the thought."

"She doesn't love us, Micu." Lola kissed the dog's ear.

"I love you. I don't love your drooling friend."

Lola made a face. "You didn't notice."

"What?"

"My new earrings." She fingered one of the dangling jewels.

"Pretty."

"Diamonds, Nat."

"A new admirer?"

"Nah. Madam Strozzi. In appreciation for the job I done."

"Blood diamonds," Natalia said sarcastically. "Nice."

"Hey, it's called working for a living. You know all about that."

"I do, and I better get back to it," Natalia said and made for the door.

Rundown apartment buildings and car repair businesses dominated the neighborhood around her Via Casanova station—no delight for eye or soul. Natalia reached her workplace, the blue CARABINIERE sign in the box above the door lighting the way to the front door. Entering, Natalia climbed the stairs. Every chair in the waiting room was taken. A small, shriveled man stood at the reception desk.

"I want to report a crime," he said. He looked like he lived in the street.

Some of the homeless eccentrics were merely lonely, a few were mad. Each was seen and heard. Every so often they provided a lucid narrative and pertinent information about a crime that led to arrests, so each was treated respectfully. The officer at the desk dutifully recorded the details of the assault on him.

Someone was sitting at Pino's desk, a black windbreaker draped over the back. For a second, Natalia thought it was a man. But when the person stood, Natalia faced a young woman not much over five feet, thin and muscular, her black hair cut punk style in uneven chunks. No one would ever take her for a Carabiniere, yet she wore the black utility uniform with red piping, slightly bulged by the armored vest underneath. Her wine-red beret lay on the out tray. The red chevrons of a corporal adorned her sleeves.

Natalia hoped she hadn't inherited a partner even more naïve than the one she'd lost, though this girl was from Sicily and a station in Palermo—no easy duty. Naples was not free of *serieta*, the ancient code of behavior expected of Italian women, but it was more seriously adhered to in Sicily. Women were expected to follow its precepts: marry young, bear many children and remain faithful to your husband. In which case she had the respect and protection of the men. Ignoring it, she forfeited even her small freedoms and couldn't so much as enter a café by herself or wear short sleeves even if the day was brutal.

A woman who defied these conventions would be accosted in the streets, harassed, ridiculed. To join an all-male organization like the Carabiniere was unthinkable. So the girl had some guts.

The kid had cleared up Pino's desk and was going through a stack of reports.

Natalia extended her hand. "Natalia Monte. Welcome to the Tenth Carabinieri Battalion."

"Cavatelli, ma'am. Angelina Cavatelli."

"Have you had the tour?"

"A Maresciallo dei Carabiniere showed me around."

"Yeah, the marshal is named Cervino. What did he say?"
Natalia got up and closed the door.

"Aside from the pleasantries?"

"Yeah."

"I got the feeling he was fishing. Who did I know in
Naples? Who did I report to in Palermo? Then something
about loyalty. That I should come to him if anyone at the
station compromised that oath. Like he wanted to recruit
me to spy. Weird, huh? But maybe he figured a newbie . . .
he could get me under his thumb right away."

"Stay clear of him. He's dangerous. Passed up for promotion more than once. Always looking for dirt. Can't stand
the idea that a woman is higher ranked than he is."

"I'm familiar with that one. Don't worry. I'll steer clear.
I did get an overview from our boss, the colonel. Seems like
a decent guy."

"He is," Natalia said, "for the most part. So who'd you
piss off in Palermo?"

Angelina laughed. "How did you figure that? You're
right, though. My superiors wanted to try out the *confinato*
on me. You know how that goes."

"*Confinato?*"

"If someone bothered Mussolini by their mere existence,
the person got charged. No evidence required. Il Duce
merely declared, '*Quest' 'uomo mi da fastidio.*' This person
annoys me. Most of them ended up on the island of Lipari.
Most didn't survive."

"You won't miss home?"

"No. It was time to go. Should I be watching my back
here, too?"

"No. But only because they're lazy chauvinist sons of
bitches."

"They?"

"You find a place to live?"

"I'm staying with a cousin until I get settled. She has a terrific place up in the Vomero."

"I'm impressed."

"Yeah, I'm going to be spoiled. My love is coming in three weeks. We'll never be able to afford anything as nice."

"What does he do?"

"She," Angelina said in a lowered voice.

"Sorry. She."

"She's a veterinary assistant. Lucky there's work here. What about you?"

"Love life?"

"Yeah."

"A recent casualty," Natalia said.

"Oh."

"Occupational hazard." Natalia glanced at the resume on her desk. "You've spent time in Naples, I see. Know your way around?"

"Pretty well—from visiting my cousin, the gynecologist. Now, hers is a nice job—delivering babies. You have kids?"

Natalia shook her head.

"Me, either. Giuletta—my girl—she loves them. If things work out, maybe we'll adopt."

Natalia tapped the resume. "I see you speak French and some English. How's that?"

"The French I took in school. I got good in English because of my mom's sister and her husband. They own a café in New Orleans. The summer I finished college, I lived with them and waitressed in their place."

"How was that?"

"A little difficult. They couldn't understand why I made such lousy cappuccinos, being from here. I couldn't understand what was so great about America."

"You didn't like the US?"

"Loved it. But the same mob lowlifes ran their neighborhood, just like in Palermo. My aunt told me to shut it. I was to bring the local gentlemen their coffee when they came by to collect and ignore their sexist remarks . . . and that they never paid. This is what they'd left Italy for, worked so hard for?"

"Pity."

"My cousin in New York went into nursing and did all right. But her brother? The hoodlums recruited him when he was sixteen. He gave up his schooling. Turned drug dealer and got addicted himself."

"That why you ended up in law enforcement?"

"Partly, yeah." She paused. "By the way, I want to thank you."

"What for?"

"I'm no good when I don't work. They were going to shelve me."

Natalia held up a hand. "Don't thank me yet."

"Yes, Captain."

"I'd like you to familiarize yourself with the cases we'll be handling."

"Yes'm. I've been reading the case notes about the two victims on the horse."

"Good. You ready to jump in?"

"Affirmative."

"I want you to interview his colleagues at the Museo Archeologico. How does tomorrow sound?"

"How about today?"

"Even better, Carabiniere Cavatelli. Go to it. I also need you to look into some domestic violence at the museum director's home about a year ago. A boyfriend the director beat up badly enough to require medical attention."

"Should I request the hospital records?"

"Yes, but find him first."

Angelina departed.

She found him at the café next to the auto repair shop. He appeared to be reading a report.

"Maresciallo."

"Officer Monte. To what do I owe the pleasure?"

"I understand you were talking to my new partner. Not your role, is it?"

"Just trying to be helpful is all. Show her the ropes. Your partner isn't from here."

"There were certain innuendos. And apparently you suggested she should come to you—as a spy. It's highly inappropriate, to say the least."

"Not innuendos, Officer Monte. Concerns. I'm not so charmed by you as the colonel. I'll say it to your face: Your friendships with certain people are in direct conflict with your role as a Carabiniere."

"My personal life is not your business."

"I will do whatever is necessary to safeguard the mission of the Carabinieri. Is that clear? Keep up with your social life and you could be putting your new partner in danger. She doesn't know the players. Let me put it to you this way." He took a sip of his coffee. "You're the nature lover. It's like throwing a baby bird into a street of cats."

"Talk to her again about my business, I'll have you up on charges of insubordination."

"You took an oath."

"Watch it, Cervino."

"On the contrary, it's you who should watch it."

She went back to the office and stormed up the stairs. "Bastard," she muttered. She tried to work, but it was difficult to concentrate. Cervino had been a thorn in her side for a long time. But he'd gotten bolder since Pino left. Jealous, of course.

Trouble was he had a right to be jealous. Slowly but surely she was being promoted, recognized. Whatever else she might think of him personally, Cervino was a dedicated officer. He lived and breathed his job. She doubted he had any interests outside of the office. And he hadn't risen despite his dedication. What accounted for that, Natalia wasn't entirely sure. She had some ideas. His personality was overbearing. He always assumed he was right. And he certainly wasn't a team player. But then neither was she.

Natalia wasn't making much headway. She completed a few reports, and it was only as she prepared to leave that she noticed the envelope slipped under her coffee mug. She opened it. Another poem from Pino copied out by hand. Mailed to the station. He was covering all bases.

> *The black and white line*
> *Of swallows that rises and falls from the*
> *Telegraph pole to the sea*
> *Doesn't console you, standing at*
> *The water's edge,*
> *Nor take you back to where you no longer are.*
> *My feelings for you remain,*

He'd written and signed it P.

It was folded between sheets of gold foiled paper, the kind Buddhists take with them in death to assure good fortune in their next life. Natalia couldn't tell if this meant that Pino accepted the end of their relationship and was preparing to move on or if he was yearning for what they'd lost. Natalia still had feelings for him as well—that she could not deny—but what path to take with regard to them, she had not a clue.

A young man interrupted her reverie. He was skinny, not yet thirty, wearing black jeans and rectangular eyeglass frames.

"Can I help you?" Natalia asked

He nodded in greeting and spoke rapidly. "I was downstairs. They sent me up here to see you, to report a missing person."

"A relation?"

"My boyfriend," he said nervously, standing in the doorway.

"Please." She indicated the chair facing her desk.

"Vincente Lattaruzzo. That's his name." He forced a smile. "He didn't come home last night, the shit."

"Sir, why don't you have a seat?"

"It's happened before. I'm pissed is all." He shoved both hands in his pockets, still standing on the threshold. "I'm sure it's a mistake, this. Sorry to waste your time."

He turned abruptly to go.

"Mr. Grappi." Natalia motioned him to come in. "Please, sir," she said. "Have a seat."

The young man sat down at the edge of the chair, eyes welling up. "He isn't . . . ?"

"I'm so sorry."

"What . . . how?"

"We aren't sure. Do you know Contessa Cavazza?"

He nodded. "She's on the museum board. They have lunch every month or so."

"He was found in her garden—shot."

His face went extremely pale. "I think I'm going to be sick."

"Put your head down," Natalia said. "Between your legs."

She got him a glass of water and moistened a handkerchief for his forehead.

"I need to see him."

"If you feel up to it. He's at the morgue. I'll have you driven over. We'll need a statement, too."

"I'll be all right. Oh, God."

"Where is he from, Vincente?"

"Cantalupo, but they're here—his parents. They own a grocery store . . . just ordinary working people. How can I tell them he's dead, their only child?"

Natalia looked at him sympathetically. "We can do that or accompany you if that would help."

"No, no. Thank you. I should tell them."

"Let me know if you change your mind. We'll be talking to them as well." She came around the desk to see him out. "Oh, one more thing. Until we find Vincente's killer, we would prefer you to stay in Naples."

"Am I a suspect?"

"Lovers are always suspect, Stefano."

Chapter 3

Naples began and ended at the sea. It spread along the waterfront, then rose to the cliffs that regarded Mt. Vesuvius across the bay. The rough crescent cliff tops were studded with cypress trees like a bowl turned on its side, Natalia thought when she was ten and saw her city for the first time from the water.

Hers was a melancholy city, its ancient stone streets, cathedrals and *palazzos* darkened by time. Yet it was also a Mediterranean city, scored with light. Palm trees sprouted around many *piazzas* and in the Comunale, a once-noble park that paralleled the docks. Tropical flora bloomed in the Orto Botanico, whose rusted gates were often shut for lack of funds.

The visiting cruise ships reminded Natalia of giant wedding cakes when she was a girl. Freighters and giant container ships loaded and unloaded goods twenty-four hours a day. Nights, they sparkled like miniature cities.

Natalia's first boat ride was on one of the passenger ferries that crisscrossed the harbor regularly. Most were en route to and from Ischia and Capri. Natalia and her parents chose Procida for their one summer vacation when she was twelve. Procida was the quieter, poorer sister island where fishermen still plied their trade, and goats wandered among scrub and lemon trees.

She tossed the remnants of her lunch to the gulls and turned away, walking inland past dingy Chinese restaurants and a handful of *trattorias* that catered to sailors and stevedores, passing hotels and a few government towers, concrete relics from the 1950s and 60s. Natalia strolled by the dingy buildings and came upon the opulent Palazzo Reale, a rosy jewel fringed by grand palm trees—the castle home of the Bourbon King Charles III, where Natalia had spent college holidays immersed in the paintings and frescoes hung in the overwhelming riches of its huge, lush rooms.

She tread past the ordinary and the extraordinary: the opulent Reale palace and along twisted streets blackened with dirt and age, the splendid glass arches of the Galleria Umberto II and then the opera house, broken down vendor carts and little *latte* trucks.

After a few blocks, grandeur faded as she tramped through her cramped but charming neighborhood in the old city's center, its humble buildings pockmarked. Laundry crisscrossed overhead, and shrines—mostly simple glass boxes with pictures of the departed flanked by votive candles—ornamented every block. The more elaborate shrines held carvings and pictures of saints surrounded by offerings of flowers amid costume gems.

The poor crowded into street-level living quarters the locals called *bassi*, half a dozen tenants to a room. In one of them, her neighbor Assunta Sanzari birthed eight children and raised them alone after her husband fled. Some humble *bassi* had been elaborately renovated and decorated for the better heeled. Plazas and weathered monuments completed the mix, relics of Bourbon rule.

Natalia recognized Tomasso, the caretaker, sweeping the sidewalk in front of the imposing *palazzo* where Director Garducci resided. Tomasso was ninety if he was a day and used to work with her father as a street sweeper.

A little early, Natalia stopped in the sundries shop on the ground floor. The proprietress played with her baby granddaughter propped up on the counter beside a hand-carved humidor. The place was unchanged. Cigars and cigarettes lay displayed in heavy glass cases with hardwood frames. Along the wall, more modern display cases filled with beauty products, their packaging yellowed and faded. Natalia surveyed the shampoos and picked up a bottle of conditioner. She was a sucker for hair products, though so far none had tamed her frizzy curls. A couple of German tourists by the door spun a creaky rack of yellowing postcards of Naples, faded black-and-white shots from the twenties.

Natalia made her purchase, tucked it into her shoulder bag, then entered the courtyard and rang Garducci's bell. His flat was on the second floor. She walked up. Garducci met her at the door dressed in designer blue jeans and a sleeveless T-shirt, his gray hair youthfully styled. A ruby stud flashed in one earlobe.

"Please. Come in. Sorry it's such a mess."

Mess? The immaculate flat was spacious, light and airy, the wooden floors bleached almost white. Everything was white—walls, drapes, floors—except a black couch. A giant cobalt blue vase held one giant white bloom. Not a thing looked out of place.

"How can I help you?" he said, inviting her to sit.

They settled on his plush couch, Garducci with his arm slung over the back, half turned toward her.

"Such a bizarre tragedy," he said. He sounded almost nonchalant.

"One of the victims, Vincente Lattaruzzo, was an employee of yours at the museum."

"That is correct."

"Carlo Bagnatti—did you know him as well?"

"No."

"You know who he is."

"Who doesn't? A distasteful creature from all accounts. Perhaps someone decided to do us a favor."

"Do you have any idea who may have resented him enough to kill him?"

"No idea. Must be quite a list. Are there any promising suspects yet?"

"One or two. How long did Vincente Lattaruzzo work at the museum?"

"Five years or thereabouts. I'll get his work record for you if that would help."

"Thank you. Perhaps later. If you will excuse my saying it, rumors have reached us. Rumors about you and Vincente Lattaruzzo. Namely, that he was preparing to leave his boyfriend to live with you, Director."

"That is . . . that was a fact. Not a rumor at all."

"So Vincente Lattaruzzo was going to reside here? With you?"

"As soon as he got things in order and got rid of his collection."

"His collection?"

"World War Two memorabilia. It wouldn't fit in here, obviously. I suggested he donate it to a museum. Not ours."

"He agreed?"

"He didn't like it. Said it was a deal breaker. But he was joking."

"How did Stefano Grappi react to the news that his lover was leaving him?"

"He was such a damn coward." Garducci fussed with his earring.

"Stefano Grappi?"

"No, Vincente."

"He hadn't told him?"

"Correct. Vincente procrastinated. He was waiting for the right time, he said. I told him there isn't one."

"Your relationship seems to have been an open secret. Your staff knew. Surely Stefano Grappi had heard of it as well."

Garducci shrugged. "You'd have to ask him."

"You were Mr. Lattaruzzo's boss—a conflict of interest at the very least. No?"

"Sadly true. He had just quit because of it. But there was plenty of freelance work offered him. And both of us had many contacts in the field."

Natalia looked up from the notes she'd made earlier interviewing Stefano Grappi and gazed at her host.

"Mr. Grappi gave me the impression he and Vincente were—aside from the usual 'dalliances,' as he put it— devoted to one another. He said Vincente had no plans to go anywhere."

"Then he is deluded," Garducci said with a dismissive wave.

"Perhaps. But what if it was you whom Vincente misled? What if he made promises he couldn't bring himself to keep? You had sacrificed your marriage, risked your career. Meanwhile, Vincente was doing well by you. Two promotions this past year, promoted to senior curator, sent to New York to bid in a major auction on behalf of the museum. The poor boy had made good."

"All totally deserved. He was extraordinarily able. No one would deny that."

"The museum faced serious budget problems, hours curtailed, people being laid off, and you assigned Vincente a new private office almost as nice as yours."

"Your point?"

"What if, after all that, he informed you he wasn't going to live with you?"

"That's simply not true."

"Really?"

"See here. Officer Monte, is it?"

"Captain."

"I suggest, Captain, you save your tactics for those more deserving—the professional criminals, for instance. Isn't that your job? You are wasting your time here. And certainly wasting mine."

Carabiniere Angelina Cavatelli went over her interview notes with Natalia in the station's canteen.

"They were a golden couple—Stefano Grappi and the victim, Vincente Lattaruzzo—until Director Garducci entered the scene. Everyone knew Garducci and Vincente were conducting an affair. Stefano took it hard. Missed important meetings, grew distracted and distant and wouldn't take off his dark glasses at work."

"So theirs wasn't a brief fling," Natalia said.

"Not according to the gift store manager, for one. She worked late a couple of weeks ago, went outside for a cigarette and practically stumbled over Director Garducci and his protégé in the sculpture garden."

"Oops."

"Yeah, kinky." Angelina closed her notebook. "Do we have a preliminary alibi for Stefano Grappi?"

"Claims he was presenting a paper of his at the university."

"And Director Garducci?" Angelina inclined her head.

"Doesn't have one. Says he was home the night Vincente Lattaruzzo died. There's no way to corroborate. According to him, he called Lattaruzzo a couple of times, left messages. We're awaiting the victim's phone records and checking his message machine."

"If Vincente had jilted Stefano, and if Vincente *was* moving in with Director Garducci after all—" Natalia paused. "—why might Garducci kill him?"

"Because his lover was also having it off with the other naked horseman sharing his midnight ride?"

"Point taken. But Grappi goes to the top of the list."

"We have the time of death?" asked Natalia.

"Dr. Agari says between ten and eleven P.M."

"Good job. You finding your way around okay? Anyone giving you a hard time?"

"Yeah, a couple of cracks about my hair, but mostly I'm being treated like a human being. If it gets out I'm gay, that could change, though."

"Angelina. It's nobody's business if you're gay."

"Right. It didn't quite work that way where I came from. Bad enough I was a female and didn't put out."

"If there's the barest hint of sexual harassment—even so much as a comment—you come to me, and we take it to Colonel Donati. Fabio Donati won't stand for it."

Angelina looked relieved.

Natalia decided to change the subject. "You think your Giuletta will adjust okay to Naples?"

"I do. She won't start work for a couple of weeks, so she'll have time to scout an apartment for us. Meantime, the Vomero is great but I don't have much privacy at my aunt's, and her teenager is on the cusp of puberty. She's a darling girl but presents a bit of a challenge."

"I can imagine."

"What's next?"

"Nothing for today. Go home and take off your bullet-proof vest. Put your feet up. Tomorrow will be here soon enough. Good work, by the way."

Angelina left to sign out, and Natalia made ready to go. The phone rang. Dr. Francesca Agari was announced on the line. Natalia punched the lit-up line button.

"Captain, I found Vincente Lattaruzzo's missing parts."

"Where?"

"In the other man."

Chapter 4

Natalia took her coffee out to the balcony. Swallows, hundreds of them, patterned the morning sky. Natalia's grandmother, her *nonna*, had always insisted they portended the future. While her floors were drying, Nonna would study their formations from the balcony, often with her granddaughter at her side. Depending on which direction they swooped, she'd make her predictions. If they veered north or west, it meant someone would come to harm. Maybe the neighbor who cheated her on a carton of eggs or the woman who stole away her first love. But if the birds winged south or east, Natalia would marry young and produce a brood of healthy children.

After Nonna's oracles flew off, Natalia got a large slice of homemade *torte di cestagno* and a warm glass of milk. The chestnuts were delivered from a childhood friend of her grandmother's once or twice a year. Those not used for the baking were roasted and taken on picnics.

Finishing her coffee, Natalia wondered whether she might have taken up divining signs, too, if she hadn't won the university scholarship. Truth be told, she'd unraveled more than one difficult case with Dame Intuition firmly by her side.

Her cell phone alarm sounded. It was nearly time for her first appointment.

"What a beautiful space," Natalia said, as the countess greeted her before leading the way to the living room, a vast space with soaring lavender walls trimmed in gold. Not much furniture: a simple wooden desk and a sleek chair and one plum-colored velvet lounge. Several crystal chandeliers caught the sunlight and shot it around the floor.

"I live simply. But I always choose good pieces. Makes life more civilized, don't you think?"

The countess looked beautiful in black linen pants and a caftan—creamy silk with a design of pale blue flowers. Drop earrings to match. Sapphires? Mariel would have known. Natalia's friend from childhood was raised in wealth. She rarely wore jewelry more flashy than a strand of pearls, but nonetheless, she could tell paste from real in a glance.

"I helped Dr. Agari design her living space," boasted the countess. "I'd be happy to consult with you."

"I'm not sure it would help," Natalia laughed. "I'm a bit of a pack rat."

"Interesting. As I get older, I value the physical world less and less."

"You mean, it's natural?"

"One de-acquisitions as one prepares to leave, I suspect, yes." The countess gestured for Natalia to be seated. "Sorry if I kept you waiting. My yoga class ran late today. She's fabulous—a Swedish girl. Woman, sorry. You're all girls to me. She has a cute studio on Vico di Pace. Either I go to her or she comes to me. If you're interested, I'd be happy to treat you to a private session sometime."

"That's kind of you, but I'm not permitted to accept such generosity."

"Of course. Forgive me. But you must have a lot of stress in your line of work. Yoga certainly helps. Nonetheless, I barely slept last night. Those young men murdered. It's so unsettling."

"I had a talk yesterday with Stefano Grappi, Vincente's boyfriend. I wanted to check something with you."

"I never had the pleasure of meeting him. I think it's wonderful these days that people are free to choose whom to love."

"According to Stefano, you and Vincente were in the habit of meeting for lunch once or twice a month. When we spoke yesterday, you told me you had met at a function for the museum and saw him at board meetings. I wondered why you omitted mentioning your luncheons."

"I didn't mean to leave you with that impression. I think I was a little unhinged is all." She shrugged. "And some of what I told him was embarrassing. That may have played a part in my being less than clear about our connection."

"So you met with some regularity?"

"Vincente was fascinated with the war, and I was able to tell him some stories, anecdotes about how it was in Naples in that period. Also I interpreted photographs taken then. Primary research, he called it."

"I've heard accounts from my grandparents. Did Vincente tell you why he was researching the war?"

"For an article he was working on that he hoped to turn into a pictorial book based on his and other people's collections of wartime artifacts and photographs. He had notions of curating a show and possibly making a documentary. I wanted to be helpful. The material deserves preserving."

"You say you interpreted photos?"

"Yes. He often didn't know what he was looking at. He had pictures, for instance, of Neapolitan women sewing from odd-looking materials. I explained there wasn't any fabric. So we made dresses from curtains, coats from blankets. I still have mine. Vincente badly wanted them for his collection. I'll show you sometime if you're interested. You and Dr. Agari should come by for lunch."

"That would be nice. Maybe when things quiet down."

"Excuse me for saying this," the countess said. "I have a habit of saying what's on my mind. It's gotten worse with age."

"Please," Natalia said. "What is it?"

"You girls. Women. Sorry. Francesca, of course. And now that we've met . . . the kind of things you are exposed to. I'm sure the work is fascinating. Compelling. Nonetheless . . ."

"Thank you for your concern. If you don't mind, what was the embarrassing part?"

"The humiliation of having been so reduced. Broken in body and mind. It is traumatic to remember the war. We had no bread, no produce. We roasted acorns for coffee. The only meat—well, innards at best. Stray cats disappeared from the streets. Then pets." She shuddered. "Can you imagine breaking into the aquarium and taking the lovely fish? My parish priest . . . the poor man was half mad from hunger. He made curios and tried to barter them for flour or military rations. Carved from human bones he had taken from the ossuary beneath his church. You can't imagine the conditions unless you were here. Girls sold themselves for food in the Santa Lucia district. We lined up for hours to get a bucket of water from the Red Cross. And then Vesuvius erupted and covered the city in ash. I fled with my parents to the family farm in Cantalupo, where I had been born."

"It was better in Cantalupo?"

"Marginally, but yes." She shook her head slowly, remembering. "A woman who had lost two sons to the war, who had nothing, insisted I take two precious tomatoes from her garden. So there were, even among these horrors, heroes and heroines—great kindness."

Natalia glanced out the window. The garden in daylight showed evidence of a firm hand. Carefully trimmed roses and hydrangeas, clearly marked paths. Lemon trees flourished along one wall. An enormous straw hat rested on a white iron chair next to a watering can. All signs of the carnage had been removed.

A pair of feral cats took up seats just outside and stared at Natalia expectantly.

"Speaking of hungry," said the countess, "do you like my babies?"

"They're beautiful. If I wasn't so overwhelmed at work, I'd love to have a cat."

"Not one of these wild things, I'm afraid. Even I can't get too close."

"Such noble looking creatures," Natalia said, "in so lovely a garden."

"My pride and joy, the garden. Designed to lift the spirit. I was so fortunate to be entrusted with this gorgeous piece of earth. Such a desecration, the murder, no?"

"Tell me about Vincente Lattaruzzo."

"He was a cultured person, self-made in many ways.

Educated at a state school, no pedigree to speak of. Worked his way to associate curator, then senior. Loved his job. A totally dedicated and dependable employee, though I can't say it always extended to his personal life."

"Meaning?" Natalia asked.

"His dalliance with the wild side. He didn't elaborate, just said it got messy on occasion."

"Did he tell you anything at all about his private life?"

"A tidbit here and there. Mostly I surmised. Sometimes he arrived out of sorts—hung over from clubbing, that sort of thing—and sore in body. I am not prurient, Officer Monte. I didn't press him for details. That said, he was a kind soul. *Simpatico.*"

"And what of Stefano Grappi?" Natalia slipped out her notebook.

"I knew of his relationship with Mr. Grappi, of course. But Vincente had at least one other friend as close—his boss at the museum."

"How did you come by that information?"

"My husband contributed generously to the museum. When he died, I was voted his place on the board. We knew a great deal about everything and everyone there."

"I'm sorry to hear of your loss."

"Well, they come to all of us, these losses. I don't erase decay from my garden. Some people prune blossoms as soon as they shrivel. Not I. The disintegration is as beautiful as new growth. My husband and I—we had wonderful years together. Nothing to feel sorry for. Forgive me. I don't have many people I talk to, so I ramble when given half a chance."

"No, it's interesting."

"A polite young woman. Anyway, what can I add?"

"You were here the night before you found the bodies in your garden? But you didn't see or hear anything."

"That's right. I was awake, too—couldn't sleep. But the villa's walls are extremely thick and the air-conditioning was on, the double-pane windows shut."

"You didn't look out into the garden at any point?"

"When I can't sleep, sometimes I make myself a cup of tea and bring it out onto the patio."

"Not the other night."

"No. Too warm and buggy."

"Would you be willing to look at some photos to see if you recognize anyone who may have been around your neighborhood yesterday?"

"Why not? Do you wish me to come to your post?"

"That won't be necessary. Either my partner or I will bring them by and sit with you. One of us will call and arrange a convenient time." Natalia put away her notebook.

"Come yourself if you can. I'll give you a tour of the house and grounds."

"That's very kind."

"Kindness has nothing to do with it. I like the company of young people."

Natalia laughed. "I'm not sure I qualify."

"Trust me. You do."

Natalia called Mariel to tell her she was running late and needed to stop at the bank.

"*Nonce problema*," Mariel said. "I'm unpacking boxes. Take your time."

Chapter 5

Natalia rang off as she passed the black-draped Funerari Sanzari emporium, then noticed the man at work across the street putting up new death announcements. Bent over, holding his pants with one hand, he dipped his brush into a bucket and slapped a large sheet of paper on the wall next to some others: a white poster with no ornamentation, only a name in bold black ink. Vincente Lattaruzzo had officially joined the revered ranks of the dead.

Natalia arrived at her bank just in time to see Lucia Ruttollo, in a chenille housecoat and sagging white socks, assisted out of the small, circular, glass enclosure where customers were scanned before entering. Natalia flashed her Carabiniere ID and stepped through, her weapon setting off beeping momentarily.

Meanwhile Maria Fanno, Lucia Rotollo's distant cousin, took Lucia's arm and walked her brazenly past ten customers queued and waiting their turn at the teller's window.

She positioned old Mama Lucia in front of a young bank clerk, then sat on one of the chairs lined up against the wall. People were grumpy and unhappy with this, but no one dared challenge Maria. Lucia opened her pocketbook with gnarled hands and took out a wad of bills. She peeled off the rubber band and counted the notes before turning them over to the teller.

Lucia Ruttollo's oldest son was *re*—king—of the Forcella district, and his mother its *madrina*, the godmother and brains behind the Camorra's operation. She ruled from a rickety wooden stool beside the cash register in the Pasticceria Ruttollo. Over the years she'd rung up sugar cakes and cannoli and ledgered untold millions from heroin. Her other son, however, hadn't made it past messenger jobs. Bad blood between the brothers, according to the neighborhood gossips. Her daughter, Suzanna, Natalia's classmate in school, had emigrated to England after a divorce.

Lucia had received the bakery from her parents' second cousins, a wedding present from the childless couple. Hers was an arranged crime-clan marriage between trusted children of the 'Nrangheta. The bakery and its hidden side enterprises remained massively lucrative. So she could well afford large-size couture, as well as a personal hairdresser, yet she stood at the teller's window looking frumpy and disheveled, her hair mussed, bathrobe tattered. She could have flaunted diamond rings on all her arthritic fingers, but Lucia Ruttollo's idea of self-indulgent pleasure was banking her money, year in, year out.

According to her Carabinieri file, she had accounts from Naples to Geneva. And piled high in a warehouse somewhere were large burlap coffee-bean bags filled with cash money in dollars, euros, Swiss marks. Twice a year she went around to check the cache and update her cryptic records.

Bank chores done, Lucia tottered out.

By the time Natalia stepped outside, clouds had over-taken the sun. She passed along Via Tribunali, the narrow, thousand-year-old, east-west main street of Neapolis in the time of the Greeks—not much wider than a chariot—and turned onto Porta Alba. A man selling lottery tickets greeted her, a blue canary perched on the edge of his box.

"Please, so we can eat!"

Natalia handed him a couple of euros and refused the ticket. She crossed the street to Libreria Arco, her friend's bookshop. Mariel dealt in art books mostly, also literary fiction, and stocked a small section devoted to foreign titles. Natalia, as always, perused the art books on display. *Napoli tra Barocco e Neoclassico* caught her eye: Naples between the Baroque and Neoclassic Era. Though she had not concentrated on architecture during her art history studies at university, Natalia basked in the magnificence of the historic buildings that made her city such a treasure, even the slummy and cramped ancient area at its center.

Natalia watched Mariel through the window shelving books, her friend looking elegant and demure in a grey cashmere sweater and forest green scarf, perfectly knotted, her sleek black hair pulled into a chignon. Natalia momen-tarily envied Mariel's tranquil nature, so unlike Lola's or hers. How had their friend come by this grace? Certainly being raised with privilege helped, though Mariel had suf-fered misfortune as well in the early loss of both her parents. Mariel didn't have to work, though. She'd inher-ited her parents' wealth and the luxurious *palazzo* where they'd lived and run their art business. Dating from the Renaissance, each of her flat's ten rooms had marble floors and carved ceilings thirteen feet high. Yet Mariel worked diligently, books and the bookshop her joy.

What was her own, Natalia wondered? She didn't possess her friend's tranquil soul, that she knew. Her job required logic and toughness, and she called on both in herself. In only one way was she like Mariel. Both were solitary at heart. But Natalia wasn't at all at peace or even content.

Entering university, her goals had been clear: to have a career as an art historian. That life upended early on. What did she seek now? Rough justice in her work? A kind of truth? Both were outnumbered and in short supply of late. Crime seemed so senior to the law. Maybe Pino was right to bow out, to concentrate on his inner self and the Buddhist's path he'd chosen. According to Pino, karma wasn't a choice but a spiritual destiny embedded in your being. He had a deep faith. Natalia? Perhaps like the Church's selfless and solitary brides of Christ, she had pledged her life to a higher calling. But all she had guiding her was her vow to the state and a government-issued nine millimeter Glock.

Natalia opened the shop door. A bell tinkled. The noise of the street diminished as she entered further. Mozart played softly on the sound system. Virginia Woolf, warming in the sun, lifted her feline self from the window display where she'd been snoozing and yawned as she stretched, seemingly doubling her length.

"*Cara!*" Mariel abandoned her books and hurried over. "Come."

She swept Natalia back outside, put a closed sign in the window and locked the door. Arm in arm, they crossed the street to their favorite local café, where their usual waiter led them to their usual table. A plate of artichokes promptly appeared, along with a saucer of seasoned olive oil and a basket of warm bread. The waiter paused to flirt with Mariel before hurrying away.

Men were easily smitten with Mariel, and she seemed

serious about a few of them, but something always interfered. Inevitably her suitors would declare themselves. When she didn't reciprocate, they grew discouraged and moved on. Perhaps the trauma of losing her parents so young prevented her from risking herself by investing them with her love. Instead, Mariel clung to her solitary routines. She hated any deviation, hated change.

"So, what's happening in law enforcement?" Mariel said.

"You might have heard about it—the double murder?"

"The curator at the Museo Archeologico and that gossip columnist?"

"Yes."

Mariel held up a tabloid. Across the front: a large photograph of the two dead men on the sculpted horse. Directly beneath it: ASSASSINIO BRUTALE. And the subhead:

"'Murdered Gay Lovers Ride Bareback in the Garden of the Contessa Cavazza,'" she read.

Natalia groaned. "Where could they have gotten that picture?"

"Bribed the police photographer?"

"Raffi? Never."

"Servants of the *contessa*? I mean, it's all over the Internet, too. What a scene—and in the *contessa*'s serene garden."

"I'm sure she'll be upset to find this splashed all over." Natalia checked her watch. "We'd better enjoy our lunch while we can. I've been assigned a new partner." Natalia sopped up some olive oil with a piece of bread.

"So soon?"

"A terrific young Sicilian woman from Palermo."

The waiter cleared the appetizer plates.

"Another female on the force. That must be nice for you."

"Yes." The waiter hovered. "I'll have the *caprese* salad," Natalia said.

Mariel smiled at him. "Me, too."

"With beautiful mozzarella," he said. "You won't be sorry."

Natalia smiled. "Never been sorry in all the years we've been coming here." He went to assemble their salads, her eyes following him. "Why are some men such sweethearts?"

"They just are," Mariel replied. "Oh, guess who's back in town after a decade?"

"I need a clue. Male or female?"

"Female. Girl with the biggest hair in tenth grade?"

"Suzanna Scavullo?"

"Ruttollo—Suzanna Ruttollo. She's using her maiden name again. According to Lola, she sounds British when she speaks in English."

Natalia cut into the creamy cheese and smeared it on a chunk of bread. "Remember when Ernesto Scavullo sent his limo to pick her up after school?"

"Yeah. Sister Fiore nearly had a stroke." Mariel squinted, thinking. "She married Ernesto when she was what, sixteen? Same year as Lola and Frankie got hitched."

"Talk about jealous. Lola had to keep house in that rented hovel, while Suzanna got to order around live-in maids in her mansion. How old was she when Scavullo kicked her out?"

"Maybe twenty-five," Mariel said. "She was like a crazy person, running down Tribunali screaming, threatening to kill herself."

Natalia brushed away a curl. "It's coming back to me now. Lucia set her daughter up with a small heroin distributorship afterward."

"Small?" Mariel said. "It had to bring in several millions."

Their waiter brought them their coffee and a plate of biscotti. "My treat," he said.

"You're wicked," Natalia said, immediately dunking one.

"Mmmmm," Mariel agreed, her mouth full. "What do you hear from the cycling policeman?"

"Pino's enjoying his leave of absence reading Dante," Natalia said and wiped crumbs from her lips. "He's staying at his uncle's farm near Airola. Does chores and repairs in lieu of rent. Wants me to visit."

"Are you going to?"

"I don't know, Em. I miss him. The other night the phone rang late. Scared the shit out of me. He'd dreamt someone was trying to harm me and wanted to come make sure I was okay."

"And?" Mariel said, her expression hopeful.

"I was tempted . . . but I couldn't, Em. Can't. You know?"

Mariel nodded. "And now he's practicing *La Smorfia*?"

"That's what I love about him," Natalia laughed.

"That he's following that old, crazy, mystical psychic numbers thing to foresee winning lottery numbers?"

"No. That he doesn't live in the real world. Monday I found this in the mail when I got home." She reached into her pocket.

Mariel read it aloud.
Hermits hide from mankind
Most go to mountains to sleep
Where green vines wind through woods enraptured
Free of what stains the world
Minds pure like white lotus.

Mariel exhaled loudly. "How come you get the interesting boyfriends? Mine are always checking their Blackberries."

"What about that German artist?"

"Franz? Who set up a studio in my living room, made my sainted grandmother's brocade couch look like a Jackson Pollock?"

Natalia smiled. "He was sexy." She handed Mariel a package. "Sorry for the wrapping."

"What's this? It's not my birthday. Have I ignored so many that I've actually forgotten the date?"

"I couldn't resist. Open it."

"Yes, Mama." Mariel unfurled a red silk scarf with Vesuvius embossed in gold. "It's gorgeous." She pulled aside her silky hair and knotted the scarf around her neck. "Perfect," she kissed Natalia. "Who needs boyfriends anyway?"

Mariel picked up the check, and they said goodbye. Natalia took out her mobile to call the countess.

"Captain?"

"Contessa, you should be forewarned. The tabloid press is running a picture of the murdered men on the sculpted horse."

The countess sighed. "Yes, I'm aware. My maid informed me of it."

"Excuse me for asking this, but do you think one of your servants might have taken the picture?"

"Impossible. There are only two, and both are dears who have been with me for decades. Besides, they are old like me and technically inept. It's all we can do to operate the toaster. No. No, it wasn't them."

Driving back to work past elite shops displaying the latest Versace and Gucci, Natalia abruptly stopped on Via Petrarca by the fountain she'd recognized as she raced past to Countess Cavazza's residence and the bodies in her garden.

The fountain's marble cherubs blew the same trumpets she had marveled at as a child, but back then they'd spouted streams of water. Now the basin was dry, the tiles surrounding it, worn and cracked. Like much of Naples, the fountain hadn't worked properly in a long time.

Chapter 6

Natalia returned to the station. She made a few calls then set out on foot to her next interview. On Via San Agostino she saw the familiar figure of Lola's boss, Bianca Strozzi, trailed by her two daughters, each pushing an expensive baby pram. She kept her distance: an unspoken agreement not to acknowledge one another in public. The ladies went single file where the sidewalk was torn up, careful not to wreck their stilettos, and entered the butcher shop.

Natalia stopped across the street and watched the clerk quickly slice an order of their favorite *prosciutto*, free of charge, while the women collected the weekly *pezzo*, their piece of the shop's revenues.

Real babies occupied the twin carriages, but Natalia was certain weapons also lay tucked somewhere under the satin coverlets near the two innocents. Bianca's daughters moved in and out of businesses along the street, collecting 500 to 2,000 euros from the shops and thirty to forty from the street peddlers. At Christmas and Easter, bonuses would be expected: gifts of gratitude for the Strozzis' benevolence and protection. Not to mention the purchase of decorations like Christmas lights from the Camorra's collectors at an absurd 100 euros a set.

Mama stood nearby in case. Collecting the *pezzo* was small time next to their trash business, but it was a traditional racket to which they remained nostalgically attached. Given the number of shopkeepers and vendors, it still came to thousands of euros from each block.

Camorristi never surrendered so much as a penny once a claim was established, and the Strozzis always exercised their right to collect their due, as they had for several generations. And their inherent right not to pay the politicians a penny of it in taxes.

Even Valentino, the drunkard, wasn't exempt. He staggered out of his folding chair as the ladies approached. Although hopelessly alcoholic, he nonetheless managed to eke out a living selling fruit to a few customers who didn't mind the occasional rotten strawberry or apricot: residents loyal to the memory of his father, who had started the business when horse-drawn carts clattered down the cobbled streets.

Further on sat Mr. Prava in a chair on the narrow sidewalk, a new bit of graffitti scrawled in blue on the ancient wall over his head. His place occupied the limbo corner where Bianca Strozzi's territory ended and Scavullo's turf began. Prava didn't look so good, with his eyes puffy, his lovely white hair uncombed, and shirt wrinkled and threadbare.

The doors to his place stood open, tables stacked on the street. The bar inside was under construction and torn up. A workman lacquered its top black. A giant television screen suspended on the far wall carried a soccer game, but Prava paid no attention. Had he fallen behind on payments? Lost the café? More likely he'd acquired uninvited partners, and they were draining him dry, helping themselves to free food and drink, forcing their knock-off booze and goods into his regular orders at jacked prices and skimming the till as they squeezed every euro out of his pockets. Scavullo showed no mercy for anyone behind on paying him.

For that matter, neither were the *madrina* and her daughters at all lenient. The ladies were running their scams and making out on garbage collection contracts as they worked their way up the criminal food chain. Meanwhile, they maintained their hold on their vendors with these traditional weekly walkabouts.

Natalia had known Mr. Prava for twenty years. She said hello. He looked past her and closed his eyes as the Strozzis passed him by, dutifully respecting the boundary of their rival.

The Strozzis were in the vanguard. With more mob men in jail, their women had moved up to take command. A Neapolitan innovation. The Sicilian mafia would never entertain the idea of having women dons. But Naples's females often stepped in when their men were sent up. The Camorra took genuine pride in their ruthlessness.

At first, not everyone in town believed they were for real. Enzo Gracci, for one. Violetta Lupe had inherited the Rione del Vasto from Papa Marco. Gracci ran a successful fish market there—wholesale and retail—maybe the largest in Naples. Thinking Violetta a pushover, he held back a couple of payments, referred to her a couple of times as "that bitch." A week later Enzo sat on a bench in Piazza Dante with his eyes gouged out, quite dead from shock.

Here were the people Natalia had sworn to protect: alcoholic Valentino; Mr. Prava; the cobbler in his dim shop
next door with a pile of broken shoes on his worktable; a
couple hugging in the shadow of the church, the woman's
lilac-colored bodice stitched with tiny mirrors that pulsed
shards of colored light where Natalia walked.

What could she realistically do? The system had ruled
since before she was born. Maybe Pino was correct in getting out before he ended up a cynic. Or worse: in a *camp ed
coj*, "cabbage patch," street slang for a grave.

Natalia crossed the road. A baby, wearing pink ice cream
on her face, sat in her father's lap as he navigated their
motorbike through traffic. An old lady yelled at them from
the sidewalk. He braked, handed the baby to a woman who
kissed it several times and got on the bike behind him, the
babe in her lap as they sped off.

Two nuns scurried into a liquor shop. A florist arranged
a bucket of tuber roses as several pigeons swooped from St.
Francis's bronze shoulders and fluttered overhead. Finally,
Natalia reached her destination and rang Stefano Grappi's
intercom bell.

She surprised him, but he was gracious, inviting her up.
He met her at the door and ushered her into his living
room. She sat and opened her dog-eared notebook.

"We're pressed for time, Mr. Grappi. Do you mind if I
just begin?"

"Not at all. I'm kind of anxious to have the investigation
over myself."

"Vincente and Carlo Bagnatti, were they having an
affair? Do you know?"

"They slept together briefly a long time ago, way before
he and I were a couple. Vincente was experimenting, just
coming out. Bagnatti was older, experienced—charming,

as Vincente put it. Not the viper the public later came to know."

"You knew him?"

"Only by reputation."

"There was nothing between them more recently?"

Stefano closed his eyes momentarily. "I don't know anymore."

"Did Vincente's collection include firearms?" Natalia said.

"Yes, several. I don't know if they work. He was always buying war souvenirs on the Internet. A year ago he stopped showing me his acquisitions. They didn't really interest me."

"Are any weapons missing from his collection?"

"Not unless Vincente removed them himself. They should all be there. No one has entered the 'War Room,' as he called it. No one ever did without an invitation. Only Beatrice. I'm not even certain I know where he keeps— kept—the key."

"You didn't find that odd? The locked room?"

"Not really. Vincente is fastidious about his possessions— about everything. Plus, he does have some very valuable articles."

"Beatrice is?"

"Beatrice Santini. She comes in to clean for him twice a month."

"I'll need to speak with her."

"She lives in the Rione Mater Dei. I have a number somewhere. But you can find her at the Hotel Neapolis."

"On Via Giudice?"

"She works there most days, yes."

The Neapolis Hotel was a floor of rooms within a grand old *palazzo* six stories high. Outside, a minuscule plaza held an antiquity: a Greek obelisk that daily drew visitors to the tiny square. Natalia took the stairs to the second floor and struggled against a heavy glass door to gain entry. The foyer was quiet, most guests being already out, traipsing through Pompeii or gasping at the art at the Capodimonte Museum.

The desk clerk's post at the front desk stood empty. A half-sandwich rested on a plate beside leather-bound menus for nearby restaurants. A case behind the counter held art books available for perusal or purchase.

The clerk returned and directed Natalia down a hall, where she found Beatrice Santini folding and stacking towels on a housekeeping cart. A stunning woman, her taut face and chiseled features resembled Greta Garbo's. The gravelly timbre of her voice, too, as they conversed in Italian.

Had Stefano and Vincente seemed like a happy couple?

"Happy?"

"Did they argue a lot?"

"They got along. At least when I saw them. But . . . who knows what goes on underneath the surface between two people?"

"Had anything changed between them recently?"

"Not that I could tell."

"Was Vincente planning to leave Stefano?"

"I wouldn't know. Mr. Vincente went out sometimes. With other men. They fought about it once when I was there."

"You cleaned the locked room where Vincente kept his collection?"

"He liked to be present when I did it—to be sure I didn't break anything."

"Do you know what a *lupara* is?"

"*Certo.* Sure I do."

"Did Vincente have one in his collection of war memorabilia?"

"I didn't see one, no. He only had a military pistol in his collection. No rifle. No shotgun."

It had only been days since her partner had come aboard, but already Angelina had scrubbed and tidied their office and revived the nearly dead African violets abandoned when Pino left. A rare flowering plant with particularly luminous petals, more delicate and sensitive than ordinary blooms. Like Pino himself.

Angelina had also commandeered two new chairs. "Ergonomic," she announced.

"We don't have the budget for ergonomic," Natalia said. "Where did you get these?"

"Don't ask," Angelina said—all mischievous grin—and picked a small Buddha figure from the shelf above her desk.

"Jade, isn't it? Yours?"

"My partner's—former partner, that is."

"Uh oh. Your partner-partner? Maybe you're not as smart as you look."

"Carabiniere Cavatelli."

"Sorry, Capitano," Angelina said, chagrined. "None of my business. Let's get to work."

"I was teasing, I was teasing."

Angelina spread a map of Naples open across her desk.

"I'm learning my way around," she explained.

"Good. How's it coming?"

"Okay," she said and tapped a spot. "What's with the Castel Dell'Ovo? Such a weird name."

"Castle of the Egg? According to legend, Virgil placed an egg beneath the castle."

"What?"

"He was big into sorcery."

"Oh."

"As long as the supernatural egg survived, Naples would as well."

"Ah, Naples," Angelina sighed. "So romantic. One of ours did the Teatro San Carlo."

"Giovanni Antonio Medrano," Natalia pronounced.

"You do know your stuff," Angelina said.

"About Naples, yeah. 'A peak of hell rising out of paradise,'" quoted Natalia.

"Virgil?"

"Goethe, according to Pino."

"Maybe that's why San Gennaro only worked his miracles in Naples. Though we could have used him in Palermo. Last report: crime rate is ten times higher in Sicily than anywhere else in our fair country."

"Are you adjusting to our Neopolitan haven?" Natalia said.

Angelina laughed. "I like it. I like not being known by anyone."

"Good. I have a task for you. Run a background check on Vincente Lattaruzzo and on the Countess Antonella Cavazza. Talk to Carlo Busto in the Municipal Building. He knows the archives like no one."

A call summoned them to the colonel's office. Fabio was standing when they entered, a copy of the day's tabloid edition spread across his desk. He pointed to it.

"We can't have this," he said. "Any idea how they got a photo like that?"

"Not our photographer," said Natalia. "Not Raffi."

Fabio pressed his index finger to the bridge of his nose. "The mortuary men?"

"Possibly," said Natalia.

"Her servants?"

"I doubt it."

"That scandal rag must have paid a small fortune for it. Damn. We'll tighten security here, and I'll look into the mortuary boys at the scene. If one of them leaked it, he'll wish he was his own client."

The man who wanted to claim Carlo Bagnatti's body wore a dark suit and lavender tie. A matching handkerchief peeped from the breast pocket. His shoes came to a point long after they should have ended.

"And you are?" Natalia asked as he took the chair alongside her desk.

"Pietro Fabretti."

"Relation to the deceased?"

"An old friend—one of his only friends, needless to say. The price of being a gossip columnist."

"Is there next of kin?"

"Carlo was an only child."

"Is there an estate?"

"Yes. Not huge but quite enough to keep a person carefree for some time. I'm the executor."

"May I know the beneficiary?"

"Sure. Vincente Lattaruzzo."

"Hmm. Pity. That's not going to benefit him now."

"No."

"And next, after the late Mr. Lattaruzzo?"

"One beneficiary: Stefano Grappi."

Natalia made an effort not to reveal her surprise.

"How much is he inheriting?"

"I hesitate to say before the testament is probated and my appointment confirmed."

"Under the circumstances, I'm afraid I have to insist," Natalia said.

"Seven hundred thousand euros, a small apartment in Rome, his two-year-old Mercedes convertible."

"How long have you known the victim?"

"Twenty years? He was seventeen when he announced himself queer. His parents disowned him. Carlo lived on the street for nearly a year. I brought him food occasionally. We started to talk. I was training to be a ballet dancer. He was curious, so one day I brought him along to a class. Turned out he had talent. Not the conventional dancer's body, but strong."

"He took up dance with you?"

"Did he ever. We lived that life for several years. But it's such a monolithic existence. And the body grows tired, even the young one. Carlo got a job in a restaurant. Out of boredom he started to observe the patrons: who was with whom, what they were saying. One thing led to another."

"He took up gossip writing."

"Not right off. He called himself a journalist at first, and then—but you know about the rest already. His star rose when he outed that Berlusconi minister. We went our separate ways, more or less. Eventually I opened a music store. Not so much tear on the body. He and I remained friends."

"Were you lovers?"

"We shared a room when we attended the ballet academy, but no. Not really." He looked away. "Do you have any idea who did this vicious thing?"

"Do you?"

"He annoyed many people, obviously. That was the idea of the job really, and he was good at it. Once or twice he became the story when people retaliated. I warned him on occasion. You know what he said?" Pietro Fabretti smiled, remembering. "'Darling, these celebrities are not the Camorra, they are pussies.'"

"Did he ever give you the impression he was blackmailing someone?"

Pietro made a face. "Not his style."

"Any idea of what particular gossip item he may have been working on most recently that could have provoked something like this?"

Pietro shifted uncomfortably. "Hard to tell."

"What does that mean?"

"It means I like my life. Good wine. Good food. Breathing."

"If you withhold information in a murder investigation," Natalia said, "you may find yourself enjoying the good life in the cells of Poggio Reale. Trust me. The wine list isn't up to your standards. Nor the food."

"No doubt true. I am not greedy, but I like my luxuries. In fact, if I had been born in another era, born to another fate, I could imagine myself as a worshipper of luxury. I would have belonged to the cult in Naples that copied from Roman customs of excess. But on the other hand, maybe not. Did you know that during the Second World War—and I mean the worst of it—when typhoid and smallpox were rampant, when people could not find even a scrap of food, there were still women of noble birth indulging in milk baths?"

"I didn't know."

"Carlo did a column on Prince Pignatelli. When the Allies liberated his *palazzo*, they found cupboards of silk stockings and flagons of Chanel perfume. He'd hoarded them to pay any girl he could lure to his rooms. Quite sordid."

For the remainder of the interview Pietro Fabretti remained evasive and said nothing substantive. Natalia showed him out. She was just returning to her desk when a call came in that Angelina picked up.

"This is Officer Cavatelli. How can I help you? Just a minute." She punched the hold button. "A gentleman wants to talk to you."

"He have a name?"

Angelina went back on the line. "May I tell her who is calling? Okay. Hold, please. He doesn't want to give his name. Sounds like a snitch. Want me to run a trace?"

"Don't bother." Natalia took the phone. "Officer Monte."

"It's about your horsemen," a voice whispered. "The ones in the garden?"

"What about them?"

"You want to find the murder weapon?" He'd lost the whisper. His voice sounded familiar, but Natalia couldn't place it.

"You have the gun?"

"I can tell you where to find it."

"Who is this?" Natalia asked.

He chuckled. "You're the detective."

"I don't have time for games," she said. "What is it?"

Usually a snitch passed information for money or a favor. But without asking for either, the caller told her outright where: a shop.

The new partners changed into plain clothes. They then left immediately. Natalia had their uniformed driver stop a block from the place so she and Angelina could walk the rest of the way and arrive undetected.

From somewhere a soccer ball landed at Angelina's feet. She backstopped it.

"*Scuzza*," a boy called and started over to retrieve his ball. Before he could, Angelina lined up on it and kicked it back.

"Another hidden talent?" Natalia said, as she watched the ball's flight.

They continued on. An overheated woman dragged a little boy with red curly hair. "Mama, *voglio fare pipi!*" he screeched, insisting he had to pee that instant.

In another block, they reached the shop. On a sidewalk table in front, a crystal rose glimmered among rusted forks and spoons, buttons, ribbons and ancient keys. On the tray alongside it were twine, a porcelain teapot and an ornate deck of cards. The display window was likewise crammed with puppets and lamps, paintings, mirrors, small sculptures, dolls.

Inside, the proprietor berated a French couple for taking his photo without offering payment for the privilege. Natalia recognized him: Ricardo Tulio, small-time junk dealer and Camorra dogsbody. Not the smartest rabbit on the planet but mean enough. Picked up for dealing stolen merchandise three years ago, he was offered a deal but refused to inform. He had served twenty months and was duly rewarded for his loyalty on release and exempted from protection payments. Natalia had interrogated him on more than one occasion, but he seemed not to recognize her out of uniform.

"Fifty euros," he said, standing too close. His large silver crucifix glinted from its bed of dark chest hair.

"Fifty euros?" Natalia put the rose down.

"Okay, forty."

"I'll have to think about it. Perhaps I'll come by tomorrow."

"I'm closed tomorrow," he said, getting irritated.

"Wednesday, then."

"I may be here. Maybe not."

Angelina, behind him, nodded at the glass counter. On

a black velvet cloth rested a small double-barreled shotgun. Natalia stepped closer to admire it.

"Nice, huh?" he said. "You don't come across too many of these. A real antique. This one is handmade. See where it's carved along the barrels? Compact. Easy to carry hidden."

"Yes."

The short barrels would make the shot go wide. Like the wounds on the two men.

"You know weapons?" he said.

"Wherever did you get this?"

"It would be unprofessional to say."

"I'm afraid I'm going to take this off your hands." She flipped open her ID.

"Fuck. You looked familiar. I shoulda guessed. How about I give you the rose and I keep the gun? A hundred euros I paid for it, for Christ's sake."

"How about I bring you in for dealing in stolen goods? You know the seller?"

"Nah. A young stud."

"I'll need a description."

"Short and muscular, long hair. Maybe twenty-five. Jesus, keep me out of it." In one motion, Tulio wrapped the shotgun in sheets of yesterday's newspaper and handed it to Natalia along with the glass rose.

"Bribing an officer is a crime."

"Give me a break, okay? I'm just a poor man trying to make a living."

"Right." Natalia shoved the weapon into her carryall. "We may need you to come in to make an identification."

She and Angelina left Tulio swearing under his breath and made their way back toward their office on foot. Clusters of pedestrians thickened into crowds that surged around the railroad terminal. A gypsy couple with a gaggle of children approached a modest café until a tattooed barista shooed them away.

"I'm glad you're getting the chance to see this," Natalia said. "Better than reading a guide book."

Every inch of sidewalk was taken, mostly by Nigerians hawking their wares. The locals were outfitted with folding chairs and umbrellas. The immigrants, more desperate, worked standing in the blazing sun. War and famine continued to churn refugees onto Italy's shores. The Camorra took advantage of their vulnerability and made a tidy profit from the knock-offs they supplied them, especially Guccis and Rolexes. Bags and watches lay on blankets.

"The police and Carabinieri could work night and day," Natalia said, "and never even scratch the surface of the labyrinthine criminal system you're seeing here."

Many had resisted, no one had triumphed. No prosecutor, judge, policeman, mayor, legislator, no president. The Camorra had subverted and compromised them all.

Her *nonna* had told her stories of Salvatore Carnevale, a socialist hero in the fifties who compelled the gentry to share with their workers the profits from their olive harvest. A real feat, approaching the miraculous. Then Carnevale had set out to organize the quarry workers: Camorra territory. A mystic of sorts, he had declared, "Whoever kills me, kills Christ."

The mafia came after him on horseback, horse shoes sparking as they struck the flinty ground. *Riding on the stars*, the terrified peasants were quoted as exclaiming. Carnevale, all of thirty-four—dumped in front of his mother's house like road kill.

Natalia and Angelina turned onto Via Casanova and continued on past the car repair shops that shared the street

with the Carabinieri station. In the foyer, the young officer
on desk duty shoved his magazine into a drawer. Natalia
clutched her carryall and walked up the two flights of stairs
to Brigadier Portero's office on the top floor.

Portero, the in-house weapons expert, was the longest
serving Carabiniere at the station. His dusty room wasn't
much bigger than a kiosk. Walking upstairs, he claimed,
kept his weight down, although all five-feet, eight inches of
him weighed well over 200 pounds.

If he hadn't come from a poor family, he might have
gone to university and become a historian. Self-taught,
he'd collected books since he was a kid. Natalia heard he
owned hundreds of them; many were treasures. He even
had a cabinet in his office with the overflow. That's what he
chose to do with his modest earnings. He never took a vacation. He never owned a car. If you had a question about
their city, chances are he had the answer. Naples during the
time of Bourbons—up until now.

So, in a way he'd missed out on his dream. Who hadn't,
Natalia thought as she approached his door. But there
were compensations being a Carabiniere: the occasional
excitement of the job, the camaraderie, the opportunity to
serve the community.

Natalia had given up mourning her own aborted university career, though she liked to think that perhaps Portero
would resume his studies when he retired. A solitary sort,
he visibly enjoyed the collegiality at the station and his
acknowledged expertise. Portero's door stood open.

"You have a minute, Brigadier?" she asked.

"For you, Captain? Always."

Natalia exposed the gun, and together they slipped it
into a plastic evidence sheath.

"Don't come across many of these," he said, studying the

weapon. "From the thirties. Hand crafted. Carvings like these I've seen maybe twice. Beautiful, aren't they?"

A peacock preened on one side of the stock, and the sun fanned out on the other. Vine etchings crept along the barrel.

"I suppose."

"A real mafia heirloom, trotted out for traditional honor killings and major vengeance. Any prints?"

"Probably clean but we haven't checked it yet."

"Figures."

Such a devastating weapon to shoot a human being. The carvings were lovely, if you could say that about an instrument intended for killing.

"Tulio had it for sale," she said.

"Ricardo Tulio is back in business?"

"It seems so, with a little help from his friends. Payment for his silence."

Portero sniffed the barrels. "Recently fired."

Back downstairs, she reported to Colonel Fabio.

"We're following a lead in the double murder at the *contessa*'s. Tulio was selling what's possibly the murder weapon used on Vincente Lattaruzzo. A traditional *lupara*."

"The bloody shirt, the traditional weapon," he said. "This has all the markings of a blood feud. Something left unaddressed from a long time ago."

"So it would seem."

"A peasant's shirt?" the colonel observed.

"Smacks of the countryside, yes sir. Why they would display the bodies in the *contessa*'s garden remains a mystery. We're investigating the victims' backgrounds . . . and the *contessa*'s."

"The *contessa*?" The colonel blinked rapidly, caught off guard.

"I know she's a personal friend, sir, but nonetheless . . . She needn't know about it at this point."

"I appreciate your discretion. Do what you need to do, obviously. And let me know as soon as you find anything, as soon as she's in the clear."

Back in her own office, Natalia rested her head in her hands for a moment, drew a long breath and called it a day. Angelina had already clocked out. Natalia needed an early night. Disrupted sleep was taking its toll.

She walked home, her feet sore and heavy, made it upstairs to her door and undid the double locks. She dropped her keys in the foyer, placed placed her weapon in the top drawer of the hall table and shed her clothes on the way to the bedroom, where she flopped into bed and slept.

She came awake as the upstairs neighbor clacked across the floor. Down in the narrow old street that fronted her building a truck transferred trash from a dumpster, winching it aboard. Metal screeched, then boomed. A toilet flushed upstairs, and the night grew quiet again.

She got out of bed, undressed and slipped on one of Pino's t-shirts and her pajama bottoms to step out onto the balcony. High clouds faintly haloed the moon. Not one star. She wished Pino were with her.

In some ways, things had improved. The latest garbage strike had been over for months. Neapolitans no longer wore gas masks in the street, and Rome had finally dispatched the militia to help clean up the aftermath and deposit large metal containers around the poorer neighborhoods to accommodate the huge backlog of refuse. But collection continued day and night, often ruining sleep.

Another victory for the Camorra gangsters. They'd

caused the problem in the first place when their Don Aldo Gambini ordered his garbage collectors not to pick up any more trash after the city proposed purchase of an incinerator to cut hauling costs. When Gambini very conveniently was shot dead, Bianca Strozzi's company won the removal contract from the city—the venture Lola ran for Bianca's gang.

A scrawny dog moved into the shadows across the courtyard. Then the burning arc of a cigarette tossed aside. Someone there walked quickly away farther into the alley. Afraid suddenly, she retreated back inside, carefully barring the louvered shutters.

Had she ruffled some felon? Was the mob keeping tabs on her? Was it some errant husband sneaking home? The possibilities were too many. In any event, pissing off the lawless went with the territory and anxiety about it went with the job.

When she and Pino worked together, they had an arrangement: They could summon one another day or night. They were natives born and bred in their dark city. They knew all the Camorra players and shared the sense of being outnumbered, often alone.

After they became lovers, it became even easier to raise the alarm or confide her fears. Almost more than missing him as a lover, Natalia missed him as her partner and protector. She slept better with him around. Ironic, since she was probably the tougher of the two. Nonetheless . . .

In the corner by Natalia's bookcase was the broom her grandmother had placed in the doorway of her bedroom when she was an infant to keep away any witches wishing her harm. Should a witch turn up, she'd be forced to count each bristle, her *nonna* said. The task would take all night until the rising sun took away her power.

Natalia collected the broom and carried it to her bedroom, leaned it on the threshold of the balcony and lay down on her bed, then took her five-shot house gun from the drawer in her night table and slipped it under her pillow.

Chapter 7

It was the day of Vincente Lattaruzzo's funeral. Bagnatti remained in Dr. Agari's custody, so far unclaimed.

After Natalia showered, she surveyed her closet for something to wear. Not much to choose from. Mariel always encouraged her to amplify her wardrobe. Maybe if she had the style sense and the means of her best friend, she might have devoted more time to shopping. Though Natalia argued that she spent a fair amount of time in uniform, Mariel insisted there was no excusing her fashion crimes.

Natalia located a black pleated skirt she hadn't worn in years. Holding it to the light, she picked off a few pieces of lint, glad her friend wasn't there to witness it. But even she couldn't have found fault with the purple silk blouse. It was still in its dry cleaning bag, untouched since the time she dated that violinist. Had it been three years?

After she finished dressing, she slathered styling gel on

her wild wet curls and combed her hair, thinking again how she had to update the antique bathroom fixtures. She was reluctant to leave. Her four-room flat with its high ceilings and glass doorknobs was her refuge from the world, the only thing she owned outright, thanks to her father. Somehow her parents had collected a nest egg for their daughter—amazing, given the paltry salary her father earned as a city sanitation worker. Her mother had augmented it from the small income she earned mending clothes. They'd never traveled, and rarely did they even take in a film. Until Natalia had treated her mother to Florence, she'd never been farther than Potenza. Natalia showed her Dante's house and explained that Galileo had trained his telescope on the heavens from a spot nearby. That evening, as they walked along the river arm in arm, the moon hung over them like a shiny locket.

Natalia felt grateful every day for her flat, her niche in the world, with its cool marble floors underfoot and thick, protective walls adorned in pale yellow brocade. It always reminded her of them and the love that had brought her into the world.

As she made her way downstairs and past the concierge's rooms, Madam Luigina's canary flooded the stairwell with song. Natalia continued down the stone steps to the ground floor of the two-hundred-year-old house. Its baroque aspect never went out of style in Naples: the inner courtyard plain, its balconies and iron banisters no more than ordinary. But on its exterior were several columns topped with decorative ribbon and floral designs that had survived the eons—a lucky happenstance when so many architectural jewels had been destroyed by Allied bombs during the war.

Overhead, bed sheets swayed on a line, awaiting the brief daily intrusion of sunlight into the shadowed space. Natalia yawned. Queen Ann's Lace and spindly weeds poked up through the cracks in the worn stone leading to the freshly painted, bright green outer door that she pulled shut with an ancient brass knocker shaped like the head of a lion.

Her motor scooter was where she'd left it, hemmed in now by several other chained *motorinos*. Luckily it wasn't too far. She could walk. Natalia pushed open the front gate. Via Giudice was nearly empty; Tribunali, quiet.

Hair wild from sleep, Cecilia Bertolli, half owner of the Bertolli fruit stall, swept the walk in front of her shop. Her husband unpacked asparagus, the cigarette in his lips burned to ash.

Natalia greeted them as she stepped into the street to avoid their boxes, then jumped back on the curb as a blue-and-white *latte* truck swayed toward her over the cobblestones, followed by a *motorino* driver with boxes of strawberries lashed to the back of his bike.

On Via Duomo, the trees along the avenue were thick and green. Several homeless people slept in a huddle in front of the cathedral's massive red doors. A white pug pulled its owner along, the leash taut. For a moment, its mistress lost her balance, her pink leggings and long, blousy top entangling with the lead until it threatened to topple her. Natalia just caught her and held her upright. The woman thanked her and picked up the dog, kissing it repeatedly.

The boutiques hadn't yet opened. Natalia ignored their window displays, instead looking at the reflected sky, hazy from the night's rain. A day for witches, Natalia and Mariel would have said when they were children. They'd grown up with stories of witches who came from the mountains of Samio south of Naples and conspired there under the walnut trees. She and Mariel were convinced the hump-backed hag who lived in a ground floor *basso* two doors from her building was a witch possessed of magical powers to communicate with the dead. Mean boys used her hump as a bull's eye for spit balls and other missiles. When she screamed at them, Natalia's mother would rush to the balcony and threaten to call the police on them.

"Shut up, *garola!*" they'd yell and flash their tiny middle fingers.

As could have been predicted, most graduated to petty crime and manual labor, except for Sandro Altra and Benni Torrone, best friends to this day, who had taken up intimidating and killing for the Forcella gang.

Undeterred by the hooligans, the crone predicted the futures of hundreds of Neapolitans and kept herself in wine with their donations.

Natalia's *nonna* had twice dragged her to the woman for readings without her mother's knowledge, then hid the prescribed amulets beneath her tiny undershirt. Her grandmother tried to keep it from her, but Natalia knew a violent end is what the old woman had foreseen.

The stormy night had deposited a carpet of pink petals on the streets of the San Carlo all'Arena district outside the Santa Maria Donna Regina church. By its entrance slept young people sprawled every which way, guitar cases and a soggy drum set beside them—giant sleeping caterpillars that, when they played their music, morphed into butterflies. Afternoons and evenings these minstrels performed on the Via San Biagio dei Librai, their songs wafting over the crowds of strollers she and Pino used to join like ordinary citizens.

Natalia couldn't imagine the lack of privacy the street dwellers endured. Two nuns came out and stepped around them. Someone had deposited a bottle of water. A passerby dropped a pastry on the ratty cloth beside them.

A girl with pink-tufted hair opened her eyes, stretched and curled back up for more sleep. Church bells tolled. A dog—part German shepherd—lay stretched out beside her. It looked clean and well fed, more than could be said for its owners. She counted five kids, two of them boys spooned together. None more than eighteen.

The stone entryway to the church was still damp. Natalia smoothed her curls and opened the small passage cut into the much larger chapel door. Stefano Grappi stood just inside, next to a confessional, eyes brimming and red. His thin wrists protruded from the too-large mourning suit. Greeting Natalia, he thanked her for coming. Either the suit was borrowed or he was losing weight drastically, as the grief-stricken often did. Natalia surveyed the crowd, astonished by a young woman in a loud orange dress. Unthinkable to wear such a bright color at such a somber event. In the while since Natalia had attended a funeral, it looked like things had changed. Someone came in behind her. "*Scuzzi.*"

Director Garducci, the consummate gentleman, greeting people, kissing women's cheeks. He at least was wearing the appropriate black suit for his lover's funeral and an obsidian and gold earring.

The thick walls kept the interior cool. Vincente Lattaruzzo's open coffin rested on a wooden bier near the altar. Beside it, his photograph on an easel. Several people gathered around the coffin. A few knelt in the pews, praying quietly. Others milled about, waiting for the mass to begin. Stefano joined an elderly couple in the front pew. Lattaruzzo's parents? Probably. She checked the sparsely occupied pews but didn't recognize anyone among the young professionals—no doubt colleagues of the deceased. Most prominent among the mourners were elderly women in black, alone or in pairs, who likely had

never known the deceased but regularly attended everyone's funeral, lonely women happy to break the solitude of
their days. A few were, perhaps, simply ghoulish or seeking
distraction. Most attended out of altruism. Their prayers,
they believed, helped speed souls out of purgatory. Their
prayers for the departed, they hoped, would be recipro-
cated by others when their time came. The grief displayed
raised the family's standing in the community, and the
departed might finally have the respect he deserved in life
but hadn't gained until the moment of his eulogy.

Funerals, like weddings, were important social affairs.
The wealthy splurged on lavish caskets. The poor on an
"uncle from Rome," usually an elderly resident of a nearby
rione or district brought in to pose as a well-off relative from
the north. Or a woman who, as the service progressed,
would wail and scratch her face bloody. These actors only
cost the family of the deceased the rental of a suit or dress,
a few euros for their enthusiasm and a glass or two of *mar-
sala* at the wake and a plate of food.

Vincente's funeral was in no way lavish. Mercifully, the
family had not resorted to professional mourners. Vincente Lattaruzzo reclined in a tasteful black casket with
silver handles—neither the pine of the indigent nor the
gold of the well heeled. Stefano had kept the proceedings
tasteful.

Angelina, sitting down beside Natalia, leaned over and
whispered. "Do you plan to confront him soon about being
the beneficiary of Bagnatti's will, after Vincente?"

"Yes," Natalia replied, "but not today."

The official period of mourning for close family was
seven years, during which black was the color traditionally
worn. Many widows still observed this, but Natalia couldn't
imagine Stefano would for that long. Unlike Natalia's *zia*

Clementina, who, when her beloved mate passed away, never wore a spot of color until the day she herself died twenty years later.

Camorra widows were another story. Often they were left widows while still young. The black might hold for a year, even two. Then color crept back. Five years later the only vestige of their grief might be a black handkerchief carried dutifully in a Chanel bag.

Old Mother Scavullo stood at the back. What was she doing there? Unlikely she and Lattaruzzo had ever crossed paths. Then again, you never knew. Renata Scavullo managed a modest criminal empire. Did she own artifacts or consult art experts about stolen pieces in the hands of her fences?

Mama Scavullo had on a fancy white dress printed with daisies. Not a trace of mourning black. Hardly funereal. A bouffant hairdo with a real daisy anchored above one ear. She looked to be attending a festive bon voyage gathering, seeing someone off on a happy journey. Or was she there to savor Lattaruzzo's demise? Gloat over some vengeance?

The priest made his way to the altar. Everyone sat. Natalia glanced back for Renata Scavullo, but the old woman had slipped off. The ceremony proceeded.

An hour later, the coffin was carried out into the intense sunlight and placed in an open hearse bedecked with ten-foot bouquets of palms and orange chrysanthemums. In this heat, the flowers would be as dead as the corpse before the procession reached the graveyard. An official car trailed behind, *Carabinieri* written large in white along its side.

The forensic techies identified a thumbprint on the *lupara* as Ernesto Scavullo's, head of the DePretis clan and boss of the Vasto and waterfront districts, among others. Natalia and Angelina changed into their uniforms, gathered up weapons and cuffs and set out. They decided to evade the district's heavy traffic and walk to the hill train. In minutes they reached the funicular station at the bottom of the steep incline leading up to the Vomero district. As they were both in uniform, the attendant waved them through, and they joined the crowd in the cool of the marble waiting room.

The cable tram whirred down. The exchange of passengers took no more than seconds, with passengers exiting from one side and passengers boarding from the other for the quick trip up in the staggered car, constructed of narrow compartments that were like joined steps which together ascended the hill.

The doors closed, and the car wrenched upward. Minutes later they stepped out at the last stop and followed the other passengers into the ritzy section high above the city.

They exited onto Via Kerbaker. Outside the station it was leafy and breezy cool. A Bengladeshi vendor assembled bouquets of roses and chrysanthemums, wrapping them in pink and orange crepe paper before setting them out to sell.

They crossed Piazza Vitelli, a vast space named, Natalia explained, for the eighteenth-century architect responsible for many of the city's neoclassical gems, and walked along a boulevard flanked by gracious apartment buildings for the two blocks to their destination. A guard posted outside Scavullo's grand estate closely examined Natalia and Angelina and said something into his walkie-talkie. Instantly the gates swung open, and he waved them in. Natalia and Angelina followed the driveway up to Scavullo's split-level villa, a virtual copy of Salvatore "the Beast" Riima's digs in Palermo, Angelina said, right down to the date palms over the drive.

It never failed to annoy Natalia the way the dons and *madrinas* added wings to their overstuffed mansions, gold toilets to their boudoirs and Ferraris to their car fleets, while Neapolitan monuments crumbled, and museums and cultural institutions cut staff and hours.

A black woman pulled out of the garage in a white Mercedes. She was a vision in pink: pink jacket, pink scarf, pink sunglasses. And a black chiffon blouse. A large topaz and a silver *cornetto* hung from a thick pink gold chain around her neck.

"The girlfriend?" Angelina said.

"Who knows? Doesn't look like the African in the file pics."

A young man opened the front door before they rang the bell.

"Paolo," Natalia exclaimed, as they stepped into the white marble foyer. "My God."

The once slim boy was beefed up, heavily muscled.

"Natalia! Natalia Monte," he said.

"Paolo." She took his hand.

"It must be twenty years, easy. You haven't changed."

"Oh, Paolo. Tell me you're not working for him?"

"Yeah . . . well. How's Mariel?"

"Still beautiful. In fact, your name came up the other day."

"Don't bullshit me."

"No, really. But Paolo, you hated this . . . business. What happened?"

"Kids happened. Unemployment happened."

"Paolo."

"What? I should have swept streets like your father? Hawked newspapers like my old man when his leather shop failed? Christ—a news*boy* at sixty? I wasn't smart like you. No scholarships here. No wealthy parents to pick up the tab like Mariel's."

Natalia said nothing.

"He's out back by the pool. You'll have to walk around. He doesn't like uninvited visitors."

"I'll bet."

"Be careful . . . Captain. He's already pissed."

"We'll try not to spoil his afternoon."

"The path is there." Paolo stepped back into the entry and resumed his post.

A few things Natalia knew about Scavullo: He was a sun worshipper, had a thing for gold jewelry and worked out religiously to maintain his boyish figure. Not only that, he obsessed over every bite of food, every sip of drink that went into his mouth. The obsession with his physique might have had to do with the fact he'd been fat as a child. Rumor had it he'd taken care of more than one boy who'd teased him back when they were kids.

Angelina and Natalia circled the huge house. Sprinklers worked their arc over a perfectly manicured lawn. There was a terra cotta deck near the back of the house, but the white leather banquettes were devoid of occupants.

They found the don face up on a black massage table beside a sapphire infinity pool. Several gold chains looped around his neck, glinting among his chest hair. A gold snake with sapphire eyes stared at them from his enormous wrist. An open yellow terry cloth jacket revealed taut stomach muscles.

He reminded Natalia of a photo she'd seen in one of the beefcake magazines Lola kept on her night table. But that porno actor had not posed with an intravenous line stuck into his arm. It dripped clear liquid into his veins from sealed plastic bags hung on a stainless steel rack.

Beside him: a glass-topped table with a cell phone, a small arrangement of miniature white roses and his morning protein shake in a yellow tumbler alongside a glass of orange juice, freshly squeezed.

A gorgeous black woman in shorts and a turquoise halter occupied the recliner beside him. He whispered something to her as Natalia and Angelina circled the pool and approached. The woman rose and strutted toward the house. A duo in matching bikinis rose from the other side of the pool and walked toward the sliding glass doors of a fully equipped gymnasium. Natalia wondered if they were twins.

A bird eyed them quizzically from its perch.

He took a sip of the chilled juice. "You're interrupting."

"Looks important," Natalia said.

"I never liked a smart-ass." He looked her over. "Maybe you should take a page from my book."

"You know what a *lupara* is?" Natalia asked.

"A shotgun, yeah. How could I not?"

"Have you operated one recently?"

"No, why?"

"We have in our possession a small, antique *lupara* likely used in a double murder, and it has your fingerprints on it."

"Those faggots on the front page the other morning?"

"Those two men," Natalia said, "yes."

"I don't know anything about those bum-fuckers—alive or dead."

"Your mother, Renata Scavullo, attended the funeral."

"Well, bravo for her. Go ask her if she gunned them down. Why are you wasting my time?"

Angelina said, "We think this shotgun with your print is the weapon used in the crime."

"Do you own a *lupara*?" Natalia demanded.

"Several but mine are in the country in a glass case."

"May we see yours?"

"I told you. They're not here. They're there."

"Where is there?"

"You can see them when I'm ordered to produce them."

"We'll get an order for you."

"Do what you gotta, Natalia Monte. Waste of time—your job, you know? You came up in the neighborhood. Could have done better."

"Right. You think you should be running the place instead?"

"We'll do a better job when we get a few more senators elected."

Natalia informed him they were not done with him. He started to answer when his cell phone buzzed.

Scavullo didn't greet the caller by name. "Yeah. A couple of bitches . . . about the faggot thing."

Natalia and her partner exchanged glances.

"Let's get out of here," Natalia whispered.

Arrogant bastard, Natalia thought as she and her partner walked away. Far enough away not to be seen but close enough to follow Ernesto's conversation, they paused.

"Yeah. Listen. I might need you to drive a van someplace. A thousand euros—you interested? No. You come here. Noon? I'll have my cook fix us something. You like chicken? I'm not eating much red meat. Pasta either. Gotta lose ten more."

There was a pause.

"Yeah, I heard," Scavullo chuckled. "It doesn't work that way. I think we need to have a meeting over this. Tomorrow night? Yeah. I told him. I warned 'em. He starts screaming and yelling, and we're gonna have to teach 'em one last time."

Quietly they retraced their steps back to the street.

Natalia could see Paolo watching them from a window at the front of the mansion.

"Nasty," Angelina said, exhaling loudly as they walked

through the massive iron gates and returned to the street. "I've dealt with lowlifes in Palermo, but this man gives me the creeps. Like he'd do his *nonna* and party after. And what's up with that place? Looks like a harem."

They moved down the block. "So what's his story?" Angelina said, walking toward the hill tram.

"Ernesto Scavullo. Mean as they come. Left school to work on the docks when he was twelve. Even though his father ran the waterfront, he expected his son to prove himself. Young Scavullo unloaded refrigerators stuffed with heroin, crated up counterfeit handbags, hid guns in cargo shipments. Ernesto worked hard and kept his eyes open. His father got busted because his son had left a tainted revolver in the glove compartment of his car when he lent it to dad. An ordinary traffic stop bagged Scavullo senior and the murder attempt perpetrated with the weapon. He stood mute and got sentenced to fifteen years. Mama Scavullo took over her husband's criminal enterprises, and young Ernesto's apprenticeship accelerated. Her husband gets out soon."

"Ernesto looked tough," Angelina said.

"He is. At thirteen he slit the throat of a stevedore. Said he didn't like the way the guy addressed him, said it was disrespectful. When he was eighteen, Mama set him up in an air-conditioned office on Via Chiaia, where he coordinated shipments of heroin from Africa, Turkey and the Middle East. No more dirt under his fingernails but plenty of blood, certainly. When his father was halfway through his sentence, Ernesto took control of the clan. Six years later he's built this. He has a villa outside Naples, too. That's where the guns live."

"A search doesn't require permission in the case of murder, drugs or suspected Camorra crimes, "Angelina said.

"True. But I don't hold out much hope when it comes to the shotgun we recovered. There's no bullet when you fire a shotgun, just pellets. There are no striations to identify the weapon that fired them, as I'm sure Ernesto Scavullo knows. Which makes the fingerprint just a fingerprint—nothing to connect it to the crime. It's not like we found the weapon at the scene."

"You make it sound like he left his print on the weapon on purpose."

"Very probably."

"Why would he do that?" Angelina said.

"Why? Because he wants it known he did it and is capable of doing even worse."

"What if we could listen in on a phone call or two?" Angelina asked as they walked.

"We have. But the bastard's clever. Talks in code. Changes phones constantly. Last time we tried a tap, the press was making a big deal about protecting people's privacy. *We* have to protect that scum's privacy?"

"Right," Angelina said. "In Palermo we usually worked around it."

"Here, too."

There had to be strong evidence that someone had committed a serious crime before permission for a tap was acquired from the magistrate. Officially if there was no authorization, any evidence gathered as a result of the tap would not be admissible in court. But often the rules were bypassed, and it was common knowledge the magistrate postdated authorization documents if necessary.

"Our stations have techies who can install listening devices, with or without authorization. But it's dangerous as hell," Natalia said. "They're more of a threat to the gangsters than a *pentito*, a snitch. Last year one of our techs was enjoying a Sunday outing with his wife at San Martino monastery. It's on top of the hill. A woman approached and asked him to take a photo of her. Thirty-five or forty, good-looking, wearing jeans with a rhinestone patch and a black T-shirt. She held up her Blackberry, asking if he would mind, and stepped back. The techie pressed the button. A bullet slammed into his brain, and she sauntered away into the crowd."

"Yeah," Angelina said. "Sounds too familiar."

After dealing with Scavullo, the streets of the fancy neighborhood seemed genteel. Women in tasteful dresses carried shopping bags with upscale designers' names emblazoned on them. A man with grey, tufted hair who, despite the heat, had a blue cashmere sweater draped around his neck, sniffed a pot of yellow fresia in a terracotta pot outside a tile shop. His russet fluff of a dog pranced toward the officers, pulling on its leash.

"Leonardo!" he called. "Sorry, ladies. He's such a flirt."

"So adorable!" Angelina crouched down and started talking baby talk to the dog.

Another one, Natalia thought. Was she the only one exempt from the charm of these miniature beings? Oh, well. She smiled at the man over her partner's body. No need to advertise herself as a misanthrope.

"He's the prince of the house," the man said. An aristocrat, his face plump and florid, nails manicured.

Angelina stood as the dog tugged him forward. "Sorry. Puppies are my weakness."

"That's okay. There are worse things."

They stopped to sit on a bench in the park that surrounded the grand *palazzo*.

"Water?" Angelina held out a bottle.

"You are prepared," Natalia said.

"You work in Palermo . . . let's just say the hottest day in Naples is spring compared to there."

People lounged on benches under the thick shade of trees. Children ran around on the grass. Natalia took a drink from the water bottle as a young man passed, his arms around two girls. He was muscled, a ring of tattoos on his biceps.

"If I ever found out another man had fucked my wife, I'd kill him," he said. One of the girls laughed.

Angelina raised an eyebrow. "He thinks it's so easy."

Chapter 8

They bypassed the office, got their unmarked car from the tiny lot and drove to the tabloid. It had offices in the financial district located in the eastern part of town. It was a neighborhood without a soul. Carpet bombing during the war had flattened its original architecture and inspired the Camorra to embark upon the lucrative building trades from excavating foundations to pouring concrete and the final wiring of high-rises. Normally Natalia avoided the area.

Large *For Rent* banners appeared on many of the buildings. Some looked like they'd hung there for years. Large businesses had run out their leases and left, clearing the way for accountants and dentists and other lone practitioners. Natalia and Angelina were waved through the lobby's security by a guard sucking on his soft drink, engrossed in a graphic novel. They got on the first elevator and pushed the button for the tenth floor. It shot them up ten stories in seconds.

The doors opened on a slight man draped with cameras: two 35-millimeter digital Nikons and a beautiful old Leica.

"Captain," he said.

"Luca!" Natalia exclaimed and reached out to touch the ancient Leica. "You're shooting actual film?"

"Somebody's gotta," he laughed, then pinched his fingertips together in front of his face.

"You take those shots of the two murder victims astride the horse sculpture?"

"I wish," Luca sighed. "I'd be in Majorca on the beach right now." He stepped past them into the elevator, hand raised in a wave as the doors closed.

Rivelare's offices were even more institutional than the Carabinieri station's at Via Casanova. Dropped ceilings made of flimsy insulation tiles that may once have been white. Fluorescent overhead lights that bathed everything in a vaguely green tinge that went well with the brown industrial carpeting and tan cubicles spread out in all directions.

Young reporters in the work stations scrolled their Blackberries and talked on phones, feet up on desks next to their computer screens. Some tapped away at laptops, others stared into their monitors as if hypnotized.

A secretary appeared to lead them to the managing editor's glassed-in window office at the end of an aisle. Natalia flashed her ID, but he had already recognized her. "Should I call my lawyer?" he joked as he ushered them in.

"Not yet," Natalia said.

He looked easily a decade older than his staff, his beard a consequence of indolence rather than a fashion statement. Pudgy around the middle, he wore a long-sleeved work shirt and blue jeans. On one wrist a thin silver bracelet. His eyes seemed sad, even when he smiled.

Though the late Carlo Bagnatti's pieces for *Rivelare* were often just titillating gossip, sometimes they contained actual newsworthy information, lifted a rock and exposed the worm beneath. Like the recent story of the interior minister and his seventeen-year-old Neapolitan girlfriend and the prostitutes and parties elected officials paid for with the tax monies of the good citizens. Although it looked like the minister's cronies would make sure he wasn't held to account, hope sprang eternal.

Franco Corso's desk was messier than Natalia's. A flaccid-looking sandwich lay in the middle, a bite or two gone, paper espresso cups heaped around it.

"What can I do for you ladies today?" He cleared a stack of papers from the couch.

"You ran a picture of a crime scene," Natalia said.

"Our Carlo and young Lattaruzzo?"

"Was one of your photographers there? It had to be someone with a police-band radio."

"Our guys monitor the band as a matter of course, but it wasn't any of them."

"Really?" Natalia said. "You must have paid a small fortune for it."

"We would have, but honestly, we paid nothing."

"How so?"

"The picture, it just arrived—appeared at our reception desk. A digital disc someone left. My assistant didn't know who it should go to and opened it on her machine. Sorry I can't be more helpful."

"Where is the disc?"

He opened his desk drawer and produced a transparent case with a disc inside. "Any leads yet?" he said and popped it into a padded mailing envelope, *Rivelare* printed across it in oversized simulated handwriting.

"Leads? I wish I could tell you," Natalia said. "You'd be the first to hear."

"Right." Corso laughed.

"We need to see what Bagnatti was working on most recently that could have gotten him in trouble."

"Yeah, I've been expecting that. We haven't touched his office since we heard."

Corso escorted them several doors down. It was surprisingly sterile, Spartan in the extreme: not a sheet of paper showing anywhere other than magazines, each tabbed with a Post-It, indicating a Bagnatti story.

Angelina fired up Carlo Bagnatti's computer while Natalia continued conversing with the managing editor.

"Was he working on anything so hot," she said, "that it might have potentially put him in harm's way?"

Corso gestured expansively, arms out like wings. "Everything Carlo was on to he said was hot and sordid and all of it a scoop. But honestly, no. It was all the usual level of nasty. Though, that said, his latest, greatest leads he kept on a memory stick that he wore around his neck like an amulet."

Bagnatti and Lattaruzzo's bodies had been stripped bare of rings, watches, chains, a bracelet and even a St. Christopher's medal that, according to Stefano, Vincente Lattaruzzo never took off. No memory stick.

"Do you know his movements the day he died?" Natalia asked.

Corso shrugged. "He left work a little early. Said he was meeting a hot source. Always the source was 'hot.' That's the last we saw him."

Natalia thanked him for his cooperation, and Corso left them to their search. "Find anything?" she asked her partner who'd been trolling the monitor.

"A slide show of a three-way at Ernesto Scavullo's with

what looks like fifteen-year-old twins. A list of lovers who frequent his residence and do anyone and everyone in the house. Copies of receipts for ruby brooches and gold pendants purchased for Scavullo's favorites, including two African beauties he beds, mother and daughter."

She rocked back for a moment, away from the screen.

"Scavullo kept sex scores on everyone, including himself, like it was a bicycle race through the mountains."

"Anything about a German nanny?"

"Mmm. No German name."

"Her last name was something like Kleinst. This would've been about a year ago. She made some mistake while working for him or witnessed the wrong thing. Died in an accident that most likely wasn't. But there was no evidence of foul play and we couldn't touch Scavullo."

Angelina shook her head. "Nothing like that here. Just a long, wide stream of sex kittens, coming and going like Scavullo was running a playboy mansion or something. Ah, here are some notes on the Garduccis paying off someone to quash a story on a liaison gone wrong. And the director's involvement with a male subordinate named . . . Lattaruzzo."

Natalia worked her way through the magazines with Bagnatti's pieces earmarked, while Angelina backed up his computer onto discs and stickered the machine *Impounded*.

"Someone will be by to pick it up this afternoon," she told Corso's secretary as they left, wending their way back through the cubicle area and to the elevators. All was quiet. The elevator arrived. Natalia and her partner stepped in.

"Maybe the techs will find something on the actual computer," Angelina said. "Something deleted they can recover."

Natalia crossed her arms, watching the floor numbers flash by.

"Corso said Bagnatti left work early to meet a source. Could the hot source have been Vincente Lattaruzzo? And if so, what would Bagnatti have heard from him?"

Carlo Bagnatti's funeral was a sad affair, with just five mourners attending, absolutely lost in a side chapel of the enormous cathedral. In the vast dark space, the chapel was lighted only by a few candles. Pietro Fabretti, his old ballet school classmate, must have sent the enormous stand of lilies that flanked the casket. Fabretti stood beside it; next to him, a shriveled-looking woman in a black skirt and sweater.

Natalia wondered if the handful of people kneeling in the pews had wandered in, unaware of the private service. Probably. Even if Bagnatti had been widely loved, people would have been loath to attend. A Scavullo victim came with a halo of intimidation. No doubt the don had emissaries among the sparse group present to mete out punishment for any misbehavior or inappropriate outbursts denouncing him. Which made Pietro Fabretti a brave man, Natalia realized, despite what he'd said in his interview.

Dark glasses in place, he made the sign of the cross, kissed the tip of his fingers and dropped a white rose into the casket, then leaned in to kiss his friend's waxy forehead. A last hymn sounded, and the coffin was rolled out of a side entrance and into a glass-sided hearse. A gold Christ ornamented the hood. The mortician arranged a bank of pink gladiolas around the black coffin.

Natalia returned to the office where Angelina was poring through copies of *Rivelare* and *La Stella*, looking for columns or feature articles that might have led to their author's murder.

"Anything?" Natalia asked.

"Not yet, but listen to this: 'Italian police say they have seized a crocodile they believe was used by a suspected crime boss to terrorize people into paying protection money. The reptile was one point seven meters long and weighed forty kilos. It was found during a search at a man's home in the southern town of Caserta, where it was kept on the terrace and fed live rabbits in full view of neighboring homes. The suspect was charged with illegal animal possession. The crocodile has been sent to an animal rehabilitation center.'"

"Lucky animal," Natalia said.

"The owner is suspected of running several protection rackets in Caserta."

"The perp have a name?" Natalia asked.

"Negative."

"Right," Natalia said. "Someone was paid off then."

"And I thought Palermo was bad."

"It is. Here, too."

"Will we ever be free of it?" said Angelina.

"Naples?"

"Italy."

"That reminds me."

She phoned the Anti-Mafia Investigations Directorate to see if they had anything new on Ernesto Scavullo. They didn't. Then she phoned the Agenzia delle Entrate and spoke to the revenue service officers about the suspiciously conspicuous affluence of one Ernesto Scavullo and asked them to look into his fleet of incredibly expensive sports cars and limousines with an eye to income unreported and taxes unpaid. She read off license plate numbers that had accrued in the past six months, all issued to Scavullo, and the makes of the automobiles. The agent thanked her for the tip.

"Not necessary," she said. "My pleasure."

If she couldn't yet arrest Ernesto Scavullo, she'd settle for annoying him.

"You're going to piss off the don," Angelina said.

"One can hope."

Mariel's living room was orderly as usual, books arranged neatly in built-in cases, surfaces polished and clear. A votive candle flickered on the low-slung coffee table, the air perfumed with lilac scent. There were no random pieces of clothing strewn around, no piled up newspapers as in Natalia's apartment. Not a speck of dust. And to cap it off, there was Mariel herself, resplendent in a rose-colored caftan, welcoming her with a goblet of wine.

"You ever think about becoming a life coach?" Natalia sank into the yellow brocade couch. "How to live graciously—in my case, on a shoestring?"

Mariel laughed. "No, I hadn't. Bad day?"

"Better now." Natalia took a sip of the wine. "Yum."

"What's going on?" Mariel sat on a sling-backed chair. One of Natalia's favorites, with its slender carved frame and crimson cushion embroidered with peacocks and gryphons. "Trouble at work? Or is it Pino?"

"That, too. The job's getting to me, Em. I'm thinking twenty more years of this, and what do I have to look forward to—assuming I make it out alive? A lousy pension."

"That doesn't sound like my favorite criminalist. What about our plans? That Christmas cruise we promised we'd take, remember?"

"I know. We'll do it yet. I'm probably just tired at the moment. Burned out on this case. It's really getting to me."

"The murder of the two men found on the horse statue?"

"Yeah."

"You have the culprit yet?"

"Not yet."

"How's the new partner working out?"

"She's great. Plus adorable. Quick on the uptake. Doesn't take any shit from the men."

"Anything you want to talk about?"

"Not really. There's possible Camorra involvement so it might not be entirely safe for you to hear me out. But thanks for asking. Hopefully by the next time I see you, it'll be solved. Oh, this might interest you. I did run into an old admirer of yours."

"Not Massimo."

"Paolo Mora."

"You're kidding."

"Cross my heart. Remember we were just talking about him the other day? How sweet he was on you, how he waited for you after school? You barely gave him the time of day."

"My parents trained me. I was not to socialize with a certain class of people."

"How did I slip through the net?"

"For one thing, you were a girl, so that helped. For another, I loved you. And they would not deny their only child her best friend. Plus they adored you. Paolo—didn't he marry that girl whose family owned the pizza place on Via Rimini?"

"That he did," Natalia took another sip. "I guess working in the pizza shop didn't do it for him."

"He was cute," Mariel smoothed her hair. "He's still cute. Are they together, he and she?"

"Probably. He did ask about you, however."

"Really? You're not just saying it because I'm making you my extraordinary seafood risotto?"

"I swear."

"What did you tell him," Mariel said, "about me?"

"That you were as gorgeous as ever. I bet you could crook your finger, and he'd come running—wife or no wife. Hey! She's blushing!"

"Am not!"

"He's Ernesto Scavullo's bodyguard."

"Christ," Mariel put her drink down. "That is depressing. So—you don't have to answer—I take it Scavullo is a suspect in the killings? God, what a slime. Enough about them. Come out on the balcony. I have something to show you."

The pigeon had made a nest in a corner next to the railing. Her eggs were incubating on a pile of dirty straw and something that looked like plastic French fries.

Natalia crouched down. "When did this mama bird arrive?"

"I'm not sure. When I went out last night to water my plants, she was there. This morning she was off the nest. There are two eggs—perfect ovals."

Natalia moved closer to get a look.

"Careful. I read somewhere they don't like you to look at them directly in the eyes."

"Sounds like some men I've dated," Natalia said.

The magnolia across the street glowed in the last of the evening light. Its creamy blossoms nestled in the full dark leaves. Mariel persuaded Natalia to stay over and lent her a pair of white silk pajamas. Natalia slipped between the satin sheets in the guest room and laid her head on the down pillow.

"Stay strong," Mariel said as the friends kissed goodnight.

"Sweet dreams," Natalia closed her eyes. "Sweet dreams, dear friend."

Chapter 9

The morning was cool. Natalia showered and dressed. Up early, she made herself an espresso in Mariel's sunny kitchen. There was a vase of fresh daisies on the kitchen table, and Mariel had left croissants in a basket and a bowl of strawberries.

Natalia partook, washed her dishes, scribbled a thank you. She slipped the note under the vase and let herself out as quietly as she could.

A block along, she bumped into a street market. Lettuce bulged from their crates. A melon that had rolled into the street had been run over, its gold pulp attracting pigeons. Two elderly women helped one another up the steps to St. Felicity for early Mass. She was in her old boyfriend's neighborhood.

As far as she knew, Gino's father was still alive, his apartment steps away. When Natalia and Gino had been together, they ate dinner with the old man once or twice a week.

Signor Valdutti lived in an ocher *palazzo*. A baroque gate opened to a stately courtyard. No mops and brooms, no laundry flapping on lines. Pink and black marble stones led to a fountain in the middle. Just inside the building a shiny brass elevator whisked them to the top floor. Everything tasteful and quiet.

His father's maid didn't live in, but she came in each day, shopping in hand, then set about to cook and serve the evening meal. There were the elegant, red, cut-glass goblets for the wine and many leisurely courses served on gold-rimmed plates. The quiet, art-filled apartment should have fostered the illusion that the fangs of the outside world could not reach in to bite you there. But Natalia always felt gloomy at Gino's father's place. Perhaps because of the massive old furniture and heavy damask drapes or the dull amber glow cast by the antique lamps.

Gino's father had started life as a humble cabinetmaker. After the war his luck changed. He started to repair antiques damaged by the bombing. Because his workshop had been destroyed, he worked on the street. He glued and clamped and curved the frames. If it wasn't raining, the pieces were left on the streets to dry. In the course of his work, he acquired many treasures sold for a fraction of their worth, given him in lieu of payment or simply abandoned when their owners died unexpectedly.

With them he started a shop. The wealthy liked doing business with him, and in a few years he himself was well off, though his wealth hadn't protected him from the loss of his beloved wife when Gino was only three. Father and son were close, despite the fact that Gino had been raised mostly by his mother's parents in Caserta.

After several glasses of wine and a couple of shots of anisette taken at the long oak table, the old man would often wax philosophical: something along the lines that when you understood life, it was over.

It hadn't made much sense to Natalia then. Did he mean it took a lifetime to understand what life was about? Or was it that a life without mystery was no longer worth living?

In the florid, well-fed man, there were traces of the hungry boy. He was never as animated as when he regaled Natalia and his son about the war. Did they know that after the war you could buy anything *sfuso*, loose? This included cigarettes, codfish, bananas, oil. Bottles were scarce. People carried their own to be filled with milk or oil or petrol. The bottles were cleaned and reused as there weren't anymore.

And he'd ruined Natalia's appetite on more than one occasion, describing a wartime meal in which someone had been fed a meal of cat.

His bedroom was taken up with his and his beloved's enormous matrimonial bed and two giant wardrobes. In one, he kept all of his wife's clothing, which he had cleaned once a year. In the lavatory, on a shelf directly over the sink, was a crystal bottle of Chanel perfume half empty, its pink rubber atomizer faded to dusky rose.

Gino found his father's shrines morbid. He'd tried to talk to him about them once or twice, told him living in the past did no good. His father needed to get on with his life, even find someone new. The man hadn't taken it well, and Gino finally realized it was of no use.

"They remind him of her," Natalia said. "What's the harm in it? It's so romantic."

"Romance," he'd answered, "the ultimate delusion."

Gino's other complaint was about her vocation. He did not want her doing such dangerous work. He wanted her instead to travel with him as he toured. As soon as they were married, she knew the objections and pressure would escalate.

Natalia's other complaint about Gino was that he was so practical, never exhibiting much in the way of impulsive behavior or romantic sentiments. That he treated her well—better than any of her previous boyfriends—was not in dispute. But the spark just wasn't there. Pino, on the other hand . . . Plus, he was a Carabinieri himself and could hardly object to her choice of professions. Though he presented other problems.

Where was the balance? Natalia wondered. Did anyone ever find it?

Outside the bank, a gypsy picked clothes out of the dumpster and laid them on the ground. A young woman wobbled by on her motorcycle, heavily weighed down with a knapsack and the two children she was delivering to school. Natalia wondered if she was happy. But maybe happy didn't have anything to do with it.

A young man pushed past Natalia and ran. He caught up to a girl in a black halter top, matching jeans and high heels. "Lara! I told you I was at work! I was working!"

"You take me for an idiot? Like your other whores?"

"Lara! That's no way to talk. Come on, sweetheart." His fedora was pushed back on his head. He put his arms around her, and she shoved him away. Natalia could see the mascara streaked where she'd been crying.

Angelina was waiting for her outside the building, as they had arranged.

"I'm sorry," Natalia said, as Stefano Grappi opened the door. "We didn't call before we came. Is this a convenient time?"

It took him a second to adjust to their uniforms. "No, it's

fine," he said and led them into the living room. It was as pristine as it had been during Natalia's last visit except for boxes piled in a corner.

"I'm organizing Vincente's collection. A couple of museums have expressed an interest. Frankly, I'm glad for the interruption. Please, sit down."

Natalia and Angelina sat side by side on a yellow-and-white striped silk chaise lounge. Natalia identified its carved frame as Victorian. She didn't remember it from the last visit.

She removed her hat. "We need to ask you a few more questions. They're quite personal. Are you okay with that?"

Stefano nodded.

They had agreed ahead of time that Natalia would take the lead in the questioning.

"Did you and Vincente ever engage in sexual games of a violent nature?"

He didn't answer right away. "Vincente . . . liked it—rough. Me, not so much. At the beginning, he dragged me to a few clubs. Finally, I refused to go anymore. I like to look at erotic art in a gallery, I told him. Simulations, even a performance piece, but the actual thing I could do without. For some reason, Vincente was fascinated with mutilation, too. I told him I thought it was self-hatred in disguise. He said it got him off. I'm pretty conservative that way. It frustrated Vincente at times."

"What did he do about it?"

"Put up with it, mostly. Now and then he went out alone. Sometimes he came back with injuries."

"What kind of injuries?"

"Cuts mostly. Not that serious. He did need stitches once."

"When was this?"

"Two years ago."

"Did he tell you who had done it to him?"

"I didn't want to know. We had an arrangement. It worked. Sort of. God—" Stefano teared up. "Sorry."

"No. Take your time."

"I'm okay. Go ahead."

"Can you tell us the name of some of these clubs where Vincente used to go?"

"Sure. Give me a minute." He went into another room.

Natalia and Angelina made eye contact but didn't speak. Angelina looked down to write something in her notebook; Natalia surveyed the room. A tidy man, Stefano—everything orderly. A mural of giant yellow blossoms adorned a wall. Beneath it a pitcher of wild flowers artfully arranged and color coordinated, the leaves stripped from the stems, not crammed in as Natalia would have done. A man who liked order and wore slippers inside to keep his floors pristine. Was he, like Director Garducci, made angry if things didn't go neatly? From the window, a view of rooftops and the cathedral across the street. Peaceful.

"Sorry," he said. "It took me a minute." He handed Natalia a sheet of linen stationery listing the clubs.

"I found receipts for the clubs and this art place—CAM, it's called. The director is—was—a friend of Vincente's. He came to a couple of our dinner parties. I don't think there was anything between them, though I'm not sure. Anyway, he knows all about the gay scene in Naples and psycho-sexual art. His gallery is at the heart of it."

Natalia folded the list and put it in her bag. "Are you aware the other murder victim, Carlo Bagnatti, left his worldly possessions to Vincente?"

"The gossip columnist?"

"Yes, the tabloid reporter."

"No."

"So you're unaware that you are the named second beneficiary in the event of Vincente Lattaruzzo's demise?"

"I'm at a total loss. Why would Bagnatti have me in his will? I've never even met the man."

"Yes, it is curious. Well, I'm sure his executor will be in touch. Thank you for your time, and I'm sorry if we upset you."

"No. It's all right. My doctor said I shouldn't repress it, so this is good. I'm trying to cope with it, you know? There are good days and bad."

Back on the street, Natalia paused at the car and looked back at Stefano Grappi's building.

"What do you think?" Angelina said.

"I don't know what to think. He's either innocent, or he's a good actor."

Natalia drove them to Casoria and the gallery that Stefano had indicated did cutting edge performance pieces involving homoerotic themes. The CAM Gallery stood tucked in between a couple of factories on a nondescript block at the edge of the financial district. Trucks occupied most of the street, but they found enough space to park right by the ornate front emblazoned with street art done in competing styles.

"What do you have to be to get in here," Angelina said, "a muscle builder?" as she tugged on a thick iron bar camouflaged amongst the scrawl of graffiti. Entering, they stepped into one large room with high ceilings—an enormous white cube. The walls appeared empty of art, other than for something hanging on the far side of the room. While Natalia answered her phone, Angelina went ahead to look. A few moments later, Natalia followed, gazing at the single art piece as she crossed the empty, open space.

It was a reverse mirror, its frame made of crushed bottle caps. As Natalia approached, her reflection receded into it until she darkened and disappeared.

"Infinity," someone said.

They hadn't heard him come up. Shorter than Natalia, the skinny man wore a ubiquitous black t-shirt and tight fitting black pants and, on his face, round tortoise-shell glasses.

"Fascinating, isn't it? It's Paolo Vertucci. He's going to be big. I'm Domenico Bertolli," he said, maintaining eye contact.

"Captain Natalia Monte. My associate, Angelina Cavatelli. We're here about Vincente Lattaruzzo . . . and this man." She held up a morgue photo of Carlo Bagnatti. "Do you recognize him?"

"Afraid not, no. How may I be of use?"

"You had a show," Angelina said and looked up from her notes. "Back in November, wasn't it? 'Homo Sapiens'?"

"Two performance pieces and the rest . . . photographic studies."

"There was some protest," she said. "A couple of officers from the municipal vice squad put in an appearance."

Domenico Bertolli looked miffed. "Yes, well, so far Italy is not a police state, try as it might. Where are we going with this? I'm quite busy today."

Angelina held up a hand. "There were images in the show involving genital mutilation. Any chance we can see them?"

"Sold out, I'm afraid. They're in the hands of private individuals. So, no, it would not be convenient."

"Convenience isn't really of consequence," Natalia said. "We'll need the names of the owners then and the photographer. According to the press coverage, he was anonymous."

"And still is. The artist prefers to remain unknown."

"Surely not to you."

"*Au contraire.* I am equally in the dark."

"How were arrangements made?"

"Through a third party. Look, I'm sure the exhibition isn't relevant to your investigation. So what's this about?"

"That's not your call," Angelina said.

Natalia said, "No artist named, no provenance. How did that affect pricing?"

Domenico shrugged. "Fifty-thousand euros a print."

"My, my. And no one batted an eyelash?" Natalia remarked. "Were you and Vincente Lattaruzzo lovers?"

She'd switched gears. Angelina cast her a furtive glance. Bertolli seemed surprised, too.

"Is that pertinent?" he snapped, irritation turning to hostility.

"What do you think?" *Asshole.* Natalia almost said it out loud. "Did you have relations with him?"

"Once or twice."

"Which?"

"I don't keep track of every dalliance."

"Any rough play?"

"None of your business. However, generally I prefer my anatomy whole, if that's what you're getting at."

"Was Vincente Lattaruzzo in any of the photographs?" she said.

He didn't answer immediately.

"Sir?"

"Yes," he said.

"You must have some record, if only a set of contact prints or Polaroids."

Domenico ushered them into his office just off the gallery and reached into his lower desk drawer. Out came an oversize catalogue.

"I want it back."

Angelina snatched it up. "We'll be in touch."

They marched back across the gallery in step like soldiers, their footfalls sounding in the hollow space.

"Creep," Angelina said as they walked out to the car. "You think he was involved?"

"No, though you can't rule him out automatically. Damn. The list of suspects is supposed to be narrowing. Instead it's growing. You want to drive?"

"Sure." Angelina came around to the driver's side. "I may need some navigational assistance."

"No problem." Natalia slid into the passenger's seat.

"I've never understood modern art." Angelina said. They snapped their seatbelts in place, and Angelina started the engine. "Am I missing something?"

"Don't judge by that. You should have had my favorite professor. Cesa loved art—the more modern, the better. Before her, I wouldn't look at anything past the Impressionists. She really opened my eyes. You should have seen the woman: combat boots, frothy blouses, wild hair. One of just a handful of female professors at the university. Her 'Sexuality in Art' lectures had a waiting list every term."

Natalia hadn't thought of Cesa in a long while. She had been pushed out by the cabal of male professors who ran the department.

"My Giuletta took some painting courses in college," Angelina said. "She's always trying to drag me to galleries. I said to her: 'What's wrong with my liking just Caravaggio?'"

"Nothing."

"Yeah. But I should try to be more open-minded, no? Broaden my horizons? Plus, maybe it would help the relationship."

"Trouble?"

"Nah. Couples are work, right?"

"I'm not sure I remember," Natalia said, as Angelina eased the car out of their parking spot. "Listen, get in touch with Vincente Lattaruzzo's literary agent and get a copy of his manuscript. And run a history on CAM and Mr. Creepy Domenico Bertolli."

"My pleasure," Angelina said. "Why is it you never hear about lesbians mutilating one another to get off?"

"Superior gender."

"Precisely, Captain Monte."

Natalia pushed the air conditioning button up a notch. "A promiscuous young man, Vincente."

"Stefano may have been in denial," Angelina said, "and jealous of Garducci. Then again, Garducci sacrificed his straight life and his marriage only to find he had committed himself to Vincente Lattaruzzo, a man still involved with his domestic partner and maybe others, like Domenico Bertolli at the gallery and the gossip columnist who shared his last moments, Bagnatti."

"You're saying maybe one of his paramours got jealous, trapped Vincente in bondage sex-play with another and took his vengeance."

Natalia exhaled, lips pursed, thinking.

"Any or all of his lovers may have felt betrayed and angered by the late Vincente Lattaruzzo. We don't even know all his partners."

"He seems like the type to have had a lot of anonymous encounters," Angelina said. "Hard to trace."

They drove through the town center, past a large building with an enormous gate. Two policemen in blue jackets and teal trousers stood guard on either side of a pole that bore a huge heraldic flag.

"Casoria City Hall," Natalia announced. "Turn here. It's a shortcut to the highway."

Angelina braked sharply, and the car veered into a narrow cobbled street that seemed to have no reason for its existence other than to show off the blue flowering vines that covered the backs of ancient houses. Two old men at a tiny café touched their caps as the car rolled past.

"Probably can't see well enough to make us as female Carabinieri," Angelina giggled. "Their hearts wouldn't have stood the shock."

"Pretty spot, isn't it?" Natalia said.

"Reminds me of Sicily." Angelina shifted and sped up.

"Miss it?" Natalia glanced over.

"It will be better for the two of us here," Angelina said. "Palermo is a fishbowl, yet so much remains hidden and will always be so."

"Don't think it's any different here," Natalia said. She thumbed through the catalogue.

"What are you seeing?" Angelina said.

"Penises and hedge clippers. Penises and razor blades. A crucified scrotum, pinned to plywood." She stopped abruptly. "Oh, my."

"What?" Angelina said.

Natalia held it up.

Angelina, driving, shook her head. "I can't look. Tell me."

"Two naked men, masked, cavorting astride a marble horse. I think the one in front may be Vincente. He's lying flat on the back of this huge stone horse, and he's got a gag in his mouth that's being used as a bit by the one behind, who appears to be buggering him."

Angelina reached over and drew the hand and catalogue closer to quickly glance. "Wow."

"It's not exactly the look of the victims in the *contessa*'s garden, but it may well have inspired the killers."

"Killers? Plural. It's official?"

"It's been pretty certain from the start if you think about it."

Back at the station, they hung up their hats and uniform jackets and examined the catalogue more closely. Most images were black and white, the tones muted, figures shadowed. Others were focused and vividly clear. One showed a crumbling wall and a niche with a skull and bones. Taken in the city's underground? Possibly. The police had become more rigorous about controlling access to the vast subterranean structures below Naples. Since the Greeks it had remained a repository of myth and bones. Modern artifacts accumulated, too, from the war years when the city was bombed, and the populace took shelter in the vast underground caverns and tunnels and the ossuaries beneath churches. Self-appointed urban archeologists snuck in regularly to search for personal articles left behind during the war, like old Zenith radios, love letters, a Doro tricycle ridden through the dank caverns by someone's child as war raged above.

Natalia remembered Marshal Cervino's story of a German couple arrested the previous summer at Fiumicino Airport. At the bottom of their luggage, wrapped in a Gucci scarf, the customs men had discovered a cache of fascist memorabilia and a child's skull.

"Incredible," Natalia said, looking at the catalogue.

"What?" Angelina leaned over to see. It was a photographic study of someone with a clerical collar—and little else—being masturbated, while a naked devil used a cross on him as a dildo. She gasped. "It's titled 'Sacrilege.'"

"Appropriately enough."

Natalia was surprised the exhibit hadn't gotten anyone arrested or stirred more controversy in the press. But could these images have gotten people killed? Were they meant as social commentary? A stab at church clergy? No wonder Domenico had been so defensive.

"I wonder how the tabloids missed this," Angelina said, coming again to the photograph of Vincente being sodomized on a marble horse.

Natalia slipped the catalogue into her desk and locked it. "Don't even whisper that in here. Walls have ears in Naples."

Chapter 10

They convened in Dr. Agari's oddly pleasant and warm office at the morgue, its air filled with the rich fragrance of coffee and chemicals. The decor colors were all warm: rust and beige, interspersed with scarlet curtains and cadmium blue cushions. Natalia and Angelina settled themselves on a comfortable couch. Angelina hated mortuaries but found the pathologist's office pleasant, she explained, in contrast to the gurneys and grim steel desks and fluorescent lights of the coroner's office in Palermo.

Dr. Agari looked lovely in a violet silk blouse and white skirt. Also exhausted and stressed.

"What's wrong?" Natalia said.

"Nothing. I just had to reattach a head. Not my favorite thing."

Angelina grimaced. "They catch the perpetrator?"

"No, no. This was from a horrendous traffic accident," said Dr. Agari. "Also, modern embalming and body preparation is so demanding. Not like the old days. They'd remove the entrails, bathe the body in lemon water, fill the body cavity with straw and were done. They didn't have to reattach many heads."

"The good old days?" Natalia said. "When I was in the Third Form, the sisters made us go down into an ossuary beneath a church. The dead were bones, skeletons fully dressed and standing upright, except for the young virgins and girl children. They lay on the ground with crowns on their heads."

"Sounds creepy," Angelina volunteered.

"So," Natalia said, "what do we have here?"

Francesca flipped open her file. "There were traces of animal blood on both bodies and in the surround."

"Animal blood?" Natalia said and took a sip of coffee.

Francesca nodded. "Pig, cow, goat . . . A lot of traces in the swabs that came back from the crime scene."

"You think they were doing animal sacrifices?" Angelina asked. "Part of some weird ritual?"

"No, Officer Cavatelli," Dr. Agari said. "I believe the two died where animals are butchered."

"A slaughterhouse."

"Right," Francesca said. "The knife used to mutilate was most likely a butcher's blade designed for dismembering cattle."

Natalia said, "Camorra are known partners in at least three abattoirs, and I'm sure they have their hooves in many more."

"God," Angelina said, grimacing. "What didn't they do to these two poor people. . ."

"The question so far avoided," said Natalia. "Sexual activity?"

Francesca glanced at her report. "Vincente Lattaruzzo suffered tears in the mucosal lining of the rectum and colon. Likewise Bagnatti, who also suffered perforations of the bowel and near the sigmoid curve at the top of the rectum that leads into the ascending colon. Both would have required emergency medical care and surgery had they survived."

"Were they raped?"

"Both men were anally penetrated but not by a penis."

"Hand balling?" Angelina said.

"What's hand balling?" Natalia asked.

"Fist fucking," Angelina said.

"The slow introduction of a hand into a body cavity," Francesca explained.

"A hand?" Natalia said, incredulous.

"By the way," Francesca said, "you did note where Vincente Lattaruzzo's testicles were found?"

Natalia balanced her cup on the wide arm of the chair. "In the other victim's mouth, yes."

"Symbolic perhaps?" Francesca said. "Maybe he talked out of turn. And the killers wanted to make their point. The cosmetics might have been a further insult and humiliation of the victims, Nat."

"Including the white dots at the outside corners of their eyes?"

"White dots?" Angelina said.

"She's still reading the reports," Natalia said. "We're keeping Corporal Cavatelli quite busy."

"Of course," Dr. Agari said. "First week on the job."

"Compared to Palermo, it's a picnic so far."

"She's still in the honeymoon phase," Natalia said. "Her boss hasn't transformed into an incompetent ogre yet."

"Don't listen to Captain Monte," Francesca said. "Hasn't ever happened. We've worked together—what?—seven years. You've done well and come far, Nat."

"Starting out late as I did, I had to try and make up for lost time."

"Which you most certainly did," Dr. Agari said.

Natalia flipped open a postmortem loose leaf on the coffee table and turned to a color close-up of Vincente Lattaruzzo's eyes. Angelina leaned forward to look.

"See?" Natalia said. "Heavy coke users once put cosmetic white dots next to their eyes to obscure the gray caste. It used to be common, a subtle sign of one's decadence. A much dated practice now."

"Were drugs involved?" Angelina asked.

"Nothing of note in their systems. Insignificant traces of cocaine and marijuana in both bodies."

"So they had no serious levels of drugs in their blood?"

"No," said Francesca. "Though they may have wished they did, given what they endured."

Angelina made a face as she skimmed through the autopsy photos. "Slaughtered in an abbatoir and delivered to the *contessa*'s garden butchered. Lovely."

"You have anything on the worker's shirt at the scene?"

"Very old, very stained with badly deteriorated dried blood. Not from either victim. Eight stab marks in the fabric: seven slits in front, one in back."

"The blood," Natalia said. "How old?"

"Decades. Half a century?"

"The sign of an old score settled?" Natalia said. "A killing avenged?"

Dr. Agari nodded. "Possibly."

It was Camorra custom for a wife and mother to remove the shirt from the slain. The women would kiss the wounds and suck at the blood of the beloved, saying, *Likewise may I drink the blood of the man who killed you.*

The shirt would be handed down from generation to

generation, preserved until the time of vengeance. Had an ancient blood debt been settled there in the *contessa*'s magnificent garden?

Natalia thanked Francesca for her time and departed with her young partner.

"So," Angelina said, as they left the morgue, "you think we have a Camorra hit? A vengeance killing?"

"An old vendetta? Could be."

"So what now, Captain?"

"Well, Scavullo is practically broadcasting his involvement, though he's made sure he's left nothing to connect him. He's not insane—certainly homophobic. But why draw attention to himself?"

"Perhaps it was business or, as you said, the settlement of an old score for someone else. That fits him more than any other theory."

"Who've we got? Who do we press next?"

Angelina stopped and ticked them off on her fingers. "Stefano Grappi? Director Garducci? Ernesto Scavullo? Persons unknown?"

Natalia squinted in the bright sunlight. "Garducci. We're overdue on a run at Garducci."

"Good," said Angelina. "I've come up with more ammunition."

A lone royal palm towered over the entrance to the museum. It had survived there for years despite the pollution from the heavy traffic on Cavour. Somehow the pink brick of the giant edifice had not been completely tarnished. Likewise the large marble columns that flanked the entrance, dirty though they were. And somehow, despite the roar of cars and motorbikes, the parked cars and hulking tour buses, Natalia always felt a sense of tranquility as soon as she climbed the steps and made her away across the tuff stone.

In the soaring vestibule, the security guards greeted them with a friendly salute. A lone tourist stashed a lime green backpack in a tiny metal locker in the coatroom as they passed through the turnstile. Some unseen docent lectured loudly in German; the halls carried her voice into the cavernous lobby.

As a student, Natalia had liked the Farnese Collection on the ground floor in the corridor of river deities and for many hours had strolled between the fountain sculptures, imagining them and the fountains as they once were, water flowing from the mouths of cherubs, angels, gargoyles, lions, dragons, the breasts of women. She'd liked the gem collection on the second floor the best.

Natalia led the way through the gift shop and out onto the courtyard's unkempt grass. Greek and Roman sculptures were placed without seeming rhyme or reason, many of them broken and eroded. Along the corridor hung large stone sarcophagi engraved with assorted mythological scenes—Prometheus, centaur Nereidi. Myths to comfort the dead, Natalia thought, long after it was of any use to them. Among the ragged greenery, she recognized a Japanese camellia, the lone bloom a sudden white glow.

"Is this where?" Angelina said.

Natalia hesitated. Where? Ah. Her partner meant the garden where Garducci and Vincente had been discovered: lovers in the darkness, away from the world.

"Yes," she said. "By the way, Colonel Fabio wants to give us Marshal Cervino to help with the case."

Angelina glanced at her superior. "Didn't you warn me against the marshal?"

"Yes. He's a great cop and a hopeless misogynist. Not a fan of women on the force."

"What's it mean?"

Natalia grimaced. "Fabio is applying pressure."

Going down a long gallery and up a graceful staircase to the second floor, they passed through a collection of Pompeii treasures and followed a wine-colored carpet down a long grey corridor to a door. They disregarded the request to knock and entered. Dr. Garducci's secretary glowed in the light of his computer screen, his dark hair curly and his eyes like coal.

"May I help you?"

"We're here to see the director."

"Have you an appointment?"

Angelina shook her head. "No."

"Oh . . . let me check."

He slipped through a heavy wooden door and disappeared, returned and asked them to follow. Director Garducci's somber office was rococo and elegant. Heavy damask drapes closed out the sun. A baroque couch and silk-upholstered chairs occupied a large corner sitting area. The director sat at an ornately carved desk, its surface uncluttered, the workspace of a perfectionist used to others taking care of mundane tasks. Behind him hung a fresco from the Villa di Giulia that Natalia recognized from another life.

He rose and showed them to chairs facing him.

"What brings the pleasure of your company, Captain, and . . . ?"

"Corporal Cavatelli," Natalia said.

"How do you do? Please, sit," he said. "I thought my part in your investigation was over." He folded his hands in front of him, a pale contrast to the hand-tooled leather blotter.

"On the contrary," said Natalia.

Angelina broke in. "Does the name Brazzo mean anything to you—Roberto Brazzo?"

"He was someone I . . . saw before I declared myself publicly to be gay."

"According to Mr. Brazzo, you and he *saw* each other a little over a year ago. You wanted an exclusive relationship, though you were still married at the time. When he declined, you lost your temper and struck him, quite severely and repeatedly. Your housekeeper and your wife got him medical attention. There was considerable blood loss and damage to his scalp and face . . . and your pocketbook."

Garducci made a steeple of his fingers but said nothing.

"Mr. Brazzo banked quite a lot of money soon after the incident. Paid down to buy his silence perhaps?"

"Are you suggesting that I, in a jealous lover's blind rage, shot Vincente dead and the other man he was apparently fucking, then hauled the two of them into Contessa Cavazza's estate in the middle of the night and mounted them atop a bronze steed in a homoerotic pose?" He dismissed the accusation with the briefest wave. "Please."

Angelina took out her folder and removed a copy of a photograph. She slid it across the empty desk.

"Are you trying to shake me?" Garducci said. "I don't have the—"

Natalia slid the CAM catalogue across to the director, held open to a page.

"This was a photographic study recently exhibited at the CAM Gallery. The exhibit drew quite a lot of attention. You may recognize someone in the piece."

"Jesus," he said, staring at the masked image of his former lover.

"You'd not seen it before?"

"No," he said, hand to his cheek.

"Something of an exhibitionist—Vincente."

Garducci didn't take his eyes from the photograph.

"You said Vincente was preparing to move in with you?"

"Yes."

"Stefano Grappi says not."

Angelina said, "Did Vincente change his mind, decide he didn't want a monogamous relationship, like Mr. Brazzo before him?"

"We've been over that," Garducci said, pushing the photo away, the ruby stud perfect in his sagging earlobe.

"We won't trouble you further then, Director." Natalia rose, Angelina following. "Oh," she said, turning back. "You may want to retain an attorney."

"I have one, thank you."

"A criminal defender." She took an envelope from her shoulder bag and passed it across. "Nearly forgot."

"What is it?" Garducci said.

"An order to surrender your passport by four o'clock today. You've been officially cited as a person of interest in the investigation of two murders. Please don't make plans to leave Naples without securing permission from us. Meanwhile, I'm officially advising you not to try leaving the country. Border crossings and airports have already been alerted. In such an event, you will be made a guest in our humble accommodations. Remand in your own custody would be unlikely. Good day."

In the elevator, Angelina checked her phone for text messages. "Your friend Carlo Busto in the Municipal Building is summoning me to the Archives."

"I'll drop you. Meet me back at the station when you're done."

Returning to Casanova, she went straight to Marshal Cervino's tiny office. His secretary, in short spandex skirt and gladiator heels, guarded the door. Cervino was the only officer besides Colonel Fabio who had a secretary. Whether because of valor in the field or a debt owed, no one was really sure.

She held up an index finger, phone cradled to her ear, applying purple nail polish at the same time. Natalia brushed past and into Cervino's lair to stand over him at his desk. A frayed oatmeal-colored carpet and a dead rubber tree were the only decorations besides a teddy bear.

Cervino looked up, unlit cigar in his mouth, and noticed her staring at the bear.

"When I was a kid, my older brother short changed Salvino Grappo two *lire* on a carton of cigarettes. Grappo shot him in the face. Manny was thirteen." Cervino picked up the bear from his desk and shook it. "This was his favorite creature. Got it on his last birthday. Battery must have run out. Too bad. He dances and says dirty words."

"Marshal, you're invading my space."

"Is this by way of a warning, Captain Monte?"

"More like a trespass notice. Keep off my patch."

"You're over your head with this double murder."

"I'll let you know when I need your help. Meantime, stay clear. Stop lobbying the colonel."

"You have a problem, Captain, whenever Camorra is involved."

"Really."

"Yes. I grew up with the same scum you did, but I never fraternized with them."

"Are you offering social advice?" Natalia said.

"It's common knowledge you bedded your partner. Maybe we chalk that up to inexperience. We were all naïve once, eh? Matters of internal security are another matter. You need to decide."

"Decide what?"

"If you are with us or them."

"Thank you so much, Marshal Cervino, for your concern and wise counsel."

Natalia returned to her desk and read the unfinished manuscript by Vincente Lattaruzzo that his publisher had emailed over. When Angelina returned, Natalia said, "How did it go?"

"You'd better look at this." Angelina tossed a sheaf of papers on Natalia's desk and settled in to wait.

Natalia read the twelve pages of history on the Countess Cavazza and the several photocopies and picked up the phone.

The same bird greeted her with a lovely five-note trill as she entered the long drive lined with magnolias that eventually led to the garden path. The countess rose as Natalia approached the patio. She wore a silver caftan over billowing white pants that set off her coloring well.

"Captain, welcome. You look so . . . official and imposing in uniform."

"Thank you for seeing me, Contessa."

"Not at all. Happy for the company. I hope you haven't eaten. I thought it would be pleasant to have a bite in the garden—some fruit and cheese?"

"Sounds wonderful."

The countess reached out and brought a blossom to her face. "What fragrance these have. You know them?" she said. "The garland of Artemis?"

A bird darted from a neighboring branch and was gone.

"Artemis of Ephaseus." Natalia said. "One of my favorite sculptures when I was a student."

"Of course," the countess said. "I remember now. In that article I read about you. You were an art history student before you became a Carabiniere. Isn't that right?"

"You have quite a memory."

"Only for what interests me, I'm afraid. So what steered you from your course?"

"It's a long story."

"If it isn't against regulations, perhaps someday you will tell me what happened. Artemis of Ephaseus," she repeated. "Sometimes I have my driver take me to see the statue on a Sunday, when all the visitors are gone. Being a board member has its perks. Did you know the Museo Archeologico was the only museum standing after the war?"

"So much was lost."

"It looked like the end of the world," the countess continued. "The price of an ordinary chicken shot up to three hundred *lire*, and soon a million *lire* couldn't have bought one bird. Then Allies bombed the port and the city. Twenty-two thousand dead. Many lived in the streets with rags for clothes. Many died from cholera. And many killed themselves. The Allies advanced. The partisans burned farms. Slaughtered innocent people."

"How awful," Natalia said.

"It was. On the twelfth of September, 1943, political fugitives who had hidden in the Ospedale Incurabili armed themselves and attacked the fascists' infantry. Ordinary citizens, Carabinieri, even children, saved the bridge over Via Sanita. As a parting lesson, the Germans torched the university and the magnificent Royal Society library."

The countess paused, remembering something.

"I was hungry but comparatively healthy even as

destitution and disease reigned. I wanted to do something for the stricken but lacked any medical training. Mercifully so, perhaps. To be perfectly frank, I am better with creatures than with people. So I took up work with the Venus Fixers. You've heard of them."

"Rescuers of art treasures."

"There I could be of use, especially after the Allies landed. I spoke French and some English. Paltry but enough, and that's how I became the liaison with the Americans. We catalogued every monument, mural, church, fresco, statue. Americans and Italians working together: artists, art historians, craftspeople. It's not like now with all the squabbling and intellectualizing. A great deal was saved. Here in Naples, only the Angevin frescoes in Santa Chiara were beyond repair, and I wept for them."

"I've only seen them in photographs," Natalia said. "A great loss."

"Enough nostalgia," said the countess. "Come."

The plush, flowery cushions on the garden chairs were surprisingly comfortable. The maid brought out a large platter with dishes of mango and pineapple and a variety of cheeses and placed them on the round, glass-topped table alongside two chilled glasses of pinot grigio and a full carafe.

"The bread basket, Ida," the countess reminded.

"Yes, ma'am." She set out individual plates and knives.

Natalia sampled the brie. "Delicious."

"How goes the investigation?" the countess said.

"Well enough, but we haven't wrapped it up as yet."

"No doubt you can't talk about it. I shouldn't have asked." She smiled. "Shameless curiosity."

"Not at all. In fact, I'm hoping to clear some up today."

The maid appeared with the bread and offered it to Natalia before setting it down.

"Thank you." Natalia took a slice and added some brie as she addressed the countess. "I can't help wondering why Vincente and the Mr. Bagnatti were brought to your garden."

"I've wondered myself."

"I also keep wondering why you omitted mentioning the extent of your friendship with Vincente Lattaruzzo."

"I thought I'd explained. I'd confided my humiliation?"

"Not association?"

"How do you mean?"

"You're originally from Cantalupo."

"Yes," the countess said, absently winding the stem of her wineglass.

"Vincente Lattaruzzo's parents were from there as well."

"Mmm. I believe that's right."

"Do you know where Ernesto Scavullo is from?" Natalia said.

"Cantalupo."

"Yes . . . so you knew that, too?"

"Most certainly. If I didn't already know, the newspapers remind us at every turn, almost as if Naples were trying to disown him."

"Apparently Scavullo's father—Gianni—was like you, barely in his teens during the war—among the region's youngest resistance members. He worked closely with your father."

"Papa was a farmer with large holdings. Gentry. He and the Scavullos didn't have much in common except their hatred of the Black Shirts and Mussolini. They conspired against the fascists. Later fought side by side against the Germans as partisans. Young Gianni Scavullo took up arms to kill fascists, which he did with great efficiency. He was a very good strategist and an even better shot."

"At twelve?"

"Twelve . . . fourteen. Somewhere in there. My father befriended him. When the Allies invaded, father took on the task of helping escaped prisoners of war, hid them. In the forests, on farms, sometimes out in the open, working as field hands. They rescued so many."

"Brave men," Natalia said.

"That they were. The Germans hung him. My beloved papa. With piano wire."

Chapter 11

Natalia returned to the station and found Dr. Agari waiting.

"I just spoke with the *contessa*," she said, as she followed Natalia into the office.

"How did it go?"

"The *contessa* is quite an amazing woman," Natalia answered, "as I'm sure you know."

"Quite a story, isn't it?"

Natalia nodded. "You knew all of it?"

"Not all. Not until I was grown. She opened up to you," Francesca said. "That is unusual. My grandmother was aware, of course," she went on. "Even though Nella rarely spoke of her father's arrest and execution or the dreadful man who denounced him to the Germans. Her mother lost her mind. She was institutionalized. An aunt here in Naples took Nella in, and she turned up one day at the school my grandmother attended. Nella wouldn't speak to anyone.

My *nonna* eventually won her trust, and she befriended me as well. We all remained devoted friends. It was my *nonna* who introduced Nella to the *conte*. They married and were happy for forty years."

"There weren't any children, I take it."

"No. What's not in the official files is that Nell, in her teens, was arrested by the Italian fascists after her father's imprisonment and discovered to be with child. She had sought solace in a wartime romance and gotten pregnant. They operated on her, aborted the fetus, and deliberately sterilized her as punishment."

"My God."

"When she came out of the anesthesia, the doctor, wearing full fascist regalia under his white coat, quoted Mussolini to her. You know, the one about those with empty cradles having no right to empire?"

"Jesus, how vile."

"You think she may have been involved?"

"She lost her father to the German fascists because of the Lattaruzzos, and now you're telling me she lost a child to the Italian fascists. I don't want to think it possible of her to wish for vengeance, but I just don't know."

"Are you adding her to your list of suspects?"

"I have no choice at the moment."

"If you could be discreet about it . . ."

"Of course."

"Have a good evening, Captain."

"You, too, Doctor," she said, wondering how Francesca would enjoy hers, troubled as she must be about the possibility her Nella was involved in a vicious crime.

The mops and buckets had been taken in. The door was open. A lone fluorescent bulb lighted the interior of the shop. Across the street, the markets were closed, their medieval arches dark.

Natalia stepped into the shop.

"*Sera, signora.*"

"*Sera,*" Natalia said as the proprietor stood and pulled her black sweater around her shoulders. She might have stayed open to catch a stray customer, but more likely she was a widow, children long flown from the nest. She must have been lonely. Hungry for company.

Natalia had also worked late, filing reports that were less than urgent. If she were honest with herself, she thought, working late was her way to avoid returning to an empty house. Peas in a pod, she thought, as the woman shifted a carton so Natalia could pass through.

She surveyed the shelves for something to buy, then settled on a container of dish soap and two wine glasses. How could this woman survive on what these purchases brought in? If the place saw a dozen customers in a day, was it a lot? Probably a money laundering operation for one of her children's illicit businesses. Lucrative for all concerned and socially conscious at the same time, providing Mama a purpose in life beyond visiting her grandchildren and attending daily mass.

The *donna* dusted each glass as if Natalia had purchased stemware of fine crystal, rather than clunky glass molded in China. Then she wrapped them in yellowing pages torn from *Rivelare.*

Natalia stepped onto her balcony as the sun slipped away, and the swallows started up. Officially the harbingers of spring, in Naples the delicate birds were evident from the first blooms of hibiscus right into the first chilly weeks of December.

The black shutters of the elegant *palazzo* on the corner swung open, revealing its high ceilings and cinnamon-colored walls. A woman on the second floor put down her packages and stepped out of her shoes. She disappeared for a moment, then returned cradling a fat, well-tended angora cat. Together they surveyed the rosy dusk.

Natalia would have imagined the countess with such a pampered creature. Odd that such a cultivated woman, with a perfectly tended garden, would exhibit such devotion to feral cats. Perhaps the deprivations of the war had softened her heart toward homeless and underfed creatures.

There was just enough light to see the next day's lessons laid out on the teacher's desk in the school across the way. Lessons left little room for ambiguity. So unlike her line of work where there were too many possible answers. Was the murder of Vincente Lattaruzzo and Carlo Bagnatti a crime of passion, or was it possibly a well-planned vendetta? She tried to imagine both scenarios as her neighbor took her cat inside and drew the curtains.

A small tremor rippled through the district. Lights went on, and people emerged on their balconies and in the street. Instantly the scene brought to mind the big quake in 1980, when the floor shook violently and the furniture danced. Nonna had screamed, grabbed her purse and rushed them both out into the dusk and a sea of neighbors, many in their nightclothes.

They hurried toward Capodimonte as streets cracked open, and buildings and trees fell. Across the Bay of Naples, Vesuvius boiled but failed to explode.

Thousands of people were displaced. Chaos reigned, and once again strengthened the Camorra. The clans rushed into rebuilding and reaped fortunes from the calamity. Their shoddy concrete resurrected whole neighborhoods. Ugly buildings sprouted like mushrooms. Artisans lost their small businesses: toy makers, porcelain craftsmen, tinsmiths. The Camorra thrived in the disaster, quickly taking over legitimate new enterprises. For more than thirty years Naples stagnated, ignored by the central government, the people abandoned. The Camorra offered the only reliable employment for many. By early '83, there were a dozen gangs; a decade later, more than a hundred.

So much faded from memory, but that day remained vivid. Her father leaving for work in the dark, as he did faithfully six mornings a week. And the world splitting open and quaking.

Tonight, as then, Mount Vesuvius sent sparks into the ink-blue sky. Experts regularly contended the volcano could blow anytime, but Neapolitans took the prediction in stride. Fatalists at heart, they believed Vesuvius would do what Vesuvius would do.

Damn Cervino, she thought. Such an unappetizing man. But he had a point. Divided loyalties were dangerous. Cervino had a right to the large chip on his shoulder, but his righteous anger against the Camorra and identifying *her* with them made him dangerous to her. She'd have to watch her back.

He'd never married and lived with his sister, a nurse at the polyclinic. There had never been the slightest whisper of scandal about him—certainly no love affair with a colleague. Moral high ground that Cervino smugly held to. He had come in as a warrant officer. Which meant that, however exceptional his police work, he'd never rise above lieutenant. Unjust certainly, but she wasn't to blame.

Being a Carabiniere was an honor, whereas Natalia had

taken the exam as a lark. And then she'd received such a high score, she was fast-tracked through the law portion of the officers' program. Marshal Cervino had been in the ranks for more than two decades when she arrived already a captain.

She had assumed she'd work five or six years before she married and raised a brood. Presumably with Gino, her cellist boyfriend. But as time went by, she'd gotten involved with her job, and little by little her career accelerated, as she was promoted from the art squad to major crime investigation in ROS.

As her fiancé's musical career heated up, his itinerary became international, so he was touring more than he was home. By the time he invited her to live in Milan with him, she'd been promoted to major investigations, and the reality of marriage to a famous absentee musician had grown less appealing.

He couldn't compete with the excitement of her job and the quiet privacy she relished after the rigors of dealing with corpses and grieving families and armed felons. Badge and he seemed incompatible.

With several childbearing years yet ahead, Natalia assumed there would be another relationship in the future and plenty of time to worry about getting pregnant and to figure out with whom. Pino had taken up more than a little of that precious time, a span she no longer could deny. In a year she would be forty.

Chapter 12

Natalia took a sip of cappuccino, enjoying the morning quiet she knew wouldn't last. She needed to catch up on paperwork, to strategize the next step in their investigation. In fifteen minutes she had to go out, but she needed a minute to organize her thoughts, to "center" herself, as Pino always advised.

A formal message arrived from the colonel. Natalia checked the seams of her stockings, smoothed her grey suit jacket and reported to his office as ordered. She found him waiting, standing at his desk, hands clasped behind his back, insignia glinting. Eyes, too. Her boss was not happy.

"The contessa a suspect? Really!" He rose from his chair to pace across to the windows.

"It's unavoidable, Colonel. The possibility is there that Ernesto Scavullo perpetrated the killings on her behalf, obligated as his family was to avenge her father. The likelihood of her initiating this crime is also present."

"A woman as genteel as she, so many years later? I find it hard to believe, I must say."

"As do I. She convincingly denies wanting vengeance so many generations later."

"Then why?"

"If she was concerned about what Vincente Lattaruzzo intended to reveal in his memoir, then this would be the moment to call in the long standing debt owed her father."

"To discourage the book's publication by removing its author?"

"Yes. There's no indication Ernesto Scavullo knew anything about the family memoir and probably could care less if he did. She did know and cares very much."

"And the murder of this Carlo Bagnatti?"

"He was widely hated, needless to say. His rumor-mongering may well have displeased and damaged someone enough that it called forth terrible retribution. Or he and Lattaruzzo may have been caught by a betrayed lover and murdered out of jealousy. Or . . . he was simply in the wrong place at the moment they pounced on Lattaruzzo."

"Hated that much?"

"Angelina is researching his pieces, working up a list. It's going to be a long one."

"What about this Fabretti fellow?" Colonel Donati asked.

"Pietro Fabretti paid for his friend's funeral. He loved Bagnatti, I'm fairly sure. But they hadn't been involved for many years. There's no motive that I can see."

"How are Director Garducci and Stefano Grappi behaving?"

"Stefano stays close to home, nursing his grief. His shock at learning of his lover's death seemed genuine, like his present depression, though both could be contrived. He turns out to be the beneficiary of Bagnatti's will after Lattaruzzo's passing, whom he succeeds as the inheritor of the columnist's sizeable estate."

"Large enough to inspire this debauched murder?"

"No, but perhaps a satisfying topping to Vincente's betrayal of him with Garducci and Bagnatti and whoever else."

"That's quite the twist."

"A surprise, for sure. Though Stefano Grappi denies any knowledge of his inclusion in Bagnatti's will, as if he were some kind of relative by extension."

"You're sure the document is genuine?"

"Yes."

"And Garducci?"

"Director Garducci has buried himself in work. He has a volatile, violent temperament, and he may have been jilted by Vincente."

"In favor of Bagnatti?"

"Possibly. Or Stefano Grappi. I haven't gotten the impression Vincente Lattaruzzo was much into monogamy."

"And Boss Scavullo?"

"Ernesto Scavullo took his mother to Sunday Mass at the Duomo. Drove her in his Lamborghini. He went on to a sports pub and met up with some cronies to watch Napoli defeat Frankfurt. The next day he lunched with his favorite Bengalese girlfriend at the Café San Felice. Outdoor table, full view from the street."

"Not a care in the world, eh? The modern day don."

"Ernesto Scavullo has five thousand friends on Facebook."

"*Jesu!* Another Camorra hero." Colonel Fabio drew himself up. "All right, Captain. That will be all."

Natalia needed air, a walk in the light away from the unrelenting pressure of the station and her job and her boss's visible pain at hearing conjectures about the countess. She wasn't so happy about her suspicions herself.

On the corner of Via Librai and Via del Duomo, the flower vendor arranged a voluminous bouquet of *girasole* and greens. The sunflowers' black velvet centers, surrounded by voluminous gold petals, seemed a reversal of the day's sun, its golden brilliance piercing in places a dark blanket of black storm clouds and matching her mood well.

Natalia walked. A young woman balanced two cake boxes filled with roses and baby's breath as she and Natalia stood side by side waiting to cross the busy street. Natalia took in her creamy neck and a blue rose tattooed there. It took her a moment to realize she knew the serious young woman with black hair. She had provided information in the Steiner case the previous year. And she'd fallen hard for Pino.

Besides the change in hair length and color, the skinny girl had filled out. And her young face was now free of piercings

"Tina?" The girl turned. "Captain Monte," Natalia said.

"Oh. Yeah." She shifted the boxes.

The light changed, and they joined the throng crossing the street.

"You left your job at the café?"

"Business was slow," Tina looked past Natalia.

Mama must have stepped in, Natalia thought. It figured. Mama was a Gracci, as Natalia had discovered when she ran a background check on the girl. Among other business ventures, the Graccis used florist bouquets to deliver drugs to special customers—socialites, businessmen, even government officials. Mostly they employed underage children for the task, but Tina's cover was nearly as good: a lovely young woman transporting flowers. Who would imagine that below the fragrant creamy petals and delicate baby's breath, several ounces of powder lay nestled in tiny satin bags? All the more perfect since Tina was pregnant.

"Everything okay?" Natalia asked.

"I got these deliveries."

"Don't let me keep you." Natalia stepped aside, and Tina disappeared into the crowd.

Natalia felt sorry for her. She hadn't noticed a wedding ring and wondered about the father. Probably a mob novice her parents had picked. Pino, besides being the object of Tina's infatuation, must have represented escape from their expectations for her life. Now the poor girl belonged firmly to the family again. But at least she'd have a baby to show for it—someone to love and be loved by—which was more than Natalia could claim for herself.

Natalia paused in front of a shop window filled with hundreds of Punicellos in jaunty red outfits who peered at her from behind black masks. For a second Natalia caught a glimpse of her own reflection in the glass: an almost middle-aged woman peering back.

She passed the Cathedral of Santa Caterina Formiello, where a gypsy woman lay prostrate beside her begging bowl, and skirted a scruffy park strewn with trash. A dog peed against the trunk of a giant plane tree while its owner sucked on a cigarette, his chartreuse shirt tucked into a pair of worn pants. In front of the benches lay a black man on a large sheet of cardboard. Not ten feet from him, half a dozen empty vials, banded together and hanging in the branches of a scraggly bush. A woman with chopped hair scratched at her face and begged for change. Her jeans were ripped, the pockets hanging out. She stumbled, caught herself, stumbled again. The park looked as ravaged.

This sad triangle of earth sheltered some homeless—mostly men from the African community who had displeased their Camorra bosses or otherwise fallen on hard times. They shared it at night with homosexuals. The locals called it *Parco Passare*—Penis Park—a popular cruising spot for gay men.

Females who expressed their love in public were cut some slack, and mothers and daughters commonly held hands, girlfriends linked arms, embraced and kissed freely. But advertising oneself as a gay man in Naples invited serious trouble. Men who had the audacity to hold hands or, God forbid, kiss in public, were routinely beaten. If a Camorra male was outed as gay, his own would handle it with unspeakable violence. Polizia and Carabinieri weren't exactly tolerant either.

Rough as her city was, she would never dream of leaving. Not for love, not for work. Ambitious as she was, promises of promotion had not lured her away. Because of her studies in art history, her first assignment had been the art squad. A permanent posting in Rome was mentioned soon after she'd recovered a painting held for ransom in a rotting cellar. But much as Natalia admired the wide boulevards and relative tranquility of the capital, she felt she belonged here among the baroque bell towers and *palazzos* of the Piazza San Domenico, the Bauhaus-inspired post office, the ancient churches, fountains, alleys, the old street market in whose shadows she bought her fruit and fish like nine centuries of Neapolitans before her.

Natalia passed a display of large sardines stacked in a silver circle, dull mussels and bloody slabs of *orate* arranged as lovingly as in a Caravaggio painting. In the next stall were topaz lemons, ruby cherries, and clusters of amethyst grapes. And beyond that, orange crabs lay belly up on crystal shards of ice, clawing the warm air.

If she managed to retire early at fifty, Natalia might still finish her art degree, publish her thesis, perhaps even return to academia part-time. Some days it seemed like a reasonable fancy. Other times she wondered who she was kidding.

Some large part of her now belonged to law enforcement, an even larger part to Naples. Better to enjoy the gardens of the Villa Floridiana and the royal porcelain in the neoclassical palace without suffering the academic pressures to analyze and publish. Anytime she liked, she could stop by Donatello's altar to inhale its beauty rather than formulate a paper. What did she have to complain about really? If she had a hankering for a quiet moment with Rembrandt or Titian, the Museo di Capodimonte stood waiting. If her colleagues at Casanova station didn't share her art obsessions, she could always talk to Mariel and her artistic friends. She had acquired a good many herself in the course of her studies and art squad investigations.

And Colonel Fabio seemed more than satisfied with her performance as an organized crime specialist. She'd even acquired a reputation as having instincts and insights about the Camorra, in whose midst she'd been born and raised and still lived.

Natalia checked her watch and headed back to the station.

Back at her desk, she opened both the fat file on Ernesto Scavullo and the enormous one for Gianni, his father, just at the finish of a fifteen-year sentence. Working backward from the present and going deep into their pasts, she read and meditated on the clan that dominated a large piece of the underworld commerce and crime in Naples. Her recollections paralleled the recorded facts and grew more vivid the further back she went, taking her finally into her youth, her school years with Lola and Mariel and Suzanna. Suzanna Ruttollo's betrothal to Ernesto Scavullo, followed by their raucous wedding and just-as-sudden break up. Then Suzanna's exile to England.

Exile. Not the norm. A temporary retreat to Florence or Milan was more usual and a long debate whether to actually divorce and suffer the Church's sanctions, followed by a return to the city. Suzanna was as Neapolitan as they come. Years away from it, from friends and family must have been hard to endure. Why did she leave, and why stay away for so long?

Natalia dialed a counterpart at the police, whose department was charged with surveillance of Camorra and elicited information about Suzanna's and her mother's movements and near term plans. The items that caught her attention were two. Suzanna Ruttollo had arrived in Rome travelling with a male companion who had remained in that city. Partner? Bodyguard? Dogsbody? Natalia emailed her colleague a request for further information on him.

The second bit of information had Natalia scrambling. Mother Lucia was just leaving for a visit with her new grandchild, going by train in an hour's time.

Near the Stazione Centrale, a man pulled ears of corn from an enormous cauldron. Flushed from the heat of the day and the steam from the boiling water, he worked in tandem with his wife, who fried eggplants and shoveled them into paper cones for travelers. Natalia was tempted by the fritters but wouldn't risk the grease. She stood on the street and scanned the throng. And there she was.

Lucia Ruttollo bore the same scar from her lip to just below her nose that Natalia remembered as a teenager. Mariel and Lola had often wondered aloud why Suzanna hadn't arranged cosmetic surgery for her mother once she had money. More likely she had offered and her mother refused, as Natalia's mother would have. That generation grew up poor and hard and considered it unseemly to toy with fate. God gave you the face you were destined to wear. Altering it was like defying Providence.

Lucia Ruttollo looked grayer and fatter than at the bank, but otherwise the same. Her ample breasts still drooped, and her attire remained unfashionable and cheap. Despite the day's heat, she wore a mousey sweater offset by an incongruous lime green scarf stamped with purple butterflies—no doubt a gift from her daughter. It was nothing she would have ever chosen for herself.

Suzanna's mother wheeled a large black suitcase, a plastic bag balanced precariously on top.

"Signora Ruttollo," Natalia said, "remember me— Natalia? Natalia Monte?"

Lucia Ruttollo hadn't recognized her in the bank and didn't immediately now. She squinted, looking at Natalia, and suddenly said, "*Si, si.* Natalia. It's been years."

"Let me help you with that." Natalia reached for the handle.

"You have time?" Lucia Rutollo slung the bag over her shoulder and surrendered the cart. Together they crossed the street in front of McDonald's and followed the crowd into the rail station. The waiting room was chaos. People stood in long lines for tickets while others dragged luggage to and from the tracks. The homeless wandered through, too. A young couple lay on the floor abutting the newsstand.

Natalia recognized a couple of con artists in the crowd, looking for a mark, and Santoro, the undercover from Casanova. The announcement board showed a lot of delays.

"My train is late."

"Let me buy you a coffee then," said Natalia.

"You have time to keep me company?"

"I do."

Natalia steered them to a kiosk with a few tables and settled Lucia at one while she bought them two cups.

"I'm going to visit my Nicky," Mama Ruttollo said. "You remember my son?"

"Of course. Nicky."

A skinny boy, uninterested in school. Fascinated with motor scooters and cars, which he boosted. Preparation for following in his family's auto-theft business.

"He opened a garage in Averso," Lucia said. "Lives there with his wife."

"Good for him."

"She just had a baby." Lucia beamed.

"Congratulations. Boy or girl?"

"Girl. What about you?"

"Children? No. You know—work and all."

"Don't worry. You still have time."

Natalia wondered if Lucia harbored hopes for her prodigal daughter producing more grandchildren.

"Little Natalia Monte—a Carabiniere. I read about you investigating those murders. We never had that when I was growing up. Men with men. God wants this?" She waved a handkerchief in front of her face to cool off. "I can't wait to tell Suzanna I saw you."

"Lola told me she's home."

"God answered my prayers. I only hope she stays. She'd love to see you. She doesn't have any friends here anymore."

"I'll give her a call."

"Your father is well?"

"No, he passed."

"Forgive me. Now I remember. I forget things these days. But you look good, Natalia."

"Thanks. You, too."

Lucia laughed. "My daughter says I look like a bag lady. Wants me to have a makeover, dye my hair. At my age? A waste of money, I told her."

The giant board clicked and rattled, updating arrivals and departures. A tiny black nun picked up her case and ran. The train to Averso was announced on track seven.

"I mustn't miss my train."

Natalia signaled to a porter to help Suzanna's mother with her bags.

"You're a good girl, Natalia," Lucia kissed her. "I'm gonna light a candle for you."

The officer on the reception desk politely pointed to a waiting visitor.

"Pino!"

"You're looking good, Captain."

"*Momento.*" She made a quick trip to the bathroom, dampened her hands and attempted to smooth her hair. Some old lip gloss helped, but there was nothing she could do about the circles under her eyes. Lola was always on her to use concealer. Even when she wasn't stressed from work and missing sleep, they were dark.

"Damn," she whispered and went back out.

"I've been trying to call your mobile," he said. "You didn't pick up?"

"It's been crazy. I've been doing interviews. Come."

She led him back to her office and closed the door.

"So nothing's wrong?" Pino said.

"No."

"I want to kiss you, but it's undoubtedly against the rules."

"What brought you back to Naples?"

"Bunnies. Uncle Ricci's closest neighbor slaughters them and sells the meat. Their shrieking didn't go so well with morning meditation. There's no perfect world, Natalia. Not there, not here."

"Is that one of your Zen koans?"

"No." Pino gathered himself and said, "I've come back to town to declare myself to you."

"Why?"

"Because I care about you, of course."

"How long have you been back?"

"A few days. Actually, I came back to open my flat for a friend . . . who needed shelter."

"Who?"

"Tina."

"She's pregnant."

"Yes. How did you know?"

"I'm a detective."

"Tina is in some trouble."

"It isn't yours."

"No, but she doesn't have anyone else to turn to."

"Of course not. Just her grifter mother and auto-thief father and many dozen underworld aunts and uncles, a hundred cousins and the child's father."

"Yeah. He wants to marry her. Her family is advocating it as well. Which is part of her problem."

"Jesus, Pino where are your brains? Don't you remember the first lecture on the first day at the Academy? If someone you've never met or don't know comes onto you, you have them vetted immediately. If there's the slightest hint of Camorra association, you report it and step away. Tina is a Gracci for Christ sake, part of Scavullo's little empire."

"She's not like them."

"They've got her delivering major dope to their finest customers. They have it brought to the door instead, from their florist."

"Six months ago she tried to hurt herself."

"That's not your problem, either."

"Why so harsh? It's not like you."

"Take her to the prenatal clinic if you're so worried."

"Natalia—"

"Tina is Camorra, born and bred."

"It's not her fault."

"No, and that's not the issue. The fact I stated is."

"We don't choose our place in the world—where we're born or to whom. Not me, not Tina. Or you either."

"What is this—a Zen thing?"

"I don't want to live my life suspicious of every little thing, everyone I come across."

"Then maybe you shouldn't be a Carabiniere."

"I'm not going to be, I don't think."

"What?"

"Not much longer."

Natalia fell silent. He was serious.

"I want us to be together, though," he said, "and I realized it would never happen if I stayed in uniform."

"What about Tina?

"She's staying with me for the moment."

Some citizen was having a tantrum at the front desk, screaming and throwing things.

"She doesn't have anywhere else to go."

"I don't have time for this." Natalia picked up her phone. "Get her out of your house, Pino, for your own good."

"Why do you always get so irrational whenever there's a little problem in life?"

"A little problem? I'd hate to see what a big problem looked like. It's you who's living in some other world, Pino. *Breathe in the gold light,*" she mimicked, "*exhale the shit.*"

He looked crestfallen. "Maybe I should go."

"Yeah, now you're thinking clearly."

"I'll see you tonight."

"Up to you."

As soon as he left, she hung up the phone and closed the door, then burst into tears.

"Do you love him?" Mariel whispered.

"Don't ask me that."

Two angels regarded them from their niche. Wings cracked, eyes vacant. At age twelve Natalia and Mariel had importuned the cherubs for the same boy to return their love. By thirteen, both questioned the existence of God. When Mariel's parents were killed, those doubts were sealed. Yet once or twice a year they still made a pilgrimage to the Church of the White Angels, as Natalia and Mariel called it, the only Orthodox church in Naples.

Nothing changed here: the same tapestries adorned the simple walls. Near the confessional, the caretaker flirted with a modern Mary Magdalene in tight jeans and a low cut sweater. A widow knitted in a pew near the altar, no doubt responsible for the yellow chrysanthemums in a tin vase at the feet of Jesus.

"Why couldn't we have a normal life," Natalia said, "living together, eating dinner together, sharing our days?"

"What did he say about the pregnancy?" Mariel asked.

"Swore it couldn't be his. Fuck, Mariel, he'll be lucky the Graccis don't deliver a wedding present."

Mariel paled. A "present" referred to cash delivered to a man who got a Camorra girl pregnant. The message: Marry the girl, and buy some china and silverware. Spurn her and it could pay for a funeral just as well.

"If Colonel Fabio finds out about Pino's involvement with this girl, he's finished in law enforcement."

"Sounds like he's done with the Carabinieri anyway."

"But I'm not. We had to break up because we'd violated policy, and here he brings me another violation the moment he's back in my life."

Mariel brushed back Natalia's hair. "What are you going to do?"

"I don't know." She kissed her friend's hand. "I haven't a clue."

Chapter 13

Normally Fionetta opened her hair salon at one on Mondays. Once a month Lola got her to open at ten thirty, though the CLOSED sign stayed up and the shades down.

Natalia rapped twice, and Onetta opened the door.

"What's the matter?" Onetta demanded. "Don't you love me anymore?"

They kissed each other's cheeks and embraced.

"I do love you, Onetta, but it's been crazy."

"Crazy here, too. Mariel was wondering where you were. Lola's already had a manicure. Blue. Blue nails, like a teenager's. And now she wants me to give the dog a manicure."

"I wouldn't let you lay a finger on my precious pooch, would I?" Lola said. "So cute!" She screeched, hugging the dog to her chest and kissing her. "Natalia, don't you love his little jacket!"

Onetta had stuck a piece of duct tape across the seat of Natalia's favorite red vinyl chair.

"What's going on? Things falling apart?" Natalia said. "We can take up a collection."

"Very funny," 'Onetta said. "When I need your help, I'll ask."

Lola and the barking Micu were dressed to kill, the former in a Dolce and Gabbana sheath, leopard skin stiletto gladiator heels and an emerald choker; the latter, in a gray knitted sweater with green rhinestone buttons.

Natalia hugged Lola and said over her shoulder to Onetta, "It's good of you to let us use your shop."

"How often do old friends have a chance to get together?"

"New friends," Lola recited, "are silver, but old friends . . ."

"Are gold," Mariel, in the chair next to Lola, finished. "Natalia, how are you?"

"Em, glad you made it. So where's the guest of honor?"

"On the way. Lola was antsy and made us come early."

"Better that way," Lola said. "Less to notice."

They'd met like this for years, and it had become second nature to keep their association semi-secret, though Natalia didn't doubt for a minute that Colonel Fabio knew. He just chose to look the other way because her contact with Lola and some others and her familiarity with the ways of Naples had paid dividends in any number of investigations. But there was always someone in the ranks or in authority, like Marshal Cervino, who objected and invoked the Carabinieri's strict rules against fraternization with what amounted to the enemy.

A lush buffet was laid out across a counter.

"What's this?" Natalia asked.

"Brunch," Lola announced. "We can't go out, so I ordered in. Scrambled eggs. Champagne. Gnocchi slathered in sour cream. And caviar, five hundred euros an ounce, from Belarus."

Onetta made a face. "Fish eggs."

Lola said, "Good thing Mama's not here. She wouldn't approve of wasting money on food. She'd serve stale bread if she could get away with it."

"My God, this is amazing," Mariel said and held out a basket of popovers and *focaccio*.

"No, thanks." Lola passed it to Natalia. "I'm forbidden to have carbs."

Natalia took a roll. "You have a trainer?"

"The boyfriend. Guess where he's taking me for a vacation? Monte Carlo. Thousand a night."

"Sounds like lust," Natalia said.

"Hope so," Lola answered, checking her cleavage.

"Where do you get asparagus this time of year?" Mariel asked.

"Chile." Lola ripped off a wedge of popover and took a bite. "So . . . what can we talk about in front of the Carabiniere?"

Mariel added food to her plate. "I have something,"

"Something exciting in books?" Lola said. "How likely is that?"

"I had dinner with someone."

"Look, she's blushing," Lola said. "A man someone?"

"A book dealer."

"Good-looking?"

"*Mezzo mezzo*—but nice."

"Then he can't be from here."

"Milan."

"Was I right, or was I right?" Lola picked up a plate, following Mariel down the line of food. "You sure he isn't married?"

Natalia's cell phone buzzed. She checked to see the caller. "Pino again."

"There a rumor Pino knocked up one of the Gracci girls."

"Shut up, Lola." Mariel said.

"Is it true?"

Natalia bit her thumbnail. "Pino says not."

Lola took out her Blackberry.

"Remember we agreed?" Mariel said.

"What? Agreed what?"

"No texting or talking on electronic devices during girl time."

"I don't know about you, *signora*, but I'm a working woman. Business doesn't stop just because I'm shooting the shit with a couple of girlfriends during working hours."

Someone knocked on the door, and Onetta went to answer. "Suzanna!" she exclaimed, "Come in, come in," and quickly closed the door behind the new arrival.

Suzanna Ruttollo strode toward her once-upon-a-time schoolmates in an orange sundress, matching heels, gold flashing everywhere, including her hair, which was beautifully styled—short now and angled over one eye.

"Suzie!" Lola squealed and rushed to greet her. Suzanna beamed and took each of them in her arms in turn, Natalia last.

"I can't believe it." She held onto Natalia's hand.

Suzanna looked better in her late thirties than she had at twenty. Skin smooth, no trace of the acne that once plagued her. Not even a hint of a wrinkle around the eyes. "Captain Monte," she said with pride.

"Good to see you, Suzanna," Natalia said, and they embraced again.

"My mother very much appreciated your kindness the other day at the rail station."

"Not at all. How is her visit?"

"She's having a wonderful time with the new baby and giving me grief that I never gave her the joy of a grandchild. Broke her heart that I never made more babies."

"You don't have anyone in your life?"

"A man? No."

"There's still time," Lola said.

"No. It's not going to happen for me."

"Are you back for good?" Mariel said.

"Not completely. I've bought a place in Naples with a beautiful view of the bay. I'll be staying with Mama for now. When it's ready, you must come by and see it."

"Terrific," Mariel said.

"Nothing like seeing old friends," Lola chimed in.

"Otherwise you're in London?" Natalia said.

"London mostly. We have businesses in Germany and England."

"Businesses?" Lola said. "Like what?"

"A variety. That's the way to go, isn't it? Pharmaceuticals. Chocolate. A line of women's sports and casual wear. Oh, and jewelry shops. We'd like to open a flagship store here."

"Good for you," Mariel said.

Lola agreed.

Natalia looked into Suzanna's grey eyes. "You're out of the family business entirely?"

"From the time I left, yes. I'm on my own. Mama helped me along. But I've paid her back tenfold. We have five divisions now and last year acquired a couple of subsidiaries."

"All of 'em legit?" Lola asked.

"Well . . ." Suzanna smiled enigmatically.

Natalia poured herself a glass of wine. "Missing London at all?"

"Only the theater. It's quite nice to be . . . home. I've missed Naples actually."

They spent the late morning reminiscing. Suzanna brought up the day they'd gone to the sliver of beach by the harbor just across Via Caracciolo. She, Mariel, Lola and Natalia were showing off their first bikinis. They'd eaten the egg sandwiches their mothers packed them and drunk wine from a thermos of an older boy in a black, cut-off T-shirt. Mariel read her latest *romanzo*, while Suzanna and Natalia sunbathed. Lola disappeared behind some rocks with the aspiring Lothario who had supplied the wine. They barely unlocked their embrace when he left to deliver pizzas, gunning his motor scooter on the walk above. Lola blew him a kiss, and he disappeared into traffic.

The girls had made their way to Mariel's house, sunburned, caked with sand. Lola proudly reported she and the boy had finished the bottle. Then she showed off her hickey. Mariel's parents were out of town at an art auction. Mariel opened a bottle of wine, and they each had a proper glass. Everyone got tipsy except Mariel, who was already served wine at dinner and used to it. On the other hand, when Natalia's mother detected the alcohol on her daughter's breath, she informed Natalia's father. First she received a lecture on the proper behavior for a young lady and then was punished with a week's isolation in the house after school.

The women were lingering over biscotti and limoncello at noon when Onetta's old Swiss clock chimed the hour.

"Twelve," Suzanna said, wistfully. "The coach turns into a pumpkin. I have to return to the world. This was great."

"Yeah," Lola said. "We're back! Look at us together again. We gotta do this more." She picked up her handbag. "Gotta go, gotta go."

They kissed and departed one by one: Suzanna first, then Lola. Mariel and Natalia lingered a while longer.

"So what's going on with Pino?" Mariel asked. "Sounds like he's pursuing you with passion. Wish I was so lucky."

"Thank your stars you're not," Natalia said. "Sometimes I think passion is overrated."

"What was that Shakespeare said? Great passion cannot survive four walls?"

"If Pino and I ever get a chance for four walls and a few years, I'll let you know."

"For a simple follower of the Buddha, that boy gets himself tangled in a lot of complication."

"That he does," Natalia said. "The Buddha Way hasn't seemed to work for him. Enough about my love life. Lola's got a new beau."

"Mmm. He bought her a mink coat."

"Mama! Are they planning to relocate to Greenland?"

"You know her. She'll ride around in a refrigerated limousine if she has to, to show it off. For a smart girl, sometimes I wonder why she parks her brains in neutral all the time."

Natalia put her drink aside. "What did you make of Suzanna?"

"Quite turned out, that one. An accomplished business woman from the look of her."

"Clothing. Jewelry. Chocolates."

"I wonder what's in the centers," Mariel said. "Cocaine?"

"I wonder what she has in mind to do here."

"You don't buy visiting mom?"

"No."

Mariel slipped on her jacket. "Do you think we'll always have to meet clandestinely, like characters in a fairy tale?"

"Until our friends get out of the rackets."

"The twelfth of never."

They slipped out the door together.

"Em," Natalia said, "did Suzanna ever divorce Ernesto Scavullo?"

"I don't believe so. No divorce, no annulment."

Natalia bit her lip. "Either one could have paid the usual gift to the Church fathers for a favorable judgment and dissolved it. But they didn't."

"Well, for all the push-up bras and other challenges she posed to the nuns, Suzanna remained faithful and observant. Ernesto, too, was religious, remember?"

"Yeah," Natalia said. "Didn't he regularly send his maker fresh souls to judge?"

"Doesn't he still?"

The friends said their goodbyes.

Natalia sauntered along Tribunali. She stopped to buy some fresh cherries. Suzanna, she mused, as the vendor weighed her fruit and threw in a few extra for good measure. Back in Naples to look after her mama. Right. What if the devoted daughter had returned to claim the territory she had left in shame years ago? Get back at Ernesto. And the others.

Funny the way Lola was cozying up to Suzanna at the beauty parlor just then. Who would have guessed? It was weird—how much Lola had hated her, insanely jealous when they were young, and now . . . But if you looked at it another way, maybe it wasn't so strange.

In the competition between the two women, for a while Lola had been ahead. While Suzanna had suffered exile, Lola gave birth to two beautiful children. And she had Frankie, who'd been nothing if not generous.

But the balance had shifted. Frankie slaughtered. And her beloved son. Businesswise, Lola had moved up the ranks partnering with Bianca Strozzi. But, face it, she worked in the shadow of her boss.

It was Suzanna who was ahead, controlling an increasingly large territory. An international star. And here she was back again in Lola's face. And Lola being so nicey-nicey. That was out of character.

Lola was up to something. Befriend Suzanna as a prelude for getting rid of her? Possible. Or was it something else? Something Natalia didn't want to contemplate.

What if her two old friends were planning to partner up? With Suzanna's clout and Lola's connections, they'd swallow Bianca's empire easily as a python ingests a mouse. They'd be in position to muscle for control of Naples. For real. Up until now Natalia's relationship with Lola had been a low-grade problem. But if her fears were founded, that would change. How could she do her job? Natalia was generally respected, even liked by her colleagues. But even now there were those who were jealous, those who would be more than happy to take her down.

Not Colonel Donati, obviously. He had her back. But even his protection could only go so far. And she couldn't blame him.

If what she suspected were true, she would be tested. Cervino would be on her ass. Her calls would be taped. She would be followed.

And, more profoundly, she loved Lola. Aside from Mariel, she considered Lola her best friend in the world.

How would she cope with her old friends moving to the top of the Carabinieri's Most Wanted list? Called on to look the other way as they bloodied the field. What would she do?

Chapter 14

The officers on night duty ate Bolognese while they watched Naples trounce Brazil at the stadium in Rome. It was edible, Natalia had to concede, though barely. They could hear people singing and shouting in the street. Then the fireworks started and the cherry bombs, each packing the explosive power of a quarter of a stick of dynamite. One went off near the station, shaking the windows.

Natalia hoped the municipal police would get the call outs. She finished drying the dishes, bade her colleagues good night and went to make up her cot in the storage room that had been converted to accommodate the station's two females. Boxes of paper records were stacked up in one corner alongside a broken chair no one had bothered to throw out. Her civilian clothes hung on a hook, preserved under filmy plastic.

As she slipped off her shoes, the duty clerk appeared in the doorway. "There's been an incident."

* * *

The club reeked of beer and greasy food from the Chinese restaurant next door. The victim reclined on a banquette. Someone must have draped a crocheted afghan over him. It had slipped to the floor. Blood speckled his blue jeans and yellow T-shirt. His black hair was gelled into a peak, the front of it askew. A skinny youth, though muscular, pretty, even with his mouth swollen and bruised. As they approached, one eye opened. The other remained sealed by the swelling. He sat up and braced himself on the round cocktail table.

"Would you like us to take you to the hospital?" Natalia asked. "You need to see a doctor."

He shook his head. She signaled the second officer to call for an ambulance anyway.

"What's your name?" Natalia said.

"Antonio."

"Do you have some identification, Antonio?"

"It's at home."

"Where do you live?"

"Santa Lucia."

"How old are you, Antonio?"

"Twenty."

Right. If he was eighteen, Natalia would be surprised, but she didn't challenge him.

She showed him a picture. "This is the man you named?"

"Yeah. He came in all the time, yeah."

"No one warned you about him?"

"They did, yeah. But he paid extra."

"Would you be willing to testify?" Natalia said. "When you're feeling better?"

"I don't know."

"Is there someone we can call for you?"

"No."

"You're sure?" Angelina said.

"Yeah."

The emergency medics arrived. The boy's anxiety rose.

"I don't want to go to a hospital," he said, holding his side. "I'll be all right here."

"Let them check you out. See if you're really okay on your own." She touched his shoulder. "All right?"

He nodded his consent. The first tech knelt down in front of him. Natalia whispered to his partner that she wanted photos of the wounds and the hospital report and the name of the attending physician. He nodded and took her card.

She left the boy and went to the bartender to show him the picture. He made the same identification.

It was a quarter to eight in the morning. Natalia gathered up Angelina and her morning coffee, and they set out for the museum. They hadn't slept a wink. Sirens wailing, lights flashing, they pulled up front and marched through unchallenged. A docent took them to where he was: a completely white gallery room with vast ceilings and walls of the palest marble designed to highlight. Mesh shades dimmed the harsh Mediterranean sun, filtering it into cool ambient light.

Garducci was alone with a giant black stone sculpture of Artemis, the Queen of Nature, Mistress of Beasts. It dwarfed him. Using his Blackberry to make notes, he paused to snap pictures of details. Carved goats, scorpions, griffins, bees. Her crown, shaped like a city wall.

The figure was covered with *pendulina*, what looked like myriad breasts but up close were actually the scrota of bulls.

Around her neck, the goddess wore a necklace bearing the signs of the zodiac. Natalia came up alongside him.

"What now?" He exclaimed. He seemed flustered, eyes flitting like he was losing it or already had.

"We've come for you," Natalia said.

"This is outrageous. I have a museum to run. I have gone out of my way to be cooperative, but you are trying my patience."

"You're quite a busy man, Mr. Garducci. And a violent one."

She raised her chin to Angelina, who held forth a phone picture.

"You recognize Antonio?" Natalia said. "Or is it difficult, given his injuries?"

Garducci flushed with fear and indignation. "He wouldn't dare press charges."

"Perhaps not, but we don't need him to. There were witnesses to the assault."

"I'm calling my lawyer." Garducci tapped the tiny keyboard of his Blackberry.

"There will be plenty of time for lawyers," Natalia said. "And lots of time to ponder your actions. But first we need to arrest you."

Angelina stepped forward and handcuffed the director's hands in front.

"The little shit," Garducci spat.

They weren't back at Casanova a second before Colonel Fabio's office summoned Captain Monte.

She found him in his favorite position: chair tilted back, glasses on the tip of his nose. His desk, a mess of papers, crumpled candy wrappers and several mugs of half-drunk coffee.

"Sir?" Natalia stood at the door.

Fabio asked after her health and ushered her in.

"You've arrested Garducci," he said.

"Yes, sir. For assault and battery of a minor."

"Does this sway your thinking concerning his possible guilt in the double murder?"

"It reinforces my suspicions about his temper and lack of control."

"Well, I will look for your arrest report."

"Yes, sir."

"*La Mattina*, by the way, has named us the new capital of homoerotic violence. Wonderful, eh?"

"That's unfortunate, sir."

"I'd like to talk to you about the *contessa*."

Natalia waited.

"As you may be aware, she is being hounded by the media. *Rivelare* has two reporters staked out around the clock outside her home. Paparazzi are practically camped at her gate, cameras trained on the house. She goes out, they rush her, shouting questions and provocative remarks, recording every second. It's unconscionable to harass someone of her age and standing."

"I'm sorry to hear of this, sir."

"Yes. Unfortunately there's nothing we can do. The *contessa*'s many prominent friends are quite upset. Until we close the case, there will be no end of prurient interest. It is as if she is the chief suspect, for Christ's sake. My dear wife suggested she stay with us until things settled down. Contessa Antonella refused, of course. It would take more than a few reporters to intimidate the woman. I had to remind my wife that it would be seen as a conflict of interest to have someone involved in a murder investigation as a guest in our home. So, you see my problem."

"I do, sir, and we are working with all speed."

"Subjecting her to our scrutiny is making life with my Elisabetta, shall we say, less than pleasant. Speaking of which, she wants to offer you a ticket to *Lucia di Lamamor* at the San Carlo. It's on Saturday."

"That's terribly considerate of her."

"She claims her sister was supposed to come but can't. I suspect it's subterfuge. She asked for you particularly. If you come, don't be surprised if my darling wife engages in some lobbying on behalf of her beloved Nell."

"Thank you, sir. For the warning and the kind offer. And thank her for me. It may be difficult to get away at the moment, even for an evening. Can I get back to you about that?"

"Of course."

Back in her office, Natalia changed into civilian garb: a cream-colored silk wrap she hadn't worn in years and hoped would keep Lola from complaining that she always looked like a slob. Off duty for the next twenty-four hours, she slipped out shortly before ten to meet Lola.

The woman who cleaned the Sanzari Funeral Emporium dumped a bucket of soapy water into the gutter. Natalia crossed to the other side of the street, navigating past locals and tourists peering through the stubby iron bars outside Santa Maria ad Arco di Purgatorio waiting to get in.

She passed between the torpedo-shaped concrete posts that divided motorbikers from pedestrians and barely avoided a bicycle with a palm tree on the back standing upright in a milk crate. A silver van followed, driven by two nuns.

A fat *nonna* slid off a tomato-colored motorbike. Natalia had never been able to coax her *nonna* to go near one.

Even when she took her for a drive in the car, Nonna made the sign of the cross and kissed her fingertips before they started out and as soon as they'd arrived at their destination.

At the end of the block, a couple embraced in the middle of a narrow sidewalk, the woman wearing purple satin pants and black boots. She reached under her blouse and adjusted her brassiere, then ran her hand over his bald head as if she were petting a cat. He took both of her hands and kissed them.

The gypsy who approached them held open a flat box with assorted key chains. She offered them to the woman first, who shook her head.

"Please," the gypsy pleaded.

"She told you, *no*," the man snapped.

The gypsy woman took a few steps away and circled back. That's when he shoved her. She stumbled. Key rings went flying. As Natalia rushed over, she rose to her feet, shaking, knees bruised and bleeding.

Natalia confronted the man. "Let me see your papers."

"Who are you?"

"Captain Natalia Monte. Casanova Station." She held up her identification.

"So, they're swearing in broads now. Better all around if everyone minded their business."

He winked at his girlfriend, who laughed.

"The public order is my business," Natalia said. "If you don't comply, I'll bring you in."

"By yourself?"

"I think I can manage, but I can always call in reserves."

"Oh. A hardass. You're making me sweat." He took out his wallet and stuck a driver's license in front of Natalia's face.

"You are Mr. Rizzi."

"You have a problem with that?"

"No. The problem is all yours."

Natalia wrote something in her notebook, handed the license back to him and proceeded to get the gypsy's particulars.

"You'll be receiving a summons in a few days. Fail to appear and a warrant will be issued, which I will personally see is executed."

She and Pino had dealt with violence against Roma on more than one occasion when they'd partnered together. Colonel Donati was only somewhat sympathetic to their plight, but most in law enforcement mirrored the hostile attitude of the public who saw gypsies as untrustworthy scum undeserving of protection.

Natalia found a cabbie a block later, parked on Via Duomo and had him drive her to a small street a few blocks from the waterfront in the Chiaia quarter where she and Lola had chosen to meet.

Arriving at her destination, Natalia nonchalantly scanned the street. A boy delivering bread wobbled past on his bicycle, fresh loaves in plastic bags hanging vertically on either side behind him. A circle of tourists listened attentively to their tour guide lecture in animated French, as she stepped off the sidewalk to pass by. No one seemed out of place, suspicious. But anyone shadowing her would see to being inconspicuous.

The heat hadn't let up. A cooling wind off the sea was needed. Instead, a blistering *vento* from inland pressed down from the hills onto the city. It made Natalia happy to take refuge in the darkened restaurant, its heavy stone walls cool even in the oppressive heat. Lola was hiding in the back behind a vine of bougainvillea growing out of the edge of the open patio, its flat stones shaded by an ancient chestnut tree and a red-and-white striped awning.

Their table overlooked the harbor. They weren't far from where as kids they'd once leapt into the cool of the bay. Lola had on a white blouse, white slacks, and white shoes, and a pair of enormous dark sunglasses. A navy blue blazer with gold buttons lay draped across the back of an extra chair.

Natalia joined her, saying, "Are you in seclusion, or do you not want to be seen with your unfashionable friend?"

"Just being discreet, Captain."

Natalia sat and tilted her friend's head, peeking past the chandelier earrings at a large bruise on Lola's cheek. "Hey, somebody hit you?"

"Nobody would dare," Lola said. "No, I had a little work done on my eyes, is all."

"What for?"

"Just updating myself."

"Last time I checked, your face didn't need updating."

"Yeah, well, I wasn't involved with a man ten years younger then."

"If your romance needs a surgeon to stitch it together—"

"Please, no lectures. Spare me. When you were bedding Pino, you rushed off to a retreat, took a vow of silence, ate lentils for days and slept on a dirt floor."

"He wanted me to understand Buddhism."

"From the ground up. Yeah, girl. That's what you said then, too—all moony-eyed and sexed up."

"Lola, it's just that I'm worried about him."

"You're worried about him?" Lola said. "Look, you're my best friend and I love you, okay? But was he thinking about you when he was fucking teeny Tina a while back?"

"Let's not go there."

"Okay, okay." Lola opened the top button of her blouse. "Look."

A ruby heart hung on a gold chain around her neck.

"Dominick. What do you think?"

"Extravagant," Natalia said.

"Right. Boy knows how to behave . . . so far."

The waiter brought them bread and took their drink orders.

"This is nice—just the two of us," Lola said. "Which reminds me: I had a visit from Suzanna after the get-together."

"Oh."

"She wanted to know if it's a problem for me—your being a Carabiniere."

"What did you say?"

"I told her no. That we didn't make a public show of our friendship, but when we were together it was just us, same as when we were growing up."

Natalia smiled. "And what did she say?"

"Nothing more about that. She switched the subject to her ex."

"Ernesto Scavullo?"

"The one and only."

"I wonder why she'd be interested at this late date? Isn't she over him?"

"Look who's talking. Obviously, she's still carrying a torch for him," Lola said. "You know, first love and all. I mean, she never remarried, did she?"

"True, but I'm not sure her curiosity about Ernesto translates as love. Though they were pretty smitten back then."

"Back then?" Lola squealed, indignant. "He started whoring around on her at their wedding and didn't let up. She toughed it out, but it couldn't have been fun."

The intensity of their young passion for one another—Suzanna's and Ernesto's—had actually alarmed Natalia at the time.

"She ask anything specific about him?" Natalia said.

"Wanted to know whether I thought Ernesto had done that to those two queers who turned up in Contessa Cavazza's garden."

"And you said?"

"That I didn't know, but a good many suspected him of being behind it." Lola lit a cigarette. "She said it would be tragic if that was true."

Natalia looked puzzled. "Of all the people he's done away with, why would she express regret about these particular two?"

"Beats me," Lola said. "Pass the olive oil, please."

Chapter 15

Via Toledo was giddy with heat. One end of the busy avenue tilted up to Capodimonte, the other down to the
harbor, changing names along the way. Natalia and Pino
stood at the intersection of Cavour and Santa Teresda degli
Scalza before it morphed into Via Pessina. Here the stairs
angled into the hill, and alleys cut into it like strands of a
spider's web.

The light changed, and the couple headed north, moving
with the crowds up the slope. Silver hubcaps glinted outside
auto repair shops where men sat coated in grease, smoking.
Canaries sang in cages set out on the sidewalk. Within a few
blocks, Natalia was out of breath from the climb.

"I'm out of shape," she said.

"I love your shape," Pino said.

"That's very forward of you, Sergeant Loriano."

He kissed her neck as they waited to cross yet another
street.

"Stop it."

"What if I refuse?"

"Insubordination, Sergeant. I can write you up."

"I'm on leave, remember? Any other reason I shouldn't display my affection?"

"We're in public."

"But not in uniform."

"All I need is to walk into Casanova with a giant hickey," Natalia said. "It would make Marshal Cervino's day."

They approached the Sanite Bridge that Neapolitans had saved from being destroyed by the retreating Wehrmacht. People streamed across, some heading into the vortex of the city, some heading away.

Suddenly there was a breeze, and Naples lay below in all its splendor. Turning inland, two worn columns marked the entrance to a small park.

There were a couple of scraggly trees and the requisite broken benches. The ground was littered with trash, a couple of needles, and a pile of broken bottles. The area reeked of alcohol, but the drunks were sleeping it off somewhere else.

They were alone except for a girl huddled under a black-and-white, polka-dotted umbrella. They sat on a bench away from her, and Pino closed his eyes. He breathed deeply. Natalia wiped her perspiring face with a tissue.

"Even the one thing invisible has a double," Pino said.

"What does *that* mean?"

Natalia got up and threw the tissue in a large metal can, although futile. One scrap of garbage attended to, while all around them lay Styrofoam containers, cigarettes, drug paraphernalia and candy wrappers.

"It means I want to kiss you."

"Permission granted. Be careful of the neck area."

"Aye, aye. I love you, Captain Monte." He kissed her eyelids and her mouth. "It's an auspicious day for us, darling."

"What did you tell Tina?"

"The truth. That I was in love with you. That she needed to relocate."

"How did she take it?"

"Fine. Better than I expected, actually. And I weakened."

"Weakened?"

"Mmm. I told her she could stay at my place until she gets her head together. Or if she needed money for a room somewhere, I said I'd help. Anything to get her away from the thug boyfriend."

"Here you go again," Natalia said, "the knight in shining armor. You sure she's not harboring any fantasies about the two of you?"

"Absolutely."

"Are you?"

"Am I what?" Pino put his arm around her shoulder.

"Harboring fantasies about that beautiful pregnant girl?"

"I want to be with you, Natalia."

"Did you get the rest of your things from your flat?"

"Here," he patted his worn backpack. "After she's gone, I'll go back and pack up the rest."

"The concierge has a key to my place," Natalia said. "I told her you'd be coming by this afternoon."

"She knows about us?"

"She's probably figured it out. We're not quiet."

Pino tickled her, and she shrieked.

"What do you mean 'we'?" he said, laughing.

"How did these get here?" Natalia asked. A vase of mimosas and violets sat on her desk.

"A corporal brought them up." Angelina grinned at her

boss. "I believe there's a note. I think they're from your Buddhist friend? It's that gold-foil paper."

Natalia flushed.

"So romantic. Reminds me of Giuletta the first night we were together."

Natalia peeled the envelope off the vase and dropped it into her bag. The last night they had spent with one another before he'd gone away, Pino had brought her the same bouquet. It was then he told her about cranes, apropos of nothing: that they represented longevity and how in Ancient Greece their cries announced the return of spring. They had been a long way from spring that night.

Tribunali was decked out with pointsettias. People scurried along the street with gifts of cakes and lavish flower arrangements, past happy families lined up in front of the pizza parlors. Liturgical music spilled from cathedrals and churches, while firework bombs went off in the alleys, celebrating a high holy day.

"Peace on earth," Natalia had joked, as she flinched from the percussions.

Pino and Natalia, soon-to-be former lovers, enjoyed their dinner together at her flat along with quite a lot of fragrant wine. Pino was supposed to go home after dessert, their future deemed impossible, but they had toasted with *Zia* Giovanna's wine glasses and fallen into bed.

It was when she'd gotten up to pee that she tripped over the wine glasses. Pino offered to get them fixed. He knew one of the few glassblowers still in business. She'd refused, annoyed at how easily he had clouded her resolve to stay away from him.

What kind of spring could they hope for? Their involvement was forbidden by regulations: She was his superior. There was little hope for both of them to remain

Carabinieri if they continued, and she knew she would not be the one to surrender her captaincy, no matter what. It meant too much to her, more to her than . . . him.

That she cared deeply for Pino only made it worse. That they were incredibly well suited as lovers and partners made it nearly unbearable. It was true: Natalia could hang out a shingle and try her hand at law. That was the degree she'd earned at officers' school in Rome. Not a very lucrative profession in Naples, where people had little faith in the legal system, and conflicts had been settled since before the Greeks by confrontation. Hell, prayers and potions were still employed to ward off the evil eye. Not to mention that lawyers were held in even lower regard than Carabiniere. Natalia was in a quandary and had leaned toward ending their affair.

The day after her night with Pino, she'd returned home to find a vase of mimosas and violets in front of her door. And a note explaining. He was gone from her life. He'd sensed her misgivings and had taken wing like one of his cranes.

It was Mariel's shoulder she'd cried on then. Mariel who'd taken her shopping the next day. Mariel who assured her Pino would be back. Her lavender silk pajamas were a legacy of their spree. That, and a gold chiffon skirt and black cashmere sweater, low cut and off the shoulder. New Year's Eve they'd splurged on dinner at the Cantina di Triunfo.

They followed the repast with La Traviata at the San Carlo.

At intermission, Mariel went to retrieve champagne. As Natalia surveyed the fancy crowds, someone tapped her shoulder.

"So, I was right," Elisabetta Donati's blue eyes sparkled. "I spotted you coming in, but Fabio insisted it couldn't be.

You should get out of uniform more often. How are you, my dear?"

"Good," Natalia said. "Where is the colonel?"

"He's having his New Year's cigarette."

"The colonel is smoking again?" Natalia asked.

"He's allowed one on New Year's and one on his birthday."

Mariel approached, a glass in each hand. Natalia made the introductions.

"The bookstore on Porta Alba, isn't it?"

"You look familiar, too," Mariel said.

"I get all my art books there. Wonderful place. Excuse me ladies, I'd better powder my nose before they start ringing those infernal bells." She kissed Natalia. "Enjoy your bubbly."

Now this second vase on her desk completed the circle. Pino was back in her heart and about to move in.

Her phone buzzed.

"Captain Monte," she answered automatically.

"Did you get them?"

"They're beautiful, Pino. You shouldn't have wasted your money."

Angelina picked up the watering can and stepped out.

"Your concierge told me to tell you she's glad you finally came to your senses. Oh, she gave us a housewarming present. I think it's a trivet. She probably used it to serve her husband his hot meals when he was alive."

"How romantic," Natalia said. "What else?"

"I rearranged some of the furniture."

"I can't talk now."

"How does butternut squash risotto sound? We can try out the trivet. When shall I expect my beloved?"

"There's a lot going on. I may have to work late."

"Eight o'clock?"

"Eight thirty."

"*Perfetto*. I don't know if I can bear taking a shower. I love having your smell on me."

"Look," Natalia said to Pino, "I have to get off."

"Understood."

"I'll see you later."

"Give the stems a fresh cut, okay? I love you."

The risotto and one round of passionate love later, Pino and Natalia faced one another in a tangle of sheets.

Pino's slim chest was tanned from working outside. Natalia imagined he'd worn nothing but yoga pants or jeans in the country. She could see him there, moving among the bees and sunlight. Natalia inhaled his scent: somewhere between clove and sex. They kissed and rubbed their faces together. Noses, cheeks, mouth, tongue.

"Is my beard scratchy? Shall I shave?"

"No. I like the rustic look."

"Oh? You like it rough?" He pushed her down. She must have fallen into a light sleep. When she opened her eyes, she found him watching her in the faint light.

"Fabio had me in for a talk," he said. "I have another month before I'm expected to report back to duty." He stroked her stomach. "So I was thinking, if we have a child, you'll need to take a leave of absence, and I want us to be able to afford it."

"A kid? You blow back into town, and now we're having a baby? What if one isn't in the picture?"

"Baby or no, we're meant to be together."

"No one is meant to be together, Pino. That's another of your romantic notions. You're on extended leave. You have no income," Natalia said.

"I know."

"Well, I'm not giving up my career, and we both can't stay in the ranks. Not serving in the same city anyway. Which would make for quite a hurdle as far as having a relationship. And when and if you quit entirely, you'll forfeit your income and pension."

"It's a conundrum."

"What are you thinking to do? We couldn't very well live on one salary."

He kissed her and said, "Turns out the *zendo* wants to add a yoga component to the practice. They need to attract more people. They're interested in my developing a following for them. They can't pay much to begin, but it's something. In a few months I could open my own studio. Good, right?"

"I don't think so."

"Okay. Well, then, Fabio and I, we're going to meet again next week to see where I might fit in."

"I thought you were done with the Carabinieri."

"Probably. But I don't want to completely close the door if there's a chance. A special post, unofficial."

"There is no unofficial," Natalia said. "You're dreaming again."

He placed her hands over his chest. "My heart is in your hands."

"So melodramatic," Natalia said.

"I love you. Don't deny your feelings, Natalia. We may not have the same opportunity in the next life."

"The next life? You sound like *Zia* Giovanna."

"Maybe she understood something about what's important in life."

"Maybe. The woman was afraid of her own shadow."

"But that's my point exactly. Fear. Look at the birds. When they take to the air, they leave the dark shadows behind."

Chapter 16

The motorcycle screeched to a halt in the alley beside San Paolo Maggiore. A girl in a gold minidress and gladiator sandals slid off the back. For good measure, her lover gunned the engine, terrifying a flock of pigeons rummaging for food.

Cleopatra pulled off her helmet. A pair of sapphire eyes appeared from behind the dark glasses she pushed up onto her forehead. Lover boy slouched in his seat. Helmets dangling, they embraced.

The couple remained glued together as she stepped around them. Nice, Natalia thought. Cupid working her tricks. Such passion. She hoped it would lead to happy days and not jealousy or death.

She wondered if she was projecting her own concerns, her fears, about the rekindled relationship with Pino. Living together was working out better than she would have dreamed, a fact she hadn't confessed to anyone—certainly not to Pino, not even to Mariel. She was more in love than ever.

And she was well aware that that put her in a vulnerable position were something to go wrong. And who was she kidding? Of course it would.

She tried to remind herself to live in the moment, to enjoy what they had. She'd never put much credence in horoscopes, but what they said about Cancers seemed to be true if Pino were an accurate example. He was a real homebody, something she hadn't appreciated before they lived together.

Two days after his return, her dingy bathroom was transformed into a sunny space with a couple of coats of canary yellow paint. Her balcony was suddenly awash in coleus plants: purples and yellows and greens. One night she returned to a candlelight dinner. Another, he swept her up to Capodimonte, and they watched the fiery sun set over Naples as they consumed chocolate and wine.

He was so spontaneous. For her, such a creature of habit, his free spirit was a delight. What was the poem Mariel had showed her once when she was dating the crazy painter? Something along the lines about being with the lover made the poet feel twice alive? Yes, that was it. Twice alive. That captured perfectly how she felt being with Pino. But when and if their relationship ended . . . how would she feel then? Twice dead?

It was the heat of the day, but the alley was cool.

An itinerant *magliare* tried his luck selling white and black socks to patrons at sidewalk tables. The headwaiter shooed him away. Undaunted, he gave him the finger and made for the café immediately adjoining.

These wandering merchants, a throwback from olden days, slipped from honest labor into shadier practices with utter ease. Now and then, they were given a low level job by the Camorra. Nothing too complicated: break the windows of a store, maim someone's dog.

They were cheap, bought for a few boxes of cigarettes, a half-dozen, knock-off designer scarves. They were also out and about and sometimes privy to useful information. Information paid a little better. Not much.

Regardless, they were loyal to the criminals who ran their districts and grateful for their hardscrabble lives. And it made sense, their loyalty. Most were without education and couldn't read or write. How else were they to eke out a living? Which is why no one ever spoke of a *magliare* operating as a snitch. Besides loyalty, the penalty of a swift and painful death kept them in line. Even if offered relocation by the authorities, that was no guarantee of physical safety. Besides, they were as wed to their streets and way of life as was Natalia. It was in their blood and hers.

Musing on this, Natalia arrived at Stefano's building. The downstairs gate swung open and a blue Fiat inched out. Natalia slipped in, arriving unannounced. The elevator was engaged, so she walked up the echoing staircase.

Using the brass sun doorknocker, she rapped twice gently. Voices murmured inside, and the door cracked open. A tan Stefano greeted her, somewhat surprised to find her at his door.

"Sorry to intrude. Is this a bad time?" Natalia asked.

Behind Stefano a slim young man in a red and white t-shirt and khaki shorts lay sprawled on the couch.

"No, not at all." He stepped aside to let her enter. "Serge, do you mind?" he said back into the room and then to her: "A friend from Paris. He's doing some research at Paestum. Seemed like a waste, this big apartment. No one to share it with. My therapist says I have to go on with my life." He laughed bitterly. "Sometimes I wonder what is the point after all?"

"You won't always feel this way," Natalia said.

"That's what I'm told. Grief makes one quite self-centered, I'm discovering. But you didn't come here to discuss my mental state, I'm sure."

"I don't want to upset you further," Natalia said.

"I'm not sure there is a further, Captain Monte. So . . ." He pulled himself together. "How can I be of use today? Or is there news?"

"Not yet. Except I didn't want you to hear that we've arrested Garducci and have you mistake that as being for the murder of Vincente. It's not. It's for another matter."

"Some days I wonder if it's better not to know. Please, come. Forgive my terrible manners. Voila—the new couch. Vincente thought white quite impractical. He'd disapprove."

Natalia wasn't sure she didn't agree with the departed curator, as she sat on the pristine white leather. "Thank you," she said. She wasn't sure how to begin the conversation and sat in awkward silence for a moment.

"Please," Stefano said, "I'm not so fragile. How can I help you?"

"I'm exploring a new theory. Do you mind a few questions?"

"Not at all."

"To your knowledge, when Vincente and Garducci were first involved, did he ever rough up Vincente?"

"Nothing more than Vincente agreed to, if that's what you're getting at. Why?"

"Did Vincente ever discuss his boss, Garducci, with you?"

"Now and then he came up. Not my favorite subject."

"And Bagnatti?"

"Nothing more than some reminiscences from when they were friends way back."

"Were you ever aware of talk at the museum about Garducci? I mean, apart from having to do with his affair with Vincente? Other involvements?"

"Way back? There was some speculation that he may have been fucking someone prominent, maybe high up in government or law enforcement or, hell, movies for all I know. The rumor was that the director was having it off with someone of note."

"And Vincente didn't know who?"

"If he did, he never said."

Back on the street, Natalia took a call from Angelina. The word had just come down from the Directorate for Anti-Mafia Investigation. Old Gianni Scavullo, father of Ernesto, father-in-law of Suzanna, husband to Renata, and the oldest Camorra head in Naples, was about to be released from prison.

Natalia turned onto Via Salvatore Tommasi. There wasn't a speck of shade. Sweaty and winded from the climb, she paused and took a deep breath.

A boy ran up the hill past her and darted into an alley.

"*Attenzione!*" someone called. A hearse maneuvered its way on the narrow street. Behind it a procession of mourners made their way to the church. Young men in dark suits, glamorous women in high heels and sleek multicolored frocks, hidden by designer sunglasses. All of them wearing long sleeves and stockings when it had to be close to 90 degrees, 32 centigrade.

It seemed summers were getting hotter. She yearned for September. Only during the rainy season would there be a respite from the baking heat. October was even better, the season of the *ottobrate*, excursions into the countryside by those who could afford to escape. For Natalia and her kin, as in many poor families, whoever could organize a car would arrange a meeting time and place. Everyone converged on the place and squeezed in.

First thing when her relatives arrived in the country, they had a sumptuous picnic and uncoiled in the sunlight to digest and rest like contented snakes. Once revived, they set out hunting for chestnuts and dandelions. Now and then they'd come across a shepherd with his flock.

The adventurous went into the woods after mushrooms that sprouted like tiny ghost villages among the moss and decay on the forest floor.

Afterwards, she and her father would lie in the fields waiting for the flights of birds heading south. Their mournful cries as they headed to Africa signaled the change of season. When the fireflies began flickering, they'd head back to rejoin the family for the trip back to town.

Unlike the other families, they didn't return triumphant with a collection of bloody carcasses. Her father had never taken to the pleasure of hunting game unlike every other male over the age of thirteen. Even during the war when food had been so scarce.

NUMBER 43, HEADQUARTERS, COMMANDO LEGIONALE CARABINIERE said the sign. The second *m* was missing. The scruffy walls were beige, and thick metal grates covered the few windows on the ground floor. Natalia pushed the bell and held up her photo ID to the video camera overhead.

The former monastery was more than four centuries old. You could see its past grandeur as the green metal door swung slowly open onto its enormous courtyard. The sudden shift in scale from portal to expanse always surprised her.

Hands behind his back, the guard greeted Natalia. "Everything okay?"

"*Si, si,*" she answered and stated her business. He led her into the reception area. The officer working intake was on his phone. Natalia studied the black-and-white photographs on the wall. Most from a long ago time. Two men came in to pick up their identification cards from the pigeonholes above the receptionist's desk as they reported to work and rushed toward the locker room to get into uniform. If they were lucky, they'd spend a quiet day fielding calls and watching some football.

Just then the officer on desk duty jumped up, slapped on his cap and jogged outside to join the entry guard. Both stood at attention, saluting, as a limousine slipped past. Their commander, no doubt. She found herself once again grateful Colonel Fabio kept the military courtesies and ceremonies minimal at Casanova. She was proud to be a member of the armed forces but could do without the flourishes, especially the formal deference paid to superiors.

The officer in reception finished his call and wrote down her ID number on a sheet of paper. He asked her to wait across the hall.

The waiting room didn't have much on Casanova either: two upright chairs with brown leather seats and a matching couch. The main difference was that there were no anxious crowds of complainants waiting to be seen. She was alone. The fact that it was a Sunday may have had something to do with it, but not all.

Headquarters was more a military installation than a working law enforcement station. The rank and file was called out for disasters and important ceremonies that were held in the courtyard. Also press conferences, award presentations and induction ceremonies for the newest recruits. But the men stationed there were more likely to be called out for deployment to war zones overseas than for police work. Currently, part of the brigade was again in the Middle East. They had lost several men during this latest violence and many more than a few during the civil war in the former Yugoslavia.

A corporal greeted her and escorted her across a wide concrete yard. A few potted plants dotted its perimeter in a feeble effort at decoration, and a single, spindly palm rose fifty feet in the air. They entered the building at the far side. Proceeding down quiet halls, she followed him to the door of the person she had requested to see.

"Thank you for seeing me."

The major greeted her warmly. He'd kept his slim figure. A few threads of silver in his mustache and hair. He still invited trust as he always had.

"Always a pleasure, Major," she said.

He'd been one of her teachers when she was in training. A decent man, one of the few who hadn't given her grief for daring to enroll as a female recruit. It was the major who had arranged for her assignment to Casanova afterward. His own father had mentored Fabio. And he himself had idolized his father and had grown up wanting to be a Carabiniere from the time he was ten.

His first posting had been to Rome, but Naples was where he'd made his name, taking on the head of the Rimaldi clan.

Major Tucci now headed internal affairs. Carabinieri in all of Naples's nearly thirty stations reported to him and him alone. No doubt he was aware of her and Pino. He knew of anyone in the ranks who fraternized or consorted with Camorra members or relatives.

The last thing Natalia wanted was to voice any suspicions about her lover, but at this point she felt she didn't have a choice.

His phone rang. He mouthed "Sorry," and took the call. "*Si, signora. Lo so. Exacto. Si, si, secorro. Arrivederci,*" he said and hung up. "Do I want to be a speaker at the celebration Friday night? No. I'd rather be home with my wife. But do I have a choice?" He laughed. "Goes with the job. In a few more years, they'll be sending you out to speak about how well you were received by the all-male contingents of Carabinieri. Or have they already?"

"Public affairs sent me to a high school last year," Natalia said. "Actually, it was kind of nice."

"Good on you. I hear only good things about you, Natalia. Bravo."

"Thank you, sir."

"So what brings you here? The Scavullo business I assume? Anything I can do to help you get him would be my pleasure. Another tap. I've got a marvelous technician working for me."

"I appreciate the offer, but we haven't the need at the moment."

"Good. So, what is it I can do for you?"

"Two things actually. The first is more of a personal nature."

A Carabiniere in black fatigues popped his head in and stopped, seeing Natalia. "You're busy."

"Give me half an hour." Major Tucci got up and closed the door. "Is Pino Loriano back from leave yet?"

"It's a bit up in the air."

"You and the sergeant made a great team, Natalia. And you're partnered now with that rookie from Palermo, Angelina Cavatelli. That's working out?"

"Very much so. You do know everything, don't you?"

"Occupational hazard." He smiled, pleased. "Given that she's from Palermo, we pay close attention. It would be just too easy to plant someone. Certain parties in Sicily would love to latch on to a piece of Naples. And, yes, we've kept an eye on Pino, too, naturally. Someone goes on indefinite leave, it catches our attention."

"Did you find a problem with him?"

"The truth? He was seen in Mergellina Park with one of the Gracci girls. Do you know anything about that?"

"Yes. They're friends. She had a crush on him a while back. He's helping her out at present. She's pregnant."

"Right. Natalia, I have no doubt about your friend's honesty. But he's naïve, in the best sense. Whether he should be allowed to resume duty given the circumstances, I can't really say. Is that what you wanted to know?"

"Yes, sir."

"Your private life is your private life. That is understood. I don't have a problem with your relationship provided you don't serve together. The situation with the Gracci girl is another matter. Be careful, Natalia. You're doing a terrific job. There's no reason you won't be promoted in due course. I'd hate to see you jeopardize all you've worked for."

"Yes, sir. The second thing I wanted your advice about is the case I'm on."

"The double murder?"

"Yes. I have several suspects, a countess among them."

"Fabio and Elisabetta's friend."

"Antonella Cavazza, yes. The bodies were found in her garden. Her beloved father was betrayed by the fascists during the war and gruesomely executed by the Germans with piano wire."

"Slow and painful."

"Yes." Natalia explained his brave work in the Resistance until he was reported by someone in the Lattaruzzo clan. And how after the armistice, the Lattaruzzos got out, fled to Naples, where eventually their grandson Vincente wound up a curator and socializing with the countess.

"Oh, my."

"Several things at the scene pointed to vendetta."

"Scavullo settling scores for the *contessa?*"

"Yes, except it was made way too obvious."

"Maybe he wanted credit for his crime," Tucci said.

"Perhaps. But I can't shake the feeling that he's playing us. That we are thinking exactly what he wants us to think."

"And now you have an added complication."

"Sir?"

"Gianni Scavullo is about to be released."

"Which presents us with a whole other set of possible Camorra troubles in Naples."

"You mean, if he attempts to resume command of the clan. Would his son stand for it?"

"Exactly."

"That's a hard one." The major described Papa Gianni's first years in the pen. He'd carried on with bravado, like nothing had changed. Furnished his cell like a hotel room. Luxury mattress, Persian carpet, easy chair, small bar. Had marble laid over the linoleum floor. Listened to opera on his stereo and watched soccer games played all over the world on his satellite dish TV. Hell, a barber came in twice a week, as did the *capos*. Twice a week Renata brought him home-cooked meals and salamis.

"He had everything," Natalia said. "Everything but freedom."

"Weekend furloughs in a facility near the prison: the

next best thing. Conjugal visits there. Then came 41-bis. You remember?"

"The program to isolate Camorra dons doing time, reduce their interaction with cronies and block their control of their gangs," Natalia recalled.

"Right. Contact was reduced to an hour a month, with the inmate in a glass cage, and communicating with visitors on handsets, all of them monitored and recorded."

"I remember," Natalia said, "but that didn't last long."

"Sadly, no. Human rights organizations lobbied it out of existence."

"And his relationship with Ernesto?" Natalia said.

"At first Ernesto faithfully visited twice a week to get his orders and update his old man. Last couple of years, he visits once a month maybe. The old guys who worked for his father, he kicked to the side of the road. Promoted young ones—muscle-builder types, not long on brains. Can't imagine Papa likes being disrespected or how his son turned out."

"Can you blame him?" said Natalia. "Ernesto is an arrogant bastard. Makes his father seem like a gentleman. In the past five years all but two of Gianni's trusted associates have been sidelined. Several of his contemporaries died, some retired, a couple disappeared, as you know."

Tucci picked up his pipe. "You mind? I can open the window."

"Go ahead, sir."

"Gianni hasn't many allies left in the organization. And Ernesto doesn't strike me as the type to concede his power. He's not going to want to be his old man's lackey again."

Natalia nodded. "But you think it unlikely Gianni Scavullo is in a position to regain control?"

"I do. But he shouldn't be underestimated either. He's

old school, as tough as they come. Even imprisoned, he had an enemy transferred to his penitentiary and put in the same cell block so he could personally kill him."

"Not like the mafia dons," she said. "Not like his son, either, who delegates most everything, running his outfit from a distance, like an executive."

"Amazing how different generations are, father and son." Tucci looked at his watch. "Come."

He treated her to a coffee in the canteen from where she could see into the window of the *basso* next door, framed by starched white curtains embroidered with green and yellow pears. Immediately she thought of stopping to see Antonietta, though a visit with her father's only remaining sister was never a simple affair. It would involve hearing about all her current and past ailments, then being fed a heavy meal. During the requisite drinking of *aurum* (a heavy liqueur never to Natalia's liking), followed by a cake made of maize flour—an interrogation would commence. About Natalia's love life.

But after leaving the major, a sense of obligation guided her to the *basso* tucked into a corner of the district.

Its tiny porch was laced with a grape arbor. From it you could see for miles out over the city and the harbor. Natalia knocked and knocked again. Perhaps her aunt was out. Natalia decided to wait.

Luckily, she wasn't in uniform, or she would never have visited. Natalia made a point never to call on her *zia* in uniform. No need to complicate matters for her with her neighbors. Nosy they were; that was a fact. If they saw her insignia, Natalia had no doubt they would be at her *zia's* door before she was out of sight. They'd pester Antonietta with questions about the Carabiniere visiting one of their own. Ironic that what went on in headquarters was hardly of interest. Headquarters had to do with the world beyond them. No matter that it was less than a hundred metres away. It might as well have been on the moon.

Nearby several women had collected on the rectangular patch of concrete behind their apartments. Their desire was to smoke and gossip. That they ignored the spectacular view of their red and grey city was not surprising. It was that familiar in their everyday lives. They felt it more than saw it. It was there and would remain. Unchanged. And what did it do for them? Time spent staring at the expanse of their city and its harbor thick with ships they considered a waste. For the majority of them, a trip to Ischia or Capri would never have crossed their minds. So what did the picturesque ferries have to do with them? They much preferred to discuss who said what to whom, who had cheated on whom. Their lives were centered within the confines of their *vici*. Here were the people they dealt with on a daily basis. Everything they needed could be found here within these cramped blocks: church, market, café, funeral parlor. Neighbors, friends, enemies.

If they needed something fixed, they rarely had to go far. When Natalia visited as a child, there was still a man in the neighborhood who repaired umbrellas. Natalia was often sent to his building with the offending item. Proud to be given the responsibility, she'd shout as loud as she could. He'd come to the window, see who was calling, then lower a bucket. She'd put the umbrella in and watch while he hauled it, swaying several stories, up to his apartment. Three days later it was her job to collect it. Good as new, she lifted it out of the bucket, placed the few *lire* in its place and was on her way, the transaction complete. An exchange based on trust and familiarity.

Even in this day and age, few locals would consider

marrying someone they hadn't known all their lives. Certainly no one outside their *rione*, their region.

Life beyond had little impact. Now and then a check arrived from a relative in America. It was duly deposited in the bank or taken to their local money dealer and cashed. Now and then there was a trip to a government office or a specialist: major expeditions, carefully planned. They did not rest easy until they'd returned. Most never yearned for distant shores. They were content. And for diversion there was always a christening, a wedding, or a funeral to attend and friendships to revisit.

On a far corner, Natalia could just see the edge of the Capellino Funeral Home. The current Capellino's grandfather had been one of the most successful coffin makers in Naples, and she remembered vividly one particular casket that he had made for show, carved and painted with gold angels and silver cupids. Natalia and her parents had accompanied her aunt window-shopping for her own among garish, factory-made boxes. When her mother suggested simpler ones, Antonietta bristled.

Antonietta's house was almost as familiar to Natalia as her own. The whitewashed walls. The plaster saints that crammed the shelves. The long table that took pride of place in the center of one of the three rooms.

On more than one occasion, Antonietta had lectured Natalia about how much better life was when the gangster Di Laura was running things. "You had a problem, he took care of it. There weren't all these troubles, like now. Man was a gentleman."

Antonietta had grown up in the notorious Secondigliano district and ridden the infamous R5 bus, which had obviously colored her view. The drivers on the route often stopped to let drug dealers off to make a deal then get back on the bus. The passengers waited patiently; no one dared complain. That the crime boss held a tight fist over the neighborhood—well, without him, they rationalized things would be a lot worse.

Natalia wondered if there were places of evil, where evil deeds were called forth. Places with bad karma as Pino would say. Places cursed. Some days she believed Naples qualified, a city under the Camorra thumb, Mount Vesuvius in the distance, ready to blow again.

Certainly Secondigliano qualified, its grinding poverty rivaling any in the south. Pozzuoli, too. And the village of Baia where Nero had murdered his mother, Agrippina, then invited his familiars to view the body. He pulled at her lifeless limbs, wanting them to judge her physical merits. They knew better than to offer compliments if they wanted to live.

Natalia had long ago given up trying to explain to Antonietta why a city operating under the thumb of a Di Lauro was not, in fact, a good thing. She made a point to emphasize it wasn't "God's will," as her aunt put it, that the mayor was beholden to a don, that even her husband had paid a *pezzo* to a local thug. That didn't sway her aunt. Antonietta's counterargument was that the money went for a good cause. Their neighborhood had the best floats when it came to festival days, times she loved. Who else would pay for that?

Her husband had been one of the last of the *pazzoriellos*. Natalia remembered him wearing his cocked hat and, accompanied by two drummers and a piper, entering shops, waving his stick about to banish evil spirits for which the shopkeeper would give them a few *lire*. People still believed life was better when they could depend on the *pazzariellos'* powers, just as they were nostalgic for the old Camorra.

It was only when she informed her *zia* that she was going to be one of those Carabinieri who fight the clans that Antonietta backed off. Natalia even convinced her to remove the photograph of Lucky Luciano and his pal Genovese from their pride of place beside the Pope.

Family loyalty trumped Antonietta's convictions about how the city should be run . . . for about a week.

Natalia's choice was foreign to her. That a woman would pursue a career was strange enough. "Why don't you get married? There's nothing wrong with you!" she exclaimed on more than one occasion.

Antonietta had never worked outside the home, though she was an excellent seamstress and sometimes took in mending, as Natalia's mother had done, keeping her family fed during the war by taking apart Allied uniforms and turning them into serviceable clothes. That these uniforms were delivered to her by Domenico Lupo's bandits hadn't fazed her. Lupo was the most notorious of the many that thrived in the wake of the war. No friend to the Camorra, he went on his own, for which the Allies liked him, even though they were well aware he was robbing them blind.

He was a saint in the eyes of the people because he would turn up now and then at a poor home with a sack of food and a thousand *lire* notes. That he had stolen the food and made the money on goods he expropriated from the armed forces that had liberated their city did not pose a moral dilemma. One did what one had to. The black market was the least of it.

And sometimes Natalia wondered who she was to judge. Her mother once confided that Antonietta's sister had been forced into prostitution during the war. She'd been among the thousands afflicted with VD. Periodically the city officials, goaded by the Allies, were forced to do a sweep—the girls hauled off to a hospital to be tested. For ten thousand *lire* a *sciaquapalle*, a ball cleaner, went to the hospital director and arranged for a bill of good health. In the case of her *zia's* sister, the result of continued employment was sterility and an early death.

Natalia's *zia* was no doubt among those who mourned when Lupo was finally taken down by a jealous girlfriend who had been shown expertly doctored pictures of him with a prostitute's naked legs encircling him. Arrested, he was transported to Poggio Reale, then to the special prison on the island of Procida and left there to rot.

The day he left their shore, a goodly number of the population joined Antonietta in wearing black.

Up until the day of Natalia's induction, her *zia* tried to talk her niece out of her chosen career. She was making a mistake, she argued. There were certain things one didn't question. You went about your business and averted your eyes from everything else. To do otherwise was dangerous. Life with the Camorra was life as she knew it. Natalia realized that for Antonietta, the Camorra was no worse than any other authority and sometimes better. She trusted none of them. Even her priest at San Carlo all'Arena, where she'd been married, where her husband had been laid out. To her *zia*, there was no difference between the clerics or the mayor or the *madrina*. They were all corrupt. And the ordinary person was therefore freed to survive through disobedience and even crime.

"*Lo stesso,*" she said. The same.

And then she threw in her trump card: Lola. Antonietta had always been fondest of Lola. She was the friend her *zia* was most comfortable with. Unlike Mariel, who seemed strange to her, almost exotic. A sophisticated little girl, polite and too quiet.

Natalia would never forget the moment of her aunt's ultimate argument against enlisting: "What about Lola? What're you gonna do, put your girlfriend in jail?"

Back then Natalia thought it was just her aunt being dramatic. But as time went on, she wondered if she hadn't been prescient.

Antonietta opened the door. She kissed her niece then made the sign of the cross and kissed her fingertips. Natalia couldn't remember seeing her aunt in anything but widow's black, which today included a saggy black sweater over her black dress.

"*Zia*, it's a hundred degrees! Forty centigrade!" Natalia exclaimed as she kissed her.

"I'm just out of the shower. You want me to catch cold? Come in, child. Come in."

Chapter 17

The day after Natalia's confab with the major, Suzanna answered the door, a white poodle snuggled in her arms. Her onyx and diamond hairband matched the dog's collar.

"Look at you," Suzanna said. "Don't you look cute in your uniform. Come in. Meet Shasha."

She held up the dog for Natalia to admire: a miniature white poodle. Natalia patted Shasha's head and followed her owner's gardenia scent down a long hallway into the living room.

Flanking the entry were a pair of onyx and white marble end tables. Across the room two green brocade couches mirrored one another, between them a Persian rug saturated with purples and splashes of ochers and greens. A baroque lamp with red butterflies gamboling on the creamy silk shade stood in the middle. Several white orchids were displayed in small gold pots on the ebony coffee table. Against the back wall a mahogany bar held every kind of liquor imaginable.

"Just abandoned my mother's place. You were there, no?"

"Once, I think. Your communion party."

"That sounds right. Marzipan angels?" Suzanna laughed.

"And almond candy," Natalia said, "coated in white sugar."

"Mama still has my dress. I was just going to treat myself to *prosecco*. Can I get you one?"

"Sounds great."

Suzanna had made a big deal out of the visit—drinks, a platter of fancy cakes on a low table between them. The dog skittered over to Natalia.

"He bother you? I can put him in my bedroom."

"No, it's fine."

While the dog sniffed her ankles, Natalia surveyed the rest of the room. Not her style, but impressive.

"Like it?" Suzanna handed Natalia a glass of pale green liquid.

"Amazing."

"First thing I did: got a feng shui expert. Rid the place of bad vibes. Helped me arrange everything. Feels harmonious right? To Auld Lang Syne."

"Cheers." Natalia and her old classmate clinked glasses.

Suzanna sat down. "You should see my mother's place. Nothing has changed, except it's all gotten dingier."

"I remember it was very large."

"Seriously, the wire's been sticking out of her cushions for the past two years. Like it would kill her to get a couple of new cushions."

Suzanna filled her in on life in London.

"You can't find a decent *prosecco* to save your ass. Plus the winters suck. But you should see my mink. I look like the original ice queen."

What was it with these women and mink, Natalia thought. First Lola. Now Suzanna. At least London was climate appropriate.

"Mama having a good visit with your brother and their new baby?"

"She and the wife don't get along—surprise, surprise. Calls every day, threatens to come home." Suzanna played with a jeweled mobile phone and handed it to Natalia.

A blurry baby's face swam into view. Enormous black eyes. Pink frilly cap.

"Cute," Natalia said. "You enjoying Naples?"

"Yeah, well." Suzanna made a face. "God, I hate this place. Everyone's in your business."

"Why'd you come back?"

"Who said I was coming back? I promised Nicky I'd check on Mama. How did she seem to you?"

"She seemed . . . the same."

"Right? Nicky's a pain in the ass. So is she. She's wearing the same old rags she wore after Papa died. Like he's going to be offended if she wears a new blouse. Uses the same rancid perfume that she got when I was twelve. I opened one of her lipsticks? It had turned to chalk. I tried to get someone in to clean, and she threw a fit. Sorry about your mom and dad," she added.

"Thanks. It's been a long time, but it still hurts."

"Sure. She drives me crazy, but when Mama goes, I can't imagine."

Natalia reassured her that with her mother's stubbornness, it wasn't going to happen any time soon. "You'll never guess who I ran into the other day. Liana Pagano. Sister Immaculata."

"Sweet Liana," Suzanna said.

"She asked after you. Wanted to know how you were doing. She'd love to see you."

"And me her. God, Liana, a nun. Jesus, the good old days, right? Only we didn't realize then."

"Yeah."

"Then came my darling Ernesto."

"We were all envious. You'd found your soul mate. Just like in the paperback romances. So what was it like being courted like that? Limousines picking you up at school? Dining out at extravagant restaurants? Flowers arriving every day? A dream wedding?"

"Dream is right. It was exciting at first. He proposed the day we met. A week later we were living together and married in another month. I had my own maid. Every morning she brought me breakfast in bed. Wheeled in on a tray. A vase with a fresh baby rose. It was amazing: pineapple and blood oranges sculpted into flowers. Chocolate croissants. The maid laid out my clothes. He wanted me to look good. We're talking Versace, St. Laurent, Halston. I wasn't allowed to lift a finger. Couldn't wash a pair of undies or a plate. Anything I wanted was mine. I admired a sapphire bracelet in Rinaldo's window, and in a blink of an eye it was on my wrist. He found out I'd never tasted caviar and ordered an iced shipment air delivered overnight to the house from Moscow."

"What went wrong?"

"First time the maid got in bed with us, I'm surprised. No, it was more like stunned and embarrassed. Shamed. But he's my husband, you know? Then he asks me to do things . . . with men he's brought home. He liked to watch and be watched. It got worse. He was into cutting."

"Himself?"

"Me."

"Jesus," Natalia said.

"It was like I was living alone after a while. Except for the times he paraded me around in public like a trophy, I never saw him. Man was never home. Middle of the night the phone rings? I answer it, they hang up. Ten minutes later, he's out the door, weighed down with cologne. I figured he was going off to one of his bimbos."

"Why didn't you leave?"

"Pride, I guess. I couldn't go back to my parents. I'd made my bed, you know? Next thing I know, I'm pregnant. He goes nuts. Accuses me of doing it deliberately, of sabotaging his life. Punches me in the abdomen and throws me out of the house."

"We had no idea."

"I couldn't let on, could I?" Suzanna leaned back into the couch, head resting on the edge. "It was sort of tolerable for a while. Until the pregnancy. When he struck me like that, I almost lost my mind. Well . . . you know."

"That was terrible," Natalia said. "Lola, Mariel—we all felt for you. But you really loved Ernesto, didn't you?"

"Loved? Yeah, I suppose so. You know how it is. I was a virgin."

"You're kidding."

"You're surprised? A good Catholic girl? Sister Benedicta had me terrified. All that stuff about hell. Underneath I still believe it—you?"

"I don't know. Probably," Natalia said. "That's when you . . ."

"Went berserk. Right. Put on quite a show for the folks on Via Tribunali. I was raving. They had to put me in a strait jacket."

"I'm sorry," Natalia said.

"Don't be. I got myself together, didn't I, Princess?" she

picked up the dog and kissed it on the mouth. "I'm in the hospital, sedated. Hubby pays a visit to my mama and papa. Suggests I'd be better looked after in a clinic abroad somewhere. Not Spain, not France, either. Not in continental Europe. It was all Lucia could do to keep my father from killing him."

"That's terrible," Natalia said.

"Don't waste your tears," Suzanna said. "I was a kid. Naïve. I left Suzie Ruttollo behind a long time ago."

"How did your father-in-law take it?"

"He was scandalized. We'd gotten along. Plus he'd been looking forward to a grandchild."

"But he didn't intervene?"

"Between an Italian husband and his Italian wife?" Suzanna shook her head. "They were very different, those two. Papa Gianni was a worker bee. Donated to the Sisters of Charity. Attended mass every day. Drove the same Fiat he'd had since 1965."

"Yes, the local hero."

"Papa Gianni was invited to every christening, every wedding. Gave a generous gift of cash without fail, even while imprisoned. He's still paying for the fireworks and floats on saints' days and holidays, though you'd never catch him riding on one. He and Renata still live in the same apartment they moved into when they were married."

"That's certainly not his son's style."

"No. Ernesto likes it fancy. And he was always a lazy son of a bitch. Don't get me wrong—he paid his dues for Papa. Killed more than a few with his own hands. Nowadays? As if you people don't know. Lounges by the pool after he lifts his weights. Pops his vitamins, counts out the grams of protein in his food. In between phone calls he screws whoever is on hand. He's big into promotion. Facebook. Twitter.

Like he's some kind of a brand. Have you heard the song?" Suzanna said.

"'The Devil Fucks Satan'?"

"I heard he paid a hundred and fifty thousand euros to this hot band in Turin to write a song about him. He told one radio deejay if he didn't play the song, he'd personally break his legs."

"Sweet," Natalia said. "What happened to your baby?"

Suzanna's face lost its color. "I . . . I'm sorry. I can't speak of it."

Natalia lay in the crook of Pino's arm. "Uncle Ricci sends his love. He's so happy I've come to my senses. Said it's time to see some children running around in the country house."

"Since when does Uncle Ricci like children?"

"He's getting sentimental in his old age. Man hasn't been in a church since the war. Now he says he'll talk to Father Mario. Arrange a church ceremony. I told him Father Mario passed eight years ago. 'Whoever,' he said. He even took a suit out of the closet. '*Zio*,' I said. 'It's full of moth holes.' 'So I'll get a new one.'"

Natalia laughed. "How did he know I wanted a church wedding?"

"You do?"

"Doesn't every Neapolitan girl? I can see it now: the photo of Lola ascending the steps of Santa Chiara. And above the headline: CARABINIERI WED, CAMORRA Attend. Seriously, I can't talk about it right now. I have a lot on my plate."

"Tell me."

"Papa Gianni's getting out, for one. We could be in for a bloodbath anytime."

"And the other?"

"I'm not at liberty to say."

"Oh, it's like that now."

"Pino, it has to be."

"Come here. Let me take your mind off your troubles."

In minutes, Pino was snoring. Natalia returned to her pillow, but sleep wouldn't come. The door to the balcony was open. The moon was silvery and full. She watched as a cloud passed over, revealing its features then hiding them in shadow.

Chapter 18

Surveillance and intelligence reports from the police anti-mafia directorate indicated that Scavullo might be losing interest in his African girlfriend. Which made Natalia think it might be a good idea to see if they could talk to her when he wasn't around and maybe shake out some information about Ernesto.

It seemed obvious he was not faithful to her. In which case, she might be willing to vent.

In any case, Scavullo would know they'd been nosing around and wouldn't like it, which made it almost worthwhile. If it led to his doing something foolhardy, it would most certainly be worth provoking him. Albeit dangerous. The woman would have to be looked after.

Natalia asked Lola to keep her posted about Ernesto Scavullo's whereabouts. Lola reported that Ernesto was en route to Gaeta to see about a football team he was interested in acquiring. Natalia quickly collected Angelina, and they once again made the journey to the mobster's mansion on the hill.

Paolo was still guarding the door, looking stylish in a black suit, black shirt and magenta tie, though the sleeves of the jacket seemed oddly short. His bulking up had contributed to this. The extra bulge of his left shoulder was courtesy of his holster.

"He's not here," Paolo said.

Behind him, a maid vacuumed the foyer. A truck pulled into the circular drive hauling fresh laundry. Paolo waved it around the side to the service entrance near the garage.

"Friendly advice?" he said. "Stay the fuck away from him."

Natalia informed Paolo they weren't interested in talking to his boss. It was the girlfriend they wanted to see. Unofficially.

"That won't be possible," he said. "She isn't here. And even if she was, I'd still need you to leave. See up under the overhang of the roof? There's a camera trained on the front door. He could be watching us right now on his computer. He likes to keep track."

"And if he sees something he doesn't like seeing?"

"You don't want to know."

"We'd like to speak to the African woman," Angelina said. "Please."

"Look, ladies. The African dame disappeared during the night. I have no idea where she went."

"Why aren't you with the boss?" Natalia asked. "You don't travel with him anymore?"

"That's not your business, is it?"

"Depends how you look at it. Maybe you stayed here because something happened to the girl, and you had to clean up the mess. Is that it? Did Ernesto lose his famous temper?"

"Nothing's happened to the girl." He got a call on his hands-free device. "What time you gonna get here?" he said into the transceiver and listened. "Okay."

A girl sauntered up behind Paolo, running her hands through a mass of dark hair. She had on a yellow tank top and white gauzy pants—no evidence of underwear. Ignoring the Carabiniere, she kissed Paolo on the ear.

"You leave me any coffee, honey?"

Paolo shook her off. "I'm working. Get it yourself, or get the housekeeper to do it."

"Love you, too," she pouted and gave him the finger as she clacked off toward the kitchen in her red stilettos.

A maid walking a tall, grey whippet made her way across the grounds toward them, circling around the sprinklers. Unleashed, the dog trotted up the steps. They made quite a pair, Natalia thought, the royal dog, pointed nose quivering, the maid in blue-and-white pinstriped uniform and a little cap.

"The dog guy is running late," Paolo said to her. "He'll do the manicure and brush him when he gets here. Give Salvatore a sponge bath in the meantime. I'll call you when the groomer gets here. Take the pooch around the back, okay? The boss noticed a couple of scratches on the floor."

Getting nowhere, Angelina and Natalia walked away toward their car. A gardener caught up to them halfway down the drive. He checked to make sure no one was watching. He was a friend of the African girl, he explained. She hadn't told him where she was going, but he thought maybe to an uncle in Naples. He had the address. She'd given it to him and told him to contact her uncle if anything ever happened to her.

* * *

Clouds sugared the sky above the dark cramped streets of the Mergellina district. Natalia and Angelina found a place to park then joined locals and dozens of tourists who drifted through the square named after poet Jacopo Sannazaro.

Africans and Bengladeshis clotted the narrow sidewalk and spilled onto the street as they waited for goods to be offloaded from hulking ships docked nearby. Shopkeepers scrolled their smartphones. A few talked on their mobiles while they sat on the sidewalk, enjoying fresh falafel oozing from pita bread.

Nigerians were eclipsed now by Senegalese and Ghanaians. The Nigerians had been the first to arrive and included the women recruited by the Camorra as prostitutes.

The Africans were loyal and came cheap, qualities the *camorristi* liked. They liked their subservience, too. It didn't hurt that the men shared a deep-seated misogyny.

As a reward for good work, a few blacks were cut into the drug trade. When the Africans grew too ambitious, they were gunned down or otherwise executed. The lucky ones fled or lay low, waiting for the killing spree to spend itself.

Those who survived stood in the blistering sun outside the train station, hawking fake Rolex watches and Gucci shoes long into the night until the last commuter train pulled out.

As the two Carabinieri approached, the soft hum of voices ceased. The pair stepped into the street and made a wide circle around some men playing soccer. A girl texted on the sidewalk. Her toddler performed a drunken walk, then sprawled, shrieking beside her. The goalie jogged over and hoisted the baby onto his shoulders. He told his girlfriend to watch the baby, or he was going to find someone else to live with.

Two African men passed Natalia hauling enormous plastic bags. The stench of body odor gripped her. No wonder. They spent countless hours in the sweltering heat. And when they were not outside they were crammed into squalid living quarters, often five to a room, minimal bathing facilities.

They were hundreds of miles from their homes, away from all that they knew and loved. Each day was grueling. Often dangerous. But in spite of that, the men often seemed cheerful. They worked together, worshipped at church or in makeshift mosques. And somehow made the best of it.

The building Angelina and Natalia were looking for they found three blocks later. The entrance to the tenement was camouflaged by a giant dumpster.

Mohammed, A. was inked onto a piece of tape stuck next to a black button. Natalia pressed it. The door clicked open just as a man passed by, resplendent in gold and purple native dress.

The halls were warm and smelled of cooking oil. She and Angelina climbed three flights and rapped on the door. The African girl opened it. She'd traded in the short shorts and gold heels for a long blue robe and printed headscarf.

Angelina proffered her ID. "May we come in?"

The three women sat down abreast on an orange plastic couch that faced an enormous plasma screen. The TV was on. The black woman picked up the remote and turned it off.

"Did he threaten you?" Angelina asked. "Miss . . . ?"

"Keandra. No, not directly. He went away on business. Someone called in the middle of the night. Said I had better get out or I would be killed."

"Did you recognize the voice?" Natalia asked.

"No."

"Male or female?" Angelina had her pen poised over a notebook.

"I couldn't tell. Most likely male."

"What happened last night," Natalia said, "before you got the phone call?"

"I had dinner in my room. Watched a movie. Then I went to sleep."

"Didn't Paolo usually accompany him when he went out of town?" Natalia asked.

"Yes."

"Why didn't you go to Paolo after you got the call?" Angelina asked.

"Paolo doesn't like me."

"Excuse me for this," Natalia said, "but you seem like a nice woman. Why were you with Ernesto at all?"

"He was a poodle, but—"

"A poodle?" Natalia interrupted.

"It's what we call them back home. A rich man who pisses his semen. He likes it wild. You know? *Ammuchiata.* Orgies. With women and sometimes men. He'd fuck a dog to get off."

"Maybe you'd had enough," Natalia suggested.

"I'm going to have a baby." She rubbed her belly the way pregnant women did. "He said we would get married. He would behave. He gave me this."

The diamond was enormous, star-cut, surrounded by tiny sapphires. "He said they matched my eyes."

At least that part was true: her pale eyes were sky blue, startling against her skin.

"You think he will?" Angelina said. "Marry you, I mean."

"No. At first, maybe I thought so. He acted so nice, like

he was pleased. Then he beat me. How dare I try to trick him with a nigger child. I'm lucky he didn't kill me then."

"What stopped him?" Angelina asked.

"He got a call."

"You know he's going to find you here," Natalia said. "When is he coming back?"

"He's due tomorrow. Don't worry. I'm leaving sooner. Ernesto wouldn't dare to hurt me in a black church in the African neighborhood. He is afraid of us." She then reassured Natalia she was leaving on the first ferry in the morning bound for Tunisia. She'd make her way south from there. Back to her mother. She'd have her baby and a new life. "Ernesto would never step foot in Africa. He thinks it's uncivilized, filled with germs!"

Natalia hoped she was right. She put in a call to Casanova and arranged for an officer to meet them at the church. He was to guard Keandra overnight. Someone would relieve him to escort her safely to the piers.

Natalia and Angelina waited while she put a few things into a bag.

"Hurry up," Angelina said as Keandra pulled a few euros out of her purse and counted them up.

"I need to leave something for my uncle."

"Okay, but you can't write a note," Angelina said, taking the paper out of her hands and crumpling it.

They walked her down to the street, keeping her firmly between them. Minutes later Ernesto's gorgeous castoff was delivered to the storefront church. The officers scanned the area for anyone too interested in them.

A wizened nun answered the door. She was expecting Keandra and pulled her inside. Natalia explained she must keep the door locked at all times—admit no one unless she knew them well. A guard would be posted on the street overnight, and another would take Keandra to the ferry in the morning.

Natalia described them. If anyone else were to come around, she was to call them immediately.

"Thank you for helping me," Keandra touched Natalia's arm as the nun closed the door. "Bless you."

"What I can't figure," Angelina said as they returned to their car, "is why she would associate with someone like Scavullo to begin with? A beautiful woman, smart—what's her problem?"

"Her problem is that she didn't want a shitty life back in her country."

"So she'd rather have a shitty life here?"

"Probably thought she had it made, seeing the house and servants and cars."

"So foolish," Angelina said.

"Let she who lives in a glass house cast the first stone," Natalia said.

"Amen."

Natalia drove to the Piazza Gesu Nuovo and parked on a side street not far from Pietro Fabretti's shop. Natalia realized she had visited the instrument maker just next door to Fabretti's frequently with her cellist boyfriend, who swore by him, claiming he was the best in all of Europe. He returned twice a year to have the man lay his hands upon his precious cello.

It was that man who one afternoon told her the story of the composer Gesualdo slaughtered in a room on San Severo a few blocks away. Gesualdo, wearing a dress, killed by his male lover. Gino had played one of Gesualdo's cello compositions for Natalia when they'd first dated.

Usually she and her ex-fiancé met for lunch or a drink

when he was in town. The last time . . . could it have been a year ago? He announced he was getting married. She'd been surprised how much the news unsettled her.

"You didn't want him, remember?" Mariel said, after Natalia had burst into her friend's bookshop, weeping. They'd settled on a flowery couch with two large glasses of wine.

"You're devoted to your job," Mariel said. "He travels all the time and wanted you to go with him. Devote yourself to him and his career. Captain Natalia Monte, groupie. Recall all that? *Cara mia*, are you suffering from amnesia?"

"Probably," she'd said. "But he seems like such a grown-up compared to Pino."

"Trust me. 'Seems like' is the operative phrase here. They're *bambini*, Natalia. Granted, some are cute—sophisticated, even. But *bambini*, nonetheless. The exception being your father."

"And I thought Lola was the cynic."

"She is. Me, I'm just realistic. Remember that Catalan poet I was crazy about when we were seventeen? When he broke it off, I thought I'd perish. Passion. It leaves a scar. Look what happened to Suzanna, to Lola."

In front of the cathedral, a forlorn guitarist played a familiar Scarlatti piece for a few tourists gathered around to listen. His tattered cap was on the ground half filled with paper euros and coins.

Fabretti's shop, Sempre Musici, was on the far side of the *piazza*. Natalia walked across. Two elderly gentlemen sat on folding chairs just inside the open door. She could hear them arguing the topic perennial with the elderly of Naples: Which native son was the better tenor—Caruso or Lucia?

In spite of the heat, they were in suits and dingy ties. No

doubt they'd grown up privileged and had led lives of comfort, idling and arguing. Idleness remained, the wealth had vanished during the war. In some way their lives had stopped then. Inside the shop time stopped as well.

Peering through the window of the shop Gino once swore by, she noted the instrument maker working at his bench. She hadn't seen him in several years. A halo of the sun played about the shadowed room. His hair whiter than ever . . . he looked like a monk bent over the stringed instrument that was taking form in his hands. Natalia sighed and continued on her mission.

She climbed two steps into Fabretti's shop. Records and crumbling sheet music were arranged on tables throughout. A *catari* played on the sound system. Its singer had a lovely, eerie voice. Natalia remembered her *nonna* had sung such a song while mending.

Fabretti was perched on a stepladder pitched against the back wall, wielding an old-fashioned feather duster.

"*Giorno*," Natalia said.

"*Giorno*," he answered without turning around.

"It's Captain Monte."

"Oh." He laid the duster on a shelf. "I'll be right down."

"Careful," she said.

"Welcome to my humble shop," he said, coming down and extending his hand. "Are you looking for something special today?"

"Is there somewhere we can talk privately?"

"Of course."

Natalia followed him into a small side room. CDs and records were stacked in neat piles on a desk along one wall, boxes lined up along the other. He pulled up two chairs.

"Sorry these aren't more comfortable. I need the space for stock." He gestured toward the boxes.

"Vinyl records?"

"Vinyl, yes. You'd be amazed how many people still want the old long-playing discs and even 78s and 45s. How can I be of service?"

"I'm after some information that might help determine your Carlo's murderers."

"Is there some new development?"

"That's just it. I'm not sure, and I've come for your help in finding out."

"How can I help?"

"I have a suspicion something is true, and I'm not even sure what it would mean if it is."

"A suspicion?"

"About Ernesto Scavullo's love life."

"Love life?"

"Yes. That's a polite term for it."

"About what goes on in his mansion?"

Natalia nodded.

"I've heard the stories, too. They make it sound like a Roman brothel."

"At the very least. Sexual orgies on a regular basis. According to what I've heard, he likes it the kinkier, the better. Males, females, animals. If he's not participating directly, he gets off on watching. He directs the scenes, makes videos, posts them on porno sites. Were you aware of this?"

"No."

"The need to advertise, almost as if he's making a point. Hiding something. Have you heard anything?"

"There haven't been rumors to that effect. None that I've heard."

"No?"

"I'll make inquiries, discreetly. Give me a little time—a

week? Come back and buy some music. I'll treat you to a Tebaldi recording. Quite rare."

"I shall. Thank you." She turned to go.

"I should perhaps tell you something about Carlo."

"Yes?"

"He, too, enjoyed the . . . how shall I put it—the sleazy, for want of a better word. One evening a few months ago, he turned up here in a blue velvet dress and high heels.

"'Bagnatti,' I said. 'Have you lost your mind?' He just laughed. Said he was mixing business with pleasure. Carlo was on his way to Forcella to cruise with the transsexuals there."

"What did he mean, mixing business with pleasure?"

"I don't know. I thought perhaps he was looking for someone in particular, trawling for material for his column. That was my impression."

"Thank you," Natalia said.

"Such a foolish boy. I miss him. Miss him terribly."

"We love who we love, sir."

Fabretti dabbed at his eyes as he saw her out. "Yes," he said, softly.

They wished one another a pleasant evening on the doorstep, and she departed. The patrol car was where she had left it, but someone had taken the opportunity to break an egg on its hood.

Chapter 19

The marshal's secretary was doing something with the coffee maker. It spluttered and started to drip.

She had a wedge of purple lipstick on one of her front teeth, an inappropriate miniskirt and a magenta push-up bra mostly visible through a filmy black blouse. The magenta heels seemed matched with the bra. Tacky, Natalia thought, but if dress up made the poor woman happy . . .

"Would you like a cup?" she said.

"Smells good but no, thank you. Is he available?"

"Just a minute." She flounced off.

Natalia took one of the wooden chairs.

The secretary returned. "He says, give him a minute."

Her cell phone played the theme from *The Godfather*. A moment later the intercom buzzed, and she pantomimed for Natalia to go in.

Without preamble, Cervino said, "Suzanna Rutollo. Lola Nuovaletta. Another woman, unidentified. And a female officer of the Carabiniere. All four met secretly a few days ago."

"Secretly? Where did this conference take place?"

"In a beauty parlor."

"Hmm. Maybe they were having their hair done. Are we investigating hair styles now?"

"Carabinieri socializing with known Camorra is mine to investigate, Captain Monte."

"We hadn't all been together in a very long while, Marshal. We went to school together as children."

"I don't care if you played doctor together."

"You must have childhood friends, classmates. No?"

"None who have pledged themselves to the Camorra remain my friends."

"How nice for you. I find friendships harder to discard. Or maybe you grew up in a better quarter of the city."

"You know the regulations on this. If you don't take steps, I'll have to report it to Colonel Fabio, ma'am."

"Do what you will, but keep clear of me and mine, Marshal."

"A threat, Captain? Must I report a threat, too?"

"You're insulting," Natalia said and walked out.

Back in her office, she found Angelina on her feet, pacing. "What?"

"I was just sending you a text. We've been summoned to a bridal shop murder."

They rushed downstairs and commandeered a car just coming off shift. By the time they arrived, the street was already cordoned off by police, and people were pushing against the tape, craning their necks to see what was going on. The locals were bad enough, but they had no patience for the curious tourists.

Natalia and Angelina identified themselves and were

signed into the crime scene. A woman in a purple house-coat grabbed Angelina's forearm and loudly informed her she was the designated mayor of the block and was going through to monitor the situation.

"No, ma'am," Angelina said.

"What's your name?" the woman demanded.

"Angelina Cavatelli, Casanova Station."

"Your boss is going to hear from me."

"I am her boss, *signora*," Natalia said. "What is the problem?"

"She's probably new, right?"

"What is it, *signora*?"

"We have an arrangement: anything happens on my block, the *polizia* call me."

"We are not the *polizia*," Natalia said. "Officer Cavatelli is doing her job properly. That doesn't include escorting you into a crime scene. Please excuse us."

Shattered glass covered the sidewalk out front. Inside the destroyed display window knelt Dr. Agari, collecting blood and tissue samples. Raffi, wearing little forensic booties, was snapping photographs of the surround.

Francesca waved a gloved hand to Natalia and pointed to a large plastic bag propped on the sidewalk against the wooden frame. Natalia zipped herself into the hazardous materials' gown, then slipped a pair of booties over her heels.

"Careful of the glass," Francesca warned as she stepped into the display.

"Captain," Raffi called out, and when she turned, the camera clicked loudly.

"What's that about?" Natalia said.

"The higher-ups want some shots of our devoted men and women at work. For the public information office."

The dead woman was propped against a mannequin. The white, crystal-beaded wedding gown soaked in blood. Bridesmaids in teal lay on the floor around her.

The victim was slender, no taller than Natalia. Blond hair in a pageboy. Blood spackled the hair, but her face appeared unscathed, eyes wide open. Death had not erased the horrified expression, however. Her scarlet lipstick was smeared, or the killer had slathered the lifeless lips with blood.

"Killed after the dress-up," Francesca said. "Slit throat. Here in the window, judging from the amount of blood everywhere. Not an easy way to go, having your wind pipe and jugular sliced through. Essentially drowned in his own blood as shock set in, and blood pressure plummeted. He suffered."

"He?" Natalia stepped closer and saw the shadow of a beard. "Fuck!"

Francesca looked up at her friend, who'd gone pale. "You know the man?"

Natalia nodded. "Pietro Fabretti. He sells music. Vintage, mostly. His shop's around the corner."

Francesca repeated the information into her lapel microphone.

"He's a friend of the gossip columnist, Carlo Bagnatti. Paid for Bagnatti's funeral, in fact. Sweet man."

"Any idea who might have killed him?" Francesca said.

"Yes. Me."

"What do you mean?" Francesca touched her arm. "Are you okay?"

Natalia nodded.

"Sure?"

"Yeah."

Just then a commotion started. Someone tried to push

through the police to get a better view. It was the lady in the purple housecoat.

"I'm sorry. No one is allowed through." A police officer had gotten hold of her sleeve. Finally he succeeded in pushing her back.

"You get your hands off me! You don't know me? You must be new."

"*Signora* . . . I'm sorry. It's the rules."

"The rules? The favors I do all of you? Since before you were born. Fuck all of you!" The sweep of her arm included Natalia and Francesca as well as the men who waited to load the body into the gurney before she stormed off.

While Francesca and her criminalists processed the bridal store, Natalia and Angelina used Fabretti's keys to enter his music shop. It was as it had been the day before.

Looking on Fabretti's desk, Angelina brushed against a button on the stereo, and Mario Lanza's voice filled the space with its golden tones. Despite several hours of searching, they turned up nothing. Natalia patted an antique violin he had on display and plucked a sad sound from its single intact string.

Whatever Fabretti might have gleaned had gone with him into the next world.

Returning to the bridal shop, they found Fabretti's body bagged and still waiting to be collected. Natalia remained with the corpse. It was finally loaded into the morgue van and driven away hours later.

Too crushed to deal with typing up the formal report, she turned for home. Halfway there, she stopped the cruiser and got out to walk along the waterfront.

The Buddhists were right, she thought, about life being a wheel. Or was it more like a medieval rack? With joy and suffering traded off as the wheel turned, bestowing its goodness and inflicting pain in equal measure.

Mariel was at a concert with her new Milanese boyfriend. Lola didn't answer her mobile; probably occupied with Dominick. Just as well. Contact with Lola was getting sticky.

A man got up from one of the benches on the promenade and started after her. She continued on a few steps and pivoted, her hand on her holstered weapon. The man calmly crossed over to the buildings facing the harbor and turned to look back. He didn't go into any of them. Just stood there staring—a short man, strong build—eating something out of a paper bag.

Natalia drove back to the station. She turned the vehicle in and started home. A slightly taller male seemed to take an interest in her, too, and she ducked into a novelty shop. The clerk behind the register was engrossed in a discussion with a woman in gold stretch pants. Natalia studied the lipsticks and packages of multicolored hair bands and glanced out at the street periodically. No one loitering.

She spent an even longer time reading the ingredients on a bottle of shampoo and finally took it to the counter. After the clerk rang up her purchase, she stepped out and checked the street carefully.

Camorra spies were everywhere. The man roasting chestnuts. The woman on the balcony stringing up baby clothes stamped with blue and white duckies. The old man on a cell phone in the doorway of the barbershop. Even the antiques dealer dusting his yellow satin Victorian chair. All or any could be reporting her passage. She took a quick look behind her. Her pursuer was nowhere to be seen.

To be sure she wasn't being followed, Natalia proceeded to the corner and dropped an index card into the red metal postbox mounted on the wall: Her pretend letter went into the left slot as if it were destined for city mail, as opposed to the right, for every other destination. She listened for footfalls. Nothing.

Closer to home, she saw her old logic professor and his wife, arm in arm, as they crept along the street. His wild hair was mostly gone. Hers was patchy, stiffly curled and dyed a strange shade that glowed the palest blue in the light of the streetlamps.

Arriving at her building, she tried to calm her breathing. Luigina had put a mattress out on her landing. Once a year Natalia's neighbor conducted an elaborate cleaning. Natalia stepped around it. Luigina was listening to a popular soap. The volume seemed even louder than usual. Natalia wondered if the dear lady was losing her hearing.

She sighed deeply and proceeded, barely managing the last set of stairs. She felt so drained. The light on her landing flickered on and off: a loose wire sending Morse messages. Scrawled in large letters across her door was another.

Morirai. You will die.

As she opened the front door, Pino rushed out of the kitchen. He was wearing an apron he must have made out of a peasant shirt. He informed her that dinner was ready, anytime "*la princesa*" desired. She said that would be delightful, although the last thing she could imagine was eating a meal.

She lay on the bed, dropped into sleep and dreamed that she and Fabretti were dancing slowly across a marble floor. A waltz. She was in a filmy gown, and he was wearing a tuxedo. Three musicians sat on velvet chairs. Gino was among them.

As they whirled by, Gino looked up, and she could see he was crying.

"*Cara!*"

Pino's voice woke her.

She tried to erase the image of bloody chiffon and sequins from her mind.

In the course of her career she'd seen death close up many times. Innocent victims as well as evil ones. She had pulled the trigger more than once. But that was because it had been necessary. To save an innocent from death. She coped because she had a role to play: to seek for justice, to hold evil accountable. And that had always sufficed. Until now.

If it hadn't been for her, Fabretti would still be alive. No question. With the death of the music shop owner, she'd crossed a line. How was she going to be able to live with that?

Chapter 20

"First there was fire," Pino said. "Then the earth—hard stone. Followed by water and sun. Near the *zendo* in Caserta you can see such stars." He was philosophical, as usual, as he was after they made love, but Natalia was distracted. Nothing felt right. Not even Pino.

She closed her eyes again and drifted. How had Angelina attained such a good balance between love and work? She and her partner had even snagged an apartment for 600 euros a month in Spaccanapoli, three blocks from Giuletta's clinic, a twenty-five minute walk to Casanova, and they were seriously talking about having a child. So ordinary, so easy. Hell, lesbians could do it. Why not she?

"Let's get married," Pino murmured. "Let's both go to Caserta, lie in the sun, breathe country air, not talk to a soul ever again. We'll be safe there."

During their first heady days of love, Pino had accompanied her to the ancient street market where she regularly

bought her food. As crabs waved their pale claws in sup-
plication, he had said, "All creatures want to live."

He believed that, in the universal scheme of things, one
would experience many lifetimes and be reincarnated in
one creature or another until reaching the state of nirvana:
nothingness. Natalia felt that you lived the life you were
born with. And that was it. No other, later lives or second
chances. Just now. She looked at him. His eyes looked cin-
namon in the flickering light of a votive candle. The same
sweet mouth. But she felt distant from him now. Maybe she
was the one who had changed.

She needed to wash away the grime. She got into the
shower and stayed beneath the falling water a long time,
letting the stopper fill the tub. Then she lowered herself in.
For several minutes the water cascaded down on her as she
quietly wept.

Her parents had assured her she could sell her flat when
the time came, meaning when she got married. She badly
wanted to sell it immediately, married or not. Take the
money and flee somewhere far, to hide in shame for what
she'd done. But she couldn't as yet. It wasn't over.

Angelina filled her in on the procedure at the morgue.
When Natalia didn't say anything, she asked what was
wrong.

"I didn't sleep well."

"Nor did I. And I have a pretty strong stomach. I've seen
plenty worse in Palermo."

"I'll bet. But this was as gruesome as it gets."

"He was gay, wasn't he?" Angelina said.

Natalia nodded.

"Came here to get away from a homophobic culture,"
Angelina said. "Thought me and my girl we were finally

free—hold hands, put an arm around one another. No one says squat. The men on the horse. I was okay with that. I'm the new girl on the block, so I deal. But this? I'd be lying if I said it didn't freak me out."

"I understand." Natalia pressed her palms against her eyes.

"My job has never been pretty and, up till now, Giuletta's been okay with it. But last night she says she doesn't feel safe and she's making noise about leaving. I tried to calm her down. Said she shouldn't be afraid. We're not dealing with a serial killer here."

"I don't think we are," Natalia said.

"She wasn't convinced. I said this could happen any-where, to anyone, gay or straight. But it happens again . . . I don't know. And not just her. Me."

Natalia opened her eyes and regarded her partner. "I totally understand. But please, don't do anything rash, okay? We make a terrific team, Officer Cavatelli. We're going to get the killer. I swear on my *nonna's* grave."

The houses reminded Natalia of tattered dowagers. Yet there were wonderful surprises that sprang up among them, like the cloistered gardens you'd come upon in the midst of a teeming, sultry street.

A fishmonger swatted away flies and directed her with the point of his enormous bloody knife. Natalia followed his directions, passing an ice cream parlor and an addict sprawled on the ground next to the door, scratching her arm as she nodded off. Maybe seventeen, she had the ashen face of an angel and heavenly prospects in her imme-diate future. Someone had bought her gelato. The plastic cup lay tipped over near her hand, and red liquid pooled by her fingers. Bitter cherry, the color of blood.

At the end of the block, clouds of flies hovered over a dumpster. Natalia crossed to the opposite side, stepping around a mattress ripped open, its stuffing pouring out as if it had been savaged.

Arriving at Paolo's father's old leather shop, Natalia peered in the window. Twenty years ago she remembered Paolo drying leather goods on the street outside. Inside, the once neat shop looked a mess. Pieces of green- and rust-colored leather lay on the worktable untouched. Sheets of paper with ballpoint and pencil sketches were tacked to the wall, alongside CDs stacked on a workbench and a boom box from the eighties. The top was marked with burns from cigarettes rested on the wood.

Paolo had dark circles under his eyes, and they looked kind of glassy. He hadn't shaved.

"You don't pick up," she said as she entered. "I left you a couple of messages."

"Yeah. I ain't been very sociable lately."

"Love life?"

"My daughter's not talking to me. Nadia, the older one."

"She'll come around. It's just adolescence."

"Maybe, maybe not. She saw something on the tube about my boss and put it all together as to what I'm doing for work."

"No," Natalia said. "I doubt it. She's known for a while. My guess is something else is bothering you more."

"Like what?"

"Cecelia perhaps."

"Who?"

"Cecelia Mina. Sixteen-year-old runaway. Shot to death on Via Formia in broad daylight. An innocent girl who didn't want to partake in Ernesto Scavullo's depravity and ran."

"I don't know about any kid like that."

"An innocent girl doesn't want to be fucked by him, and he takes it as rejection, goes into a rage. Figures no one's interested enough in Cecelia to miss her. So he erases her with a bullet. She was a child."

"I never did nothing like that."

"No, because you have a code. Because your workaholic father raised you to live right. Ernesto grew up different—a criminal in the making. He had real guns for toys. He killed Cecelia, then her kid sister. She was Nadia's age."

"That doesn't sound right."

"You know it's the truth, Paolo. Why are you hiding your head in the sand here? Someone disrespects him, they're dead. Then for the fun of it—he seizes their mother, a brother or sister. And just to teach everyone a lesson, he kills that person, too."

"Crazy rumors." Paolo looked uncomfortable. "That's all they are."

"They're not, and you know it. He kills people with the drugs he provides, uses the most strung-out street dwellers as guinea pigs to test new product, to make sure the junk won't kill paying customers. Why am I wasting my breath? You know all this already."

"What do you want me to do, reform him? Rat him out?"

"No. You never would."

"What then?"

"Do something for me, Paolo. For once in your life, make Nadia proud. Find me the right moment to get close to him."

"Why? What are you gonna do?"

"Don't ask. You don't want to be an accessory."

The voice came through the message machine. "Hello? Natalia? Are you there?"

"I'm here, Pino." Natalia said and interrupted the recording. "Just got home. Where are you?"

"At my place. I needed to get a few things. Perfect opportunity. I explained to Tina she couldn't stay here anymore."

"How did that go?"

"She was weepy but seemed okay with it. I wished her luck. She started packing. I told her to drop the key in my mailbox."

"Good."

"Maybe. I went to the *zendo*, figured she could use the space. On the way back, I stopped by again to pick up some more things. The key was there, and she left a note that she'd be at her mother's for a few days."

"So, what's the problem?"

"My gun. It's missing."

"God, Pino. You have to turn it in next week. Find it. What if she took it?"

"I'll go over to her folks place tomorrow and talk to her."

"Get it back. I mean, you lose your weapon, and you'll never work in law enforcement again."

"I'll look around here some more and then I'll go to her folks' tomorrow and talk to her."

"Why would she take it?"

"I don't know. To annoy me. Worry me. Make me beg."

"First thing in the morning."

"Right."

"Like dawn, Pino. This is serious. Worse than losing your badge credentials."

"I know, I know. I'll get it back."

"I've got to go. I'm meeting the girls."

"Say hi to Em and don't give my regards to Blondie."

"See you later."

She put down the phone. Fuck, now what?

* * *

A flock of squawking seagulls argued overhead as they glided in the deep blue sky. The women had gathered at the old jetty on the far side of the Mergellina, where they had played as children. They were far from prying eyes, but to be on the safe side they'd traveled in separate cabs.

Mariel was in her signature white blouse and charcoal skirt; Lola in aqua velour track gear and matching cap. Natalia in a plain dress from her undercover closet and a slinky blonde wig that hid her curls.

Lola raised her face to the sun.

"I thought you were worried about your skin," Mariel said. "Direct sun's the worst thing for it."

"I look better with a tan. I'm only doing five minutes. God, I'm in the mood for seafood. Anyone hungry?"

"I'm not so hungry," Natalia said. "Something cold to drink maybe."

Natalia closed her eyes and listened to seagulls squawk overhead.

"Pino moves in, and you stop eating?" Lola teased.

Natalia sat up. "You promised you wouldn't tell," she said to Mariel.

"She wormed it out of me. Besides, you said you were going to tell her anyway."

"So is it true," Lola teased, "you're back with the boy-man?"

"You jealous?"

"If I want someone with straw between his ears, I'll let you know."

"Don't listen to her," Mariel said. "Pino's a great guy. More mature than her Dominick, for sure."

"Yeah, Pino's such a swell guy, he got the Gracci girl with child?"

Natalia winced. "They're still saying that? They're lying."

"Maybe," Lola said.

"Enough," Mariel said. "We're celebrating."

"Right. I forgot myself. To love—whoopee."

"Girls," Mariel rapped her book for attention. "What would you like to drink? I'll go to the vendor's cart over there. You have choice of lemonade, lemonade, or lemonade. I'm having lemonade myself."

"I'll have a lemonade, too," Natalia said.

"Make it three. So you've let Pino move in," Lola said. "Are you sure then?"

Natalia pressed a cool water bottle to her cheek, squinting in the sharp light. "I know what I'm doing, okay?"

"Uh oh. Girl's in love," Lola teased. "How does that song go? 'Love is just a four-letter word.'"

"I didn't say that I was in love."

"You better be, *cara mia*."

"Lola," Mariel warned as she returned.

"Guy's gonna test her. I want to make sure she's got her eyes open about him, Em. That's what friends are for."

"Time out," Mariel said.

"I'm gonna wash my hands in the bay," Lola announced.

"I wouldn't consider that water too clean," Mariel said.

"It's salt, Smarty. Watch my bag." She put down her clutch. "I got myself this cute little Ruger six-shot automatic that Bianca raved about. Initials in diamonds. Make me sick if someone tried to take it."

"Who stuck the thorn in her butt?" Mariel said, as Lola sauntered away. "You okay?"

"Barely. But, yeah, I'll cope."

Returning, Lola dried her hands on a napkin. "Truce?" and leaned in to kiss Natalia on both cheeks. "Don't mind me. Woke up with this shitty headache."

"Truce," Natalia repeated and returned the embrace.

"So," Lola said. "Lover boy is living at your place and you pay all the bills? Sounds peachy."

"God, did I hear truce?" Mariel said. "I must be hallucinating in this heat."

"He's going to resign from the ranks," Natalia said.

"Really?" Mariel said, sounding concerned.

"Yes. He's going to teach yoga at the *zendo*. They've already asked him. He's thinking about opening his own studio."

"That's perfect for him," Mariel said.

"Isn't it just?" Lola sneered. "Sits on his ass all day envisioning rainbows while you put your life on the line."

Natalia bristled. "What's with the attitude?"

"Just what it sounds like."

"You're so bitchy today," Mariel said.

"Sorry. My man's getting bossy, is all. Like I'm expected to account to him for my time. I might as well be back with the late great husband." She took out her Blackberry and touched the screen.

Mariel went off to fetch more lemonades from the vendor's cart.

As Lola scrolled, Natalia closed her eyes and inhaled the salt air. She wished she could put her problems on hold. Keep the world at bay at least for a little while.

"Oh, this is interesting," Lola tapped her leg.

"What's interesting?" Natalia opened her eyes.

"I was curious about something so I checked it out."

"Do I want to know?"

"You do. You do. Listen to this. Last night Papa Gianni hosted a get-together with his old cronies at the social club on Baiano. It was like the Queen of England holding court. A receiving line with fifty retired soldiers kissing his hand."

"Sentimental reunion," Natalia said. "What's that about?"

"Sentimental? I don't think so. Word is he's seeing if he has enough loyalty behind him to take over again."

"You think? Gianni's kind of old for a power play."

"True. He is. Maybe it was just for old time's sake. Plus Ernesto. Bloodbath if someone tried to take over. Even so, Papa might be tempted. But I don't know. There aren't too many of the old farts around anymore. And the ones who are—well, a lot of them wear diapers, if you know what I mean."

"What's really bothering you?" Natalia said.

Lola lay back and draped an arm over her eyes. "Just a bad dream."

"What?"

"I can't remember much of it, except a hand at my throat. You remember what that means?"

"Same as a bird flying into your house. Someone's going to die."

Natalia's phone vibrated. A call on the emergency line from work. It was Angelina. They'd been called out to investigate a suspicious death in a Camorra household.

"Right," Natalia said. "I'll be right there."

"Going?" Lola asked.

Natalia sat in disbelief.

"What's the matter?"

"The pregnant girl, Tina. She's dead."

Whatever was happening, it was happening too fast. Natalia needed her brain to catch up, but it kept straggling. She had to get in front of events if she was going to figure out what was happening.

There were three buildings built around a narrow courtyard. Several defunct *motorinos* rusted quietly in a corner.

No need to wonder which building it was. The middle one already had candles burning by the entrance and a few bouquets on the ground. A bunch of daisies in clear cellophane rested against a life-sized statue of the Queen of Heaven. A long-stemmed rose rested across her outstretched hands. Several pigeons preened on the Virgin's head; her crown, a slim string of electric lights.

Natalia paused in the forecourt before attempting the stairs. A billboard photo gazed down from where two of the buildings met: from the looks of it, a memorial for the man who had probably met a brutal death.

Graccis had ruled the quarter since horse-drawn carriages clattered down the narrow streets. Half its residents were unemployed. To survive, many did the Graccis' bidding, and the rest tithed the Camorra.

A woman in a purple robe and slippers came out of a ground floor *basso* and put out a plate of scraps. If she noticed Natalia, she didn't let on. This *signora* no doubt faithfully mopped her balcony every morning, scrubbed the family's clothes and kept their rooms spotless. No telling if, while cooking in her humble kitchen, she bagged cocaine while the water boiled for pasta.

If she was reluctant to engage in the drug trade, consequences could be unpleasant. If she refused outright and talked about it, they were likely lethal. Eight months ago the father of an eleven-year-old boy agreed to spill family business and saw his son kidnapped. No ransom note ever arrived. A half-year later the boy's strangled body turned up in a vat of acid that had failed to complete its job.

Tomorrow would be a new day, but the sun would not make even a rare and momentary visit to this dark place, moving only across the tops of the buildings and a slice of the street.

Natalia began her climb past bags of garbage that cluttered the landings. Doors opened a crack and immediately closed. She caught sight of a cheek, a nose, an eye and little more. On the fourth floor, a large man in sunglasses and a pork pie hat stood guard outside a steel door. A serpent and several skulls frolicked on his enormous biceps.

His desert camouflage trousers contrasted sharply with his hot lime T-shirt. He stepped forward, menacing. This didn't surprise Natalia. A dead girl in the house would only make the Carabinieri less welcome than usual. The last thing they'd want was her help.

"Get out. This is private business."

"Sorry, *signor.* Can't oblige." Natalia showed her ID, hand on her gun. He reluctantly let her pass.

She followed an orange and brown rug along the hall and into the living room, occupied by a glass coffee table, gigantic lounge chair and a plaid couch with two slouched men watching Brazil's footballers beating Mexico on the TV.

In their youth, they had probably been among the *tifosi,* the crowds at the Stadio San Paolo, jeering at the opposing team to celebrate victory or to incite a brawl to exorcise a defeat. Approaching middle age, they looked on in virtual solitude.

"Sit down," the lighter man on the couch commanded.

"Where is she?" Natalia asked.

He pointed down the hall. Natalia found the bedroom and pushed open the door. A girl's room. The girl asleep on her bed. Only she wasn't asleep.

Tina's hair, combed and arranged around her shoulders, didn't quite cover the piece of her skull where it stuck out. Clotted in some places, some strands had been cut away. Her grey cheeks were rouged. Her mother, weeping, sat on the bed holding her daughter's hand.

Never had Natalia seen a head shot victim so tidy. Usually blood and brains were everywhere. Where was the
mess? The soiled clothes? Furniture? Walls? Tina Gracci
looked so small, so innocent. Whatever destiny she had
dreamed for herself and her unborn child would go unre-
alized. Unwanted pregnancy? Unwanted girl? What was the
story here?

"*Signora?*"

Tina's mother looked up, face bleary as Angelina
entered in uniform, followed by Dr. Agari. Both quickly
took in the scene and stopped.

"I am sorry, *signora*," Natalia said, "we have to ask you
some questions."

Angelina took out her notebook. Francesca stood silent,
making no move toward the corpse. Which, Natalia knew,
meant she surmised suicide.

"You don't have to tell them anything." They hadn't realized Tina's cousin had entered the room. "She's lost a
daughter. Vultures, that's what you are."

"*Signor*, we need to speak to her in private."

"Fucking vultures," he said as his aunt waved him away.

Natalia waited until he retreated, then closed the door.

"I am sorry for your great loss, *signora*," Angelina said.

A hard woman, Emelinia Cora Gracci. It was common
knowledge she'd passed verbal messages from her jailed husband ordering assassinations and beatings. Both she and her
husband had grown up in the Secondigliano underworld.

"Can you tell us what happened?" Angelina said.

"She called me, said she was coming home for a few days."

"When was that?" Angelina asked.

"Yesterday afternoon."

"She was living where?" Natalia asked.

"In Santa Lucia, with her fiancé."

Angelina made a note. "His name?"

"Francesco Matta."

"Has he been informed?" Natalia asked.

"He's not in Naples."

"Where is he?"

"Genoa. On business."

"Do you have a number for him?"

"No."

Natalia scanned the room. A pink teddy bear sat on a white vanity table. A poster was taped above the bed. Also taped to the mirror: several photographs of a family wedding and a man dancing with a younger Tina. Natalia recognized a young Loredana. The soccer star had been linked to the crime family once upon a time.

"Can you go over what happened this morning?" Angelina flipped a page.

"She was sleeping. I went to wake her to get ready for work. She kissed me. 'In a minute, Mama,' she said. 'I want to finish my dream.' I left to pay a bill and stopped for early Mass."

"What time did you get home?" Angelina asked.

"Just before nine. I put away my groceries, made a couple of calls. Then I went to clean her room and . . ."

Emelinia started to cry.

"It's okay, *signora*," Angelina said and murmured something Natalia couldn't hear.

"What time was that?" Natalia said. "When you went to her room?"

"I don't know. She was on the floor . . . over there." She pointed to the far side by the bed. Francesca peered over.

"You picked her up by yourself?" Natalia asked.

She nodded.

"Cleaned the blood?" Natalia said.

"Yes."

The room was tidy. No evidence of forced entry or a struggle. Then again, Tina's mother must have mopped up, cleaned her daughter, gotten her into the yellow nightgown and into bed and scrubbed for several hours to remove the stains.

"Is the room otherwise as you found it?" Natalia said.

"Yes."

"What did you do with the clothes she was wearing?" Angelina asked.

"I took them to the trash."

Hearing this, Angelina slipped out to have a word with the other officers in the hall to retrieve the garments and shoes.

Natalia tried to appear nonchalant. "What did you do with the gun?"

Signora Gracci didn't answer.

"Do you know what happened to the gun?" she repeated.

"What gun?"

"The one that shot Tina."

The mother merely shrugged.

"Do you know where Tina keeps her cell phone?" Angelina asked.

"She has a backpack. It's probably in the closet."

The cousin reappeared in the doorway, looking to complain some more.

"Beppe, please," Tina's mother implored. "Go and watch TV," she said and smoothed her daughter's hair.

Francesca opened her carryall and pulled out a pair of gloves and a pristine lab coat.

"She's not going to the morgue." Emelinia blocked her path. "You're not taking her away."

"We don't plan to take her anywhere, *signora*. But I need to verify the circumstances of your daughter's death so I can issue a certificate. It is the law. I need to look. It would be better for you if you wait outside. We'll call you as soon as we're through."

Emelinia Gracci made the sign of the cross and kissed her daughter's lips.

"Oh, Mrs. Gracci," Francesca said. "Was she right-handed or left-handed?"

"Right-handed. She's right-handed."

"Thank you."

As Emelinia Gracci opened the door to leave, the stadium crowd on TV cheered.

"Some gathering out there." Francesca pulled on her rubber gloves.

"Graccis and Giulianos," Natalia said. "Quite a Camorra cocktail party."

"Corporal Cavatelli, would you take notes?" Francesca asked.

"Certainly." Angelina took out her miniature recorder and moved closer.

"Dr. Francesca Agari," the pathologist said, identifying herself. She then stated the date, time, location and the names of Captain Monte and Corporal Cavatelli. She followed with Tina's particulars as she gently lifted her hair and studied the wound. "A gunshot to the right temple, exiting in back."

Francesca signaled for Angelina to turn off the tape. Some blood had pooled on the sheet in a slowly forming halo. "It's a miracle she didn't blow her face off," Francesca said. "I wonder if the slug is in the wall somewhere. Take a look, Angelina, will you? Never mind, I'll do it."

She moved to the wall on the far side of the bed, then scanned downward, looking for the hole where the bullet went. She found it at about waist high and knelt for a closer look.

"Suicide?" Angelina asked Dr. Agari who'd gotten up and was looking in her bag for something.

"I can't give a definitive answer yet, but it's looking that way, yes."

"Is there any likelihood she may have been murdered?" Natalia asked. She took Francesca's place by the wall, clearing away white debris from the opening with a finger. When she was sure no one was paying attention, she poked at it with a pencil, until the shiny metal of a slug was visible when she shone her small flashlight into the channel. She glanced back to make sure she was blocking their view of it.

"Murder?" Francesca said, pondering. "Doubtful, wouldn't you say?"

"Yes." Natalia breathed a sigh of relief.

Francesca pulled open the dead girl's cramped hand. Several dark spots were clearly visible along the palm, findings which she reported aloud into the recorder.

"God," she said. "Terrible. When they're young, they have no idea that they're not going to wake up again and find everyone sorry and repentant for whatever wrong they'd done the suicide."

"Is there a note?" Angelina said.

"If there was, Mama probably disposed of it," Natalia said and pushed the pencil hard against the slug while manufacturing small noises with her free hand and squeaky boot to cover the sound of the spent bullet clattering down into the hollow space behind the plaster. The slug was entombed in the wall.

Francesca felt along the girl's body. "Pregnant and showing. In this day and age, I wouldn't have thought that was a motive for killing oneself. Any idea where the gun might be?"

"Gone missing," Angelina said.

"Mama again," Natalia said.

"Why?"

"Why do you think?"

"Oh, of course. The consecrated burial. No high mass and no interment in hallowed ground if her child killed herself."

"And the baby," Angelina added.

"Yes. The Church would deny her its rites if it's suicide, and Tina would be doomed to a long stretch in Purgatory." Francesca stretched her stiff lower back for a moment. "Maybe after the funeral the gun will reappear?"

"That's what I'm thinking," Natalia said, back pushing the point of the pencil until it went right through into whatever was on the other side. "Are you almost through?"

"A few minutes more." Francesca pulled Tina's hair aside and studied the wound with a magnifying glass. "Interesting," she said.

"What?" Natalia turned away from the wall.

"Her wound appears consistent with a round from a largish caliber. Heavy for her to fire."

"There must be an arsenal in this house," Angelina said. "Do you want me to do a search?" she asked Natalia.

"Not today."

"I guess she used whatever was at hand. Okay, the crucial test next. Gunpowder residue." Francesca lined up her materials. "There's a green folder in my bag, Angelina, with a blank death certificate in it. Would you mind?

"Not at all."

"Trouble is," Natalia said, "we rule it a suicide, and Tina Gracci is denied her final rites."

"I know," Francesca said, as she initiated the test for the presence of expended gunpowder on Tina's hands. "It would be a shame. But suicide it may be."

"Angelina," Natalia said, "you have a nice touch with the woman—talk to her—see if you can get any sense of what happened here."

"Yes, Captain." Angelina put the certificate on the bed and stepped out.

"Francesca, I need you to delay your ruling until the girl is buried, or I'll never get the weapon."

"Would twenty-four hours do?" Francesca peeled off her gloves.

"It will have to. Thanks." Natalia willed herself not to show the overwhelming relief surging through her.

"I might manage that, but only if the residue test is positive. Otherwise, I'll be compelled to conduct a full autopsy, and my preliminary call will be homicide. You know the drill."

"Yes."

Francesca leaned over Tina's right hand with a magnifier. "Positive. She's recently fired a revolver, poor child."

"Good work, doc."

"Any luck excavating for the slug?"

"Not much. It punched right through to the adjoining room."

"It's there?"

"We're gonna take a look."

Angelina returned, and the officers proceeded to the room adjacent to Tina's. Images of Jesus suffering on his cross were mounted on each wall. They were outnumbered only by photos of Graccis jammed on the bureau.

Signora Gracci's matrimonial bed abutted her daughter's wall.

"A museum piece," Angelina said, running her hands over the elaborate carving.

They each took a post and dragged the bed a few inches

from the wall. Natalia squeezed in and pretended to do a search.

"Nothing here."

"That's too bad," Angelina said. "The walls are thick. Not like the shit they put up these days. We'd need a sledge to get through there. Worth a try?"

"Maybe," Natalia said. "Not today. Mama's traumatized as it is."

They reported their lack of findings to Francesca.

"Well, let me know if you find it. Though I suppose it's less crucial as we have the positive residue test. Still, it's odd. No note, no bullet, no gun."

Francesca packed up and left, and Emelinia Gracci returned to her daughter's side. Beppe could be heard arguing with one of his cousins. Natalia asked Angelina to wait for her in the hall.

Emelinia stroked her daughter's face. It sounded like she was singing a lullaby. She'd birthed this child. Raised her. Loved her in her own fashion.

"*Signora,*" she said. "Excuse me. If your child is to have a church funeral, I must have the gun no later than the day after tomorrow."

"What are you insinuating?" The grieving mother had given way to the *madrina.*

"Absolutely nothing," Natalia said. "I'm stating hard facts. You need to hear them again?"

"No."

"Then we have an understanding?"

The woman nodded.

"Okay. You must see to your daughter's immediate burial."

"Three days from now, *si.*"

"No. Tomorrow. No later than tomorrow. Or you will not be able to have what you wish for her."

"Tomorrow," the woman said, hand to her face, concerned. "But out-of-town relatives are coming, some by train."

"Tell them to take an express. Tomorrow is all the time there is. There is no more. Understand?"

"Yes."

"And the day after tomorrow, you will see me again. I will be back for the gun."

Silence.

"Say you understand."

"I understand," Signora Gracci replied mechanically.

"Good," Natalia said. "Good."

Out on the street, she didn't call Pino on her mobile, not entrusting their conversation to remote transmission. She needed a landline and drove to the rail station on the way back to Casanova to find a pay phone. Pino answered on the first ring. From the tremor in his voice she knew he had already heard.

"She is, isn't she?" he said.

"Yes. Early this morning. Pino? Are you there? Are you okay?"

A nun rushed past dragging an old leather suitcase. Natalia spotted a colleague undercover. He took off after the nun, making sure one of the dozens of lowlifes didn't try something before the good sister was safely aboard her train. He'd be back in minutes, and he'd wonder what she was doing there.

"Pino. I can't stay on the phone here."

"It's my fault. I should have done something to save her."

"Like what? You're all powerful? The girl was a mess. A moth headed to a flame. She was carrying a child. A very selfish thing she did."

"If I'd secured my gun . . ."

"She didn't need your gun. Her parents place is an armory by all accounts. For Christ's sake, she had her own arsenal. I don't know why she took your piece. To get back at you probably. For not loving her enough."

"I should have never gotten involved."

"It's too late now, Pino. It's over."

"When is the funeral?"

"Tomorrow. Promise me you won't go. The one thing you mustn't do is attend the funeral."

"I need to."

"No, you don't, and you won't. They see you there? It could get the family wondering."

"I don't know."

"I do. You will not go."

"Maybe I should turn myself in."

"You won't do that either."

"But the gun, my prints are on it. They'll find it. Forensics will tie the bullet to the Glock and me. I'm done."

"No bullet's been recovered, and we'll have the gun shortly. Hopefully, Francesca will quietly rule it a suicide right after the funeral, and it will all be over."

"Not for me, Nat," he said. "Not ever."

"Look, the kid wasn't yours, was it?"

"Of course not."

"It's sad. Without a doubt. But life goes on."

"So hard, Natalia. It doesn't sound like you."

"And what about you? Shacking up with a teenager? Leaving me to clean up the mess?"

Natalia sat on a bench to collect her thoughts. Never in her career would she have imagined she would tamper with evidence. Up until recently she had understood her role clearly. She had killed in the line of duty. But only when necessary to protect the innocent. Things were getting murky. She had caused the death of one innocent man recently. Now she'd violated her oath as a Carabinieri in order to protect her boyfriend.

She'd once sailed a course where good and evil were clearly delineated. Suddenly the weather had changed, the clarity obscured as the sky over the rim of Vesuvius when the earth shifted and molten lava surged from its bowels.

Moral ambiguity had been a pet phrase of Sister Benedicta's. The good Sister often lectured about the toxins released when one made a sinful choice. They used to make fun of the portly Sister, Lola and she. Even Mariel. But now?

She wished she had her mother's rosary beads. They were safely at home in their velvet case in the back of her drawer. Perhaps when she got home she'd finger the cool pearls, say a simple prayer.

Chapter 21

The chapel off Via Caracciolo wasn't far from the altar to Neptune, a niche decorated with sculpted conch shells. Borne on the shoulders of six burly men, Tina's white coffin reminded Natalia of something that had drifted in from the sea as well. She watched as they climbed the steps of the church and, in slow motion, disappeared into the dark beyond. She wondered if Pino was among the mourners streaming in.

Outside the church, several limos idled. Angelina, shaded from the powerful sun by a dilapidated red umbrella, sipped her cappuccino, snapping photos of the mourners with her cell phone as they entered the church. Despite a sea breeze, the scent of garbage was strong.

Tina's white coffin led every online news story of her passing. Newspaper sites had it on their digital front page, and it led the late morning news on RAI and two other channels.

Camorra bosses and underlings, the Archbishop had announced, could no longer stand as godparents at baptisms or first communions. They could not act as witnesses at weddings and were no longer welcome congregants. But so many churchmen were cozy with the *camorristi* who provided funds to repair crumbling sacristies, financed overseas missions, bought them new sacramental robes and cases of aged whiskey for the priest's residence. Camorra funded church day care centers and subsidized widows who would otherwise go hungry. Judging from the ceremony for Tina, the Archbishop's decree was not being heeded. As with government announcements in this vein, there was no enforcement.

Natalia and her partner had agreed to rendezvous a few blocks from the chapel after the service was over. Angelina was waiting for Natalia, and they proceeded together to Casanova.

"Quite a spectacle," Angelina said. "We could have made some good arrests back there."

"If only," Natalia took out a pair of dark glasses. "The sun's getting to me."

The partners checked in at the station. They climbed to their office and sat down for a brief meeting.

"I've been reviewing Scavullo's files," Angelina said. "I had some time yesterday."

"Good girl. Anything I should know? Wait a minute." She closed the door.

Angelina took a swig of water. "Past couple of years all but two of Papa Gianni's trusted advisors have been sidelined. Several died. Mostly they were old, but a couple disappeared under mysterious circumstances."

"Good work. How's domestic life?"

"It's a modern miracle we ever got together." Angelina rocked her water bottle. "Two days after she moves in, I hardly recognized my own place. The woman's amazing. My underwear is now color coded."

Natalia had to smile.

Angelina assumed a thoughtful expression. "You know, I keep thinking Ernesto seems so familiar."

"How so?"

"He's more like a mafia don than a Camorra clan leader."

"How's that?"

"Aside from the obvious lowlife factor?" Angelina said. "They both start out doing their own killing, slaughter being part of the apprenticeship. As you know, Camorra bosses are expected to keep doing the physical stuff. Hands on is very important. Mafia dons, the higher they rise, the less they do that will dirty their hands or expose them to serious felony charges."

"Ernesto stays squeaky clean?"

"Exactly. He has his boys get bloody. From what I can piece together, after he killed the dockworker—you know, when he was a kid?—There were a couple of incidents, but it was like he retired from active service. We're talking years here. One of his enemies gets done, the authorities go to question the don and he's practicing his golf swing—pink shirt, white gloves, for Christ's sake. They got him for dicing up some ex-girlfriend's poodle, which *mafiosi* might do, but it was an isolated incident."

"You are good."

"That's what Giuletta tells me."

"Look at the time," Natalia said. "I can't be late. Gotta run."

She scampered out front for a quick getaway on her *motorino*. Dodging traffic, she reached Picoletto I Pontenuovo, which was torn up more often than not. Today was not the exception, with workmen drilling into the cobblestone. The orange plastic mesh had become a permanent fixture.

Natalia reached the end of the alley and crossed onto the street. The market was bustling. Enormous loaves of bread and wheels of cheese were displayed in the windows of several shops. Enough to feed a family of twelve. Mops and brooms, whirligigs, toys and shovels on the sidewalk in front.

Women already weighted down with bags of food crowded the vendors. Whiny children tugged at their arms. A slim girl in a pink rhinestone jacket maneuvered her *motorino* through the crowds. The wind zipped through her hair.

Natalia found Ernesto's father at the Falcone, the café from which he had ruled his crew and business ventures before prison. His hair was white now—freshly trimmed—and his barber had given him an expert shave.

Papa Gianni Scavullo had always been well groomed but never a peacock like Ernesto. Not even when he was young.

His first day out, he had on a beige shirt and brown pants. You could've easily mistaken him for the neighborhood shoemaker he had once been. During the time he'd been away, not much had changed in his appearance, except he'd gotten plump. Strange to see him with a cell phone. Spotting Natalia, he finished his conversation quickly, got up and pulled out a chair for her.

"You're Captain Natalia Monte?" he said when she'd showed him her ID.

"Yes."

"And they sent you to give me a talking to?" he laughed. "I've been out less than twenty-four hours. Give me a chance to get into some trouble here."

They sat.

"These new phones are something," he said, "Know who I was talking to? The wife. Reminding me to pick up the *mortadella* Ernesto likes. I'm home for the first time in what—twenty years? She makes a bigger fuss over her son comin' to dinner, you believe it? What can I get you, a coffee? Or is that not permitted these days?"

"Coffee, please."

"Good." He flicked his hand, and the waiter hustled over. "Something to eat?" he slipped on a pair of glasses and perused the menu.

"No, thank you," Natalia said.

"All you girls are watching your figures. And my son. Won't even go near caffeine. Me, it doesn't interest. Two coffees," he said to the waiter, "and bring me a *sfogliatella.*"

The waiter bowed and took away the menus.

Gianni folded his glasses and stuck them in his shirt pocket. "It's great to be out, you know?"

"I can imagine," Natalia said.

"No, you can't. Not unless you've been there. Look at this." He indicated his mouth. "Went in with a full set. You'd think with my connections I could've gotten a decent dentist. Anyway you didn't come here to talk about my teeth."

"No."

"I knew your father, by the way, back when we were kids. Ran into Carmelo when I had an office in the Galleria. A real hard worker. Handsome. A full head of hair, I remember."

"He didn't mention he knew you."

"He wouldn't, would he?"

"I suppose not."

"A bird watcher, right?"

"Yes," Natalia said.

"I tried to get him to work for me, but he turned me

down. In those days he had a small kiosk on a main drag and was selling sundries. Some outfit put the arm on him for protection money. He took off his apron and walked away. Took a job sweeping streets rather than pay."

"I never knew that," she said.

"Yeah. He never changed. Same guy as a kid when we were running messages for the partisans."

"He carried messages during the war?"

"He never told you?"

"No."

Papa Gianni had a good chuckle. "Typical." He waved off a hovering waiter. "So what can I do for you this fine day?"

"You need to do something about your son."

"Pardon?"

"Ernesto. He's always been vicious. Worse since you got sent away. You know better than I do."

"I see."

"I won't have it in my jurisdiction. I just wanted you to know from me what's going to happen."

"That's quite a threat you're making, young lady."

"It's not a threat. He's over the line. Either the System deals with him or the Carabinieri will."

"Just what do you think he's done?"

"He sliced up teenage girls if they didn't want to have sex with him. Slaughtered their families if he wanted to make a point. A couple of days ago he slit the throat of a sweet man named Fabretti. Man sold music in a shop near Gesu Nuovo. Never harmed a soul in his life. Ernesto hung, castrated and shot two men dead, and displayed them in Contessa Cavazza's flower garden."

"I read about the double murder. But why would my son do that?"

"For you, ostensibly. Make us think he was fulfilling a

long-standing obligation. The bloody shirt, it was like he was advertising the vendetta."

"That's your theory?"

"That's what he wanted us to think."

"It's not true?"

"Bagnatti, the gossip columnist, was the real target. He was about to run a critical story on Ernesto that would have cost him dearly. Lattaruzzo was the cover and decoy. I can't prove it, but I suspect Director Garducci put him up to it, revealing Bagnatti's upcoming piece that would expose Ernesto's homosexuality, plus identify the two of them as lovers. Lattaruzzo would serve as the perfect diversion from all this: the wrong avenged after half a century."

"I see."

"It's gone too far. I'm sure you would have stopped it had you been here, but you weren't and couldn't. You are now. He's been butchering people. Something you'd never countenance. He's overstepped the bounds of the Camorra and the civil community."

"You're quite something, Captain Monte. You sure are your father's daughter. I wish I'd been as lucky. How did my son learn of my rescue during the war by the *contessa*'s father?"

Natalia fixed him with her glare. "What do you mean? From you, of course."

"I never told him. The Lattaruzzos fled before anyone in my family did anything."

"From your wife or his grandparents, maybe an aunt or an uncle."

Scavullo leaned forward. "His grandparents passed in the late 40s. Ernesto never met them. My brother knew better than to talk about it, because my wife and I did not want the story handed down and some innocent become the target of a vendetta."

"Somebody knew," Natalia said.

"Secrets," he said and pushed back his chair. "I always enjoy talking to a pretty lady. If you'll excuse me." He touched the rim of his cap.

The waiter escorted him into the street. Trying to get his ear.

What to make of him, Natalia wondered as she took the last sip of coffee. Truth teller or not, Papa Gianni appeared to be relaxing in his twilight years, doing nothing more taxing than spending time with his old pals, consuming coffee and pastries. She was certain, as the swallows returned in the spring, that he'd paid off some priest—sponsored a new roof, a fancy piece of furniture—to insure his place at mass and communion. No doubt he was doubling up on confessions to make sure his exit and whatever came thereafter were sanctioned by God. He certainly showed no interest in ruling his once-empire again. He was old. Tired. Maybe Ernesto was right that his father was over the hill. He'd lost his edge during the years in prison. The enterprise required someone vital and alert and a youthful crew to see after the day-to-day.

Pity, she thought. And unfortunate, because from here on Ernesto appeared to be her problem.

In the afternoon, Natalia drove to the police firing range and knocked down twenty out of twenty targets on the live fire range and then did target firing for an hour.

Returning to Casanova, she cleaned her two pistols and reloaded the four magazines. Then went to Dr. Agari for the official ruling on the cause of Tina Gracci's death.

"Suicide," Francesca said. "No surprise there."

"I can't thank you enough for your help yesterday," Natalia said.

Francesca gave her a long, hard look.

"Job getting to you?"

"You could say that."

"I've been there. More than once. Mind if I say something?"

"Of course not."

"A few years ago I had to see a therapist. I don't usually tell people this. I'm tough, you know? But I am human. First you get sick seeing people eviscerated. Then you grow numb. I'm not sure which is worse. Talk to someone. Take a day off. See a friend. You'll be surprised. The world won't come to an end."

"Yes."

"And listen, if something funny is going on in a case, come to me, okay? We've all been there. The men cover each other's backs. We should do the same, yes?"

When Natalia got home, she found Pino sitting on the floor of the balcony by a large potted plant, his head buried in his arms.

"You all right?"

"No," he said.

She found a bottle of Chivas in the back of the cupboard and got down the two cut-crystal glasses she owned. She brought everything out to the little terrace and poured out two stiff ones. They sat beside one another not talking. Pino knocked back his. She sipped.

"I'm sorry I got you into this."

"Yeah, well. It's done. Some of it was just my job."

"I'm hoping Tina's mother surrenders the gun tomorrow," Pino said.

"Me, too."

She poured him a second round and splashed some in her glass, too.

"I need you to do something, no questions asked, Pino."

"Like what?"

"Go to your Uncle Ricci. Stay there for a while."

"Go when?"

"Tonight. Take the late train. Keep off your mobile phone."

"You'll tell me why someday?"

"Someday, sure."

"I can't. I just can't right now."

"Pino, please. Listen to me."

"No," he said, and with that he rose and left.

Chapter 22

Rain pooled in the cracks of the black stone. Blessed rain, Natalia thought. She hadn't bothered with an umbrella, and the light drizzle felt refreshing. She turned her face upward, "catching blessings" as her grandmother called it. She passed the Teresa Calfonieri School. She could hear the girls reciting their sums. No doubt impatient for lunch, to be free of the classroom, of the day's lessons as she and Mariel and Lola had once been. And itching to grow up, so that their real lives could begin.

They didn't realize that their lives were already fully underway or that, for many, these school days might be the best life would offer. Before they were weighted down by men and screaming infants or careers.

"Did you ever consider using an umbrella?" Francesca said as she opened the door and welcomed her colleague. Natalia shook the water from her curls and slid in. The silver Miata was sleek and small.

"How do you get your long legs into such a tiny car?" Natalia said.

"Vanity. Last year I needed some cheering up. I'll spare you the details. And this baby just stole my heart. Problem with an engine? Take it to a mechanic. With a man?"

They laughed.

Natalia had to admit it was a thrill to zoom along the waterfront in such a snazzy car.

Antonella Cavazza, waiting for them at the entrance to her mansion, reminded Natalia of a heron. She waited while Francesca parked, then shared her large black umbrella with Natalia as the three women walked together slowly up the driveway of her mansion. Francesca led the way, her taupe umbrella flecked with gold moons.

Not only that, she had a pair of stylish rain boots—with heels. Natalia could feel the water squishing into her flats. The countess did her best to avoid the puddles and keep the cuffs of her black capris dry.

"This is such a treat for me that you took time from your busy schedule to come out. I'm sorry for the foul weather."

"How cute!" Francesca said.

Two amber-colored kittens tumbled from the bushes.

"Looking for me to feed them," the countess said. "I'll bring them something after we dry off. I don't know what I'd do without them. I depend on them as they do on me. They say cats aren't loyal. Not true. They are my babies. Can you imagine? During the war the *scugnuzzi* hunted them down and killed them. The same street urchins also stole petrol from the Allies, soaked rags in it, tied them to bats they'd trapped, set them ablaze and let them fly. It looked like fireworks going on all over the city. Come, we're going to get soaked if we stay out here."

There were three places set at one end of a long dining

table. A wine-colored damask cloth covered it. Two vases of wildflowers—purples and reds. The *contessa* insisted Natalia dry herself with a large fluffy towel. She even provided a pair of jeweled flip flops. "A gift," she insisted. "I probably have ten pair. What do I need with ten pairs? Come, get comfortable."

The maid brought in platters of grilled sardine. Then *pasta al forno* and a basket of *focaccia* just out of the oven.

"This is amazing, Nella. You went to too much trouble."

"Nonsense, Francesca. I always feed myself very well. And I like to extend that civility, if you will, to those I care about. I never take it for granted—the privilege of being fed. During the war, all we thought about was food," she said as they served themselves. "And I was one of the fortunate ones. But I never take the next meal for granted. We had a handyman. A lovely man, part of the family, you might say. He contracted TB. And it was too dangerous to take him for medical help. He survived the winter. In the spring he was a living skeleton. I asked if there was anything he wanted, anything I could bring him. And you know what he wanted? Cherries. We had several trees on the property—gorgeous things. I prepared a basket for him and brought it to his room. He was able to eat at most half a dozen. The next week he was dead."

Francesca passed the bread to Natalia. Through an open window they could hear the rain's gentle patter.

"I made a conscious decision then that life was too short to waste being miserable," the countess continued. "At least personally. But then can we will ourselves to be happy? Foolish to use the term 'happy' perhaps. Accepting might be a better term. Everything passes—good and bad. I understand your case is officially closed?"

"Not yet," Natalia said. "For the moment we seem to have reached a dead end."

"Funny how things seem to be at an end when you don't even realize it. And then when you think they are, well . . . they never are—not entirely. Case in point—the war. Am I going on too much?"

"Not at all," Francesca said. "Please."

"All right. At the end—but we didn't yet know it was the end and weren't sure we would survive to see it—the Germans were desperate. They killed innocent people, children included. Rape was the norm, if you can imagine such a thing. Change your mind yet?"

"No," Natalia said. "Please. Go on."

"They burned farms. Slaughtered innocent people. But every afternoon without fail I read to a group of neighborhood children in our garden. I was determined to have something of ordinary life, something beautiful."

"I never knew that," Francesca said. "How brave."

"Brave? I don't know. Forgive me for saying it, but I worry about you girls. The kinds of things you are exposed to. I suppose the work is interesting."

"That it is," Natalia said.

"Fascinating, actually." Francesca took a sip of wine.

"Not morbid?" the countess asked.

"That most definitely," Francesca laughed.

"Not my business, but do you have boyfriends, if they still use that term?"

"I do, but I suspect I won't much longer," Natalia said. "Not the present one anyway. I can't speak for my colleague."

"I'm between boyfriends." Francesca dabbed her mouth with a linen cloth and pushed back from the table. "This is fantastic, Nella, but I'm afraid I have to eat and run. I'll come back when I can spend more time."

"On Saturday? No time for coffee?"

"Afraid not. Barbaric, isn't it? I have to check on

something at the morgue. Never a dull moment." She kissed the countess's head. "I'll call you tomorrow."

"What about you?" she asked Natalia as the maid saw Francesca out.

"I'm in no rush."

"Terrific. I'll have my driver run you home."

"That's not necessary," Natalia said.

"No, absolutely. I insist. I'm so glad I haven't bored you. Plus I have these terrific *dolci*. I hope you like caramel. They make them for me specially."

The women repaired to the living room for coffee.

"This is nice. Having female company. Don't misunderstand me—my husband was a wonderful man—he understood me. But one advantage—perhaps the only advantage of being a widow, I've found—is that I can do what I want to do, when I desire. Quite a luxury. No one to answer to. It almost, but doesn't quite, make up for the loneliness."

"Gianni Scavullo was captured," Natalia said, suddenly changing gear. "You didn't mention that when I spoke with you about Cantalupo."

"Only because I didn't think it was relevant. Yes. Papa saved him from arrest. It was sheer bravado. He shamed the Germans into releasing him, protesting that he was just a boy. But the Gestapo grew suspicious of my father and took him for interrogation."

"Painful memories," Natalia said.

"Yes, they are."

"I'm sorry."

"Don't be sorry. I am not as fragile as I may appear."

"They imprisoned him on information provided by another local, a dedicated fascist named Lattaruzzo," Natalia continued.

The *contessa* didn't immediately respond, merely sat thinking.

Natalia said, "According to Vincente's unpublished manuscript, your land holdings were confiscated and awarded to the Lattaruzzos. You were evicted, alone, at fourteen."

"Yes."

"But you survived."

"I was among the fortunate. I was provided a roof over my head, flour and eggs."

"You had the protection of the Resistance," said Natalia.

"In the form of the Scavullos. Yes. My father had saved Gianni Scavullo. The family in turn risked all to try and rescue my father. But they couldn't." She put aside her tea. "My father was a man of principle. There weren't many such men left in our world then. The times made for odd alliances—communists, democrats, monarchists, liberals, devout Catholics, clerics, Sicilian mafia, and of course, Camorra."

"That's a partnership hard to imagine," Natalia said.

"Believe me, if it hadn't been for *camorristi* like the Scavullos or libertarians like Papa, we would still be giving the fascist salute and celebrating Il Duce's birthday."

"Might Ernesto Scavullo have been avenging your father in killing Vincente Lattaruzzo and the other unfortunate man?"

"I can't imagine . . . certainly not on my account." She paused mid-breath, visibly distraught. "When I was young, I dwelled on revenge. At that age, you think you are powerful and obligated by family. Time eroded my pain and the anger. The actual culprit is long dead. I grew up. I met a man I loved." She sipped her water glass. "Vincente wasn't even born yet."

"Were you aware Vincente Lattaruzzo intended to

include some of his family's history in his book on the war—his grandfather's fascism, the help from the Camorra you and your mother received after the Armistice that paid for your farm's restoration?"

"No."

"He was given to sensationalizing. He even included the story of your father's betrayal by his own grandfather. Also your meeting him, all these years later . . . and your long-standing relationship with the Scavullos. The loan of funds back in the 40s, invitations you accepted to their weddings and christenings, your faithful visits to Don Gianni Scavullo in prison twice every year of his imprisonment."

"They were close—Gianni and Father. I felt indebted and grateful."

"I understand, but would you have wanted that made public? The media in your driveway, tabloids railing about your family's ties to the Naples underworld?"

The *contessa* sighed and sat back. "I see your point. You think Gianni Scavullo may have exacted retribution for the sins of a previous generation, ordered Vincente Lattaruzzo and his companion delivered by his son's associates to my garden like . . . a trophy?"

"Something like that. Possibly, yes."

"And all along I've taken it as a heinous crime committed by someone with a deep hatred of homosexuals, a sociopath. Or a deranged lover cast aside. But Gianni Scavullo?" She shook her head in disbelief. "I can't believe that."

"Ernesto qualifies as both homophobic and brutal, I assure you," Natalia said.

"A blood debt repaid. Well . . ." Countess Antonella Cavazza looked away. "But it's true. The war did things to us. Inhuman things." She suddenly stood. "A blood debt," she repeated. "Crushing, if true. I'll confess something:

When Vincente appeared at the museum board, the past came rushing back. I could barely stay in the same room with him. I thought God was taunting me. Yet he was so young, completely charming." She recovered her glass and took a sip. "Upset as I was, I felt no anger toward him. He had no responsibility for his grandfather's deeds, after all. If you live long enough, you find the soul itself becomes a kind of palimpsest . . . the distant past, shimmery and vague."

Chapter 23

Natalia turned onto Arcangelo a Baiano. A third of the way up the block, one of the men from the social club got off his chair and sauntered up the street behind her. The lookout. Checking on where she was going, who she was talking to. And reporting it to the next in the chain of command.

Someone was playing "Polvere di Stelle" in the apartment below Tina's parents' flat. The vinyl was scratched, but the voice was unmistakable: Hoagy Carmichael. A legacy that remained decades after the Americans were long gone.

Natalia pushed the bell. Nothing. She knocked hard. Someone looked through the peephole. She waited as several locks were disengaged.

A tall, well-built woman opened the door. Her concession to mourning: black toreador pants, stilettos, and a grey and white silk blouse. The blouse, off the shoulder, a black brassiere strap taut on her plump, bronzed skin. Signora Gracci appeared.

"Oh, it's you." She sounded tired. She looked exhausted, eyes bloodshot from crying.

Natalia stepped into the foyer. "Can I speak to you alone?"

"Go into the kitchen a minute," she urged the glamorous visitor. Natalia wondered who she was.

The TV was off. There didn't appear to be anyone else in the apartment.

"What do you want?" she said. "We're in mourning here. People will be coming over to pay their respects. I was just going to lie down."

"I know you've had some hard days, and I'm sorry to bother you at this time."

"What is it now?"

"It's about the gun, Signora Gracci. You wanted your daughter properly buried in Church ground. But I'm afraid, even when a death is ruled a suicide, we need—"

"My Tina didn't kill herself."

"Then all the more reason we need the gun."

"We prefer to handle it ourselves." Her chin wriggled. "It would be better if you left. For your own sake."

"Tampering with evidence is a felony, *signora*. Haven't you suffered enough already?"

"Like I said, the gun isn't here."

"We had an understanding."

"We had nothing. Get away."

Natalia punched in Lola's number. She could meet Nat at the Communale in fifteen minutes. Natalia slipped on her helmet and turned the ignition key. The bike erupted as she revved the engine and took off, zipping through the streets.

Natalia got there first and sat waiting on the bench

nearest the fountain. The air was pungent with jasmine. Lola appeared in a baseball cap with rhinestones and black velvet hoodie. They hugged and sat down.

"What's going on with you?" Lola said. "You got me worried."

Natalia told all—the parts Lola was not already privy to, which was most of it: the gun going missing from Pino's flat, turning up in Tina's, Tina's committing suicide no doubt using his issued weapon, her own tampering with the slug and obstructing the course of justice by pushing it into the bowels of the ancient walls. Emilinia refusing to relinquish the gun.

"So she killed herself with Pino's Glock?"

"I think so."

"But he wasn't present."

"No. God, I hope not."

"And you don't think he killed her?"

"No, I don't. But if the bullet comes out of the wall, if it comes out that I knew all along it was his gun that killed her, I'm done. Unless I get the piece back, process it into the system, and carry on like it never left Pino's hands, we are both done being Carabinieri."

"You've tampered with evidence, withheld evidence. You could be looking at the end of your career. Fuck, you could be facing jail."

"I know."

"And what if it wasn't suicide and somebody murdered her? The Graccis have been doing and being done to for years."

"What am I going to do?"

"Pick a grown-up for a boyfriend next time around."

"I don't need a lecture here, Lola."

"Look, you're my best friend and I love you, okay? But he wasn't thinking about you when he fucked Tina. True?"

"True."

"He's dragging you down, Nat. Your little Buddha boy-friend."

"So what do I do?"

"Who else knows besides us?"

"No one."

"Excellent. Second, if you get the gun back and turned into the armorer, Pino will be off the hook."

"And how do I do that?"

"You don't. I'm going to—try to, at least. I'll call you as soon as I know."

Back at the station an hour later, Natalia's mobile went off. She excused herself to take the call in the fire stairs corridor.

"I located it," Lola said.

"What a relief."

"Not really, hon. Gracci doesn't have it anymore."

"Who does?"

"Ernesto Scavullo."

Chapter 24

The phone chimed again as she drove back home. She had to pull over to answer it.

"Oooh," said a male voice. "I get hard just hearing your voice."

"Who is this?"

"You don't recognize me? You're breaking my heart here."

"Scavullo."

"We haven't had a proper conversation since the wedding. Weren't you a bride's maid?"

"Yes, Ernesto. I'm surprised you remembered."

"The bad witches is what I remember: you, Lola Nuovoletta and the lovely bride herself, my sweet Suzanna Ruttollo."

"What's this about?"

"It's about keeping your nose out of my business. It's about your boyfriend's government-issued pistol. The one he used to kill the Gracci girl he knocked up."

"What do you want?"

"You in my pocket, warm and safe, baby."

"I'm hanging up."

"Oh, no, sweetie. I have a great need to see you. Calabritto Palace. Half an hour."

"Why should I come?"

"Because I have it, and you want it—bad."

He broke the connection.

When she got to the palace, the guard warned, "We close in forty-five minutes."

A straggly line of tourists lined up loading onto a last bus departing the lot. Two female statues flanked the entrance. Natalia entered and paid her admission. Paolo stood just inside, holding a Nortel transceiver. He approached, still talking into it. "I'll call you back," he said and tried to take her by the elbow. She pulled her arm back from his touch.

"We're not friends anymore?"

"We haven't been friends for a long time, Paolo."

"You're breaking my heart, *lattaia*." Milkmaid. His pet name for her when they were kids. It had started when she turned thirteen and celebrated the arrival of breasts.

"Don't call me that," she said.

"No? What should I call you? Captain? We knew each other long before all this. Once upon a time, remember?"

How could she forget? They'd driven to Sorrento in a low-slung, yellow convertible that a cousin had shipped over from New Jersey. Something named after a horse. Top down, wind wild in her hair. Natalia closed her eyes on the hairpin curves and felt her stomach lurch from the excitement. In another hour, they reached the glittery blue ocean.

Of course she remembered.

When she got home, she was sunburned in embarrassing places. Her father broke open several tea bags, soaked them and made a poultice for her face and back. A day later her flaming skin was nearly normal again.

"Paolo," she said, "where's Scavullo? I don't have all day."

"Okay," is all he said, "okay," and ushered her into the Lion Room, then stood a respectful distance away. The guard had been paid off or felt intimidated by the Camorra men—or both—and left them to conduct their business.

Ernesto's back was to her. He appeared to be studying the massive black marble lion that was centermost in the hall.

"What do you think?" he said. "Nice, huh?" He turned around. "I'd like to do my bedroom like this." He indicated the refurbished hall. "You promise not to open your big mouth, and I'll tell you a secret. I paid for restoring this fucking gallery—you believe that?"

"Does it matter if I do?"

"The director is a pussy. Like all of them. The director's assistant works out with me sometimes. Tells me how much it would do for me if I financed a civic good deed. Talks me into it. Okay, so it's chump change, but I figure the least the fucker could do is put up a plaque with my name. Maybe with those lights over it, you know?"

"I'm happy for you," she said. "You'll be immortal."

"Not happening is what the head guy tells me. The prick gets the money, then says it would be bad public relations for my name to be associated with my donation—the money *I* put up."

"How awful for you."

"Isn't it? I thought about having the little shit topped. Might still. Maybe after he gets me this dynamite painting he's promised me. They lend them out to major donors like library books. If he comes through before Mama's birthday, maybe I'll reconsider."

"No place on the board for Ernesto?" she said. "Life has been so unfair to you."

"Ain't that the truth. They don't think I'm good enough to sit on their effing board is what it is, but when they're short of cash to meet the payroll, my dirty money suddenly smells sweet."

The lights blinked on and off a couple of times. She glanced back at the entryway.

"Don't worry. It won't close until I say." Ernesto patted the lion's flank.

"Who exactly approached you for a donation?"

"Fancy boy. Their friggin' director."

"Garducci. Really?"

"Surprised?" Scavullo touched his crotch, like he'd adopted the mannerism from his elders: something they did to ward off evil intent.

"Garducci contacted you himself?" Natalia said.

"We had some people in common."

The lights flickered again.

"What is it you want, Ernesto?"

"To have you as my A number one bitch, of course."

"You have a foul mind."

"That's what my nigger girlfriend said. But my new one, the Brazilian hottie? She loves it. The dirtier, the better. In fact, I'm thinking it might be fun to fuck her with Pino's rod. Stick a condom over the barrel. What do you think?"

"I think you give animals a bad name."

He played with a diamond on his pinkie. "Here I am, trying to be nice on our first date."

Her phone beeped: Lola.

"Monte," Natalia said.

"Scavullo bring the item?"

"We're discussing it now," she said and hung up. She turned to Scavullo. "So where is it?"

"Don't be that way, Natalia. What are we, vendors transacting?"

"What do you want for it?"

"Ooh, let me think. I think I want . . . you."

"You can't have me."

"Think I don't own you already?"

"Say what it is you want."

"Natalia, Natalia. What's your rush? You're gonna develop symptoms from all the stress if you keep this up."

"I didn't know you cared," she said. "What've you got to tell me?"

"You been to Paolo's place?"

"Not since we were kids, why?"

"No, not that sad-ass hovel. I bought him this duplex with a real nice view of the harbor. Just had his master bathroom redone in malachite. You know what that is?"

"Yeah, I know what that is," she said.

"That's green jade is what that is. I gifted him a BMW last December, too."

"Such a Father Christmas you are."

"If he does an extra-nice job for me, he gets a reward."

"Like a trained seal?"

"A weekend in Paris, five days in New York . . ."

"Out of the goodness of your heart, eh? What is he carting for you? Are you sending out money for laundering?"

"Sometimes. Sometimes he's got just an errand or two. Maybe a message to our American cousins that needs to be delivered personally. Or just a well-earned break for Paolo and his family."

"How nice for him."

"You still into art? You like modern stuff? Do this right and you could be looking at a Picasso on your own wall."

"No, thank you."

"Hard or easy, your choice. No matter which, I am going to have my way with you, Captain Monte."

"The gun. What's the price?"

"Your virginity."

"Meaning?"

"Information when I need it. Advance warning of what's coming my way from the forces of law and public order. Names of snitches who might rat me out."

Threats to snuff out, he meant. Natalia said nothing.

"How it's going to work is, I keep the gun, and for now you don't have to worry about Pino's uncle contracting anything lethal or Mariel's shop burning down, what with all that combustible paper and book glue she's got."

"It's not going to happen."

"Oh, it can absolutely happen and will unless you get me taken off the suspects list for the double murder of those fags."

"My bosses aren't about to do that."

"Now, now. You'll figure out how to pull it off, I'm sure. You were always the smart one. If you don't . . . hell, your dear Mariel's life gets barbecued. Pino's uncle, too, most likely. Obviously Pino himself. That understood?"

Natalia stood silent.

"Good," he said. "Anytime I snap my fingers, you will produce for me. You deliver: the names of any witnesses against me that they're developing. Any suspicions that crop up about my corrupting Carabiniere and police who work in my districts." He smiled. "What do you think?"

"A work of genius, Ernesto. Really."

* * *

As soon as she was out of the building, she rang Pino.

"Sweetheart," he said.

"I just had a lovely visit with Scavullo."

"Ernesto Scavullo?"

"Yeah. Bad news. He has it."

"Shit. How?"

"From Mama, obviously."

"I'm sorry I got you into this."

"Yeah, well. It's done. Are you at home?"

"Almost."

"Good, I caught you. Stop right where you are. Don't go there—not to your flat either. Pick up nothing. Turn off your cellphone the minute we're done and keep it off. Any future calls, use a pay phone. Right now you have to go to the rail station. I mean, immediately. Don't buy a ticket with your credit card. Make the purchase with cash—on the train, if you can—but for some stop beyond where you're getting off. Get on the next one. Go to your Uncle Ricci."

"Why?"

"Scavullo says he's keeping the thing for insurance, but I don't trust him. He made a threat about torching Mariel's shop."

"And me? Christ. A threat to off me."

"It didn't go well. He offered me a trade—the Glock—for my loyalty to him."

"Maybe he's just bluffing. About the gun."

"He's not."

"He wouldn't dare target Carabinieri."

"Listen to me. He needs to show the other bosses and his father who the real man is. He'll target anyone he needs just to demonstrate. You need to get away tonight."

"If he has ordered a hit, being at Uncle Ricci's won't do

me any good," Pino said. "I can't put my uncle in danger like that. I'll go to my place."

"Pino, you don't have a choice right now. Don't go to your uncle then, but get out of Naples this minute."

"You're serious. He'd risk going after Carabiniere?"

"Without a doubt. He'll do anything to prove himself. If you want to stay alive, go. Please."

They hung up. She imagined Pino setting out on foot for the train station, his lovely eyes troubled, the sun playing on his dark tousled hair.

Chapter 25

"You can't kill him," Lola exclaimed, slapping the steering wheel so hard the horn bleated.

"Why not? You and yours do it all the time."

"I'm not a captain of the Carabinieri."

"So?"

"You're the good guys."

"And he's a bad guy. The worst. He's been slaughtering the innocent for years. Getting away with it. And he's getting away with it again. We can't prove anything on the horsemen. Not on Fabretti either. He set it up. Fed us false evidence. And now he has Pino's gun. He wants to own me, Lola. I might as well wear his tattoo."

"Fucking Pino," Lola said, pumping the horn as she cruised through a light.

"He'll kill Pino. He threatened to burn down Mariel's store."

"He said that? Okay, take him down."

"I may need some help getting to him."

"We'll do it together."

Natalia shook her head. "It's too dangerous. You're a mother, Lola, remember? You promised you wouldn't take any foolish chances."

"You chickening out?"

"No. I'm going to take care of it alone, that's all."

Lola idled and pushed the curls from Natalia's face. "You're not nearly nasty enough for this, *cara*." She put her foot on the accelerator. "You need me there."

Without Natalia's realizing it, they'd come out of the narrow streets and were rapidly climbing to the Vomero section. Soon the cacophony of Naples was far below them. She could see islands in the distance, and the sea twinkled. How peaceful everything seemed. Soon they'd be on the road that connected Naples to Sorrento.

"Where are we going?" Natalia asked.

"Nowhere. I'll turn around in a minute. Safer to keep moving. Even though I have the car swept every day for bugs—I'm paranoid, you know? I bug my own house, for Christ's sake. The glamorous life, right?"

"Dominick doesn't mind being on tape?" Natalia said.

"He doesn't know."

"So he's not getting involved in your business life, I take it?"

"Only my bed life."

Natalia laughed.

"For now."

Lola pulled off the road into a roundabout, and they got out of the car. A white butterfly danced around a clump of green foliage. Someone had spray painted *Forza Italia!* in purple on a concrete wall.

They conferred for a few moments then Lola reversed direction and dropped her a few blocks from the Casanova station. Natalia walked the rest of the way and reported in for the afternoon shift.

Angelina was engrossed in her computer screen and talking on the phone at the same time. Natalia passed by on the way to her office and closed the door. Concentrating was difficult. The phone rang, and Natalia answered with her name.

"Captain," Francesca said, "when is Tina Gracci being interred?"

"Hi, doc. She was buried this morning. Raffi photographed the mourners for the intelligence people."

"Okay, then. It's officially ruled a suicide."

"That's it? Simple as that?"

"Unless the gun turns up," Francesca said, "and we find otherwise. This is my first suicide in twenty years without a note left behind. Wait, there was Maria Martelli and her husband. A suicide pact."

"The couple that informed on the Giuliano clan?"

"Good memory. What a crime scene. He blew her brains out. Then his. Actually, it was quite like the Tina Gracci situation. No gun found. But the gunpowder marks on the hand? Pretty conclusive."

"What were you offered to rule their suicide pact an accident?"

"It opened at a thousand euros, stopped when I turned down fifty. Any luck getting the weapon from Mama Gracci now that her daughter rests in holy ground?"

"Not as yet."

"No surprise there, I suppose," Francesca said. "Tough as she is, the woman can't face the truth. We'll never know what the daughter was thinking. So sad, her being born to that gang that passes for a family. She didn't have much of a chance in life."

"That's what Pino says."

"Your Sergeant Loriano, he knew her?"

"He and I both, from a previous case."

"What's going on with you two, anyway? Wait! Forget I asked. Not my business. Gotta go."

Francesca hung up.

"When I figure it out, I'll let you know," Natalia said into the dead phone.

Natalia signed out to patrol along the docks, hoping to let the sea air clear her muddled brain. She called Lola again on her private line. *We are otherwise engaged*, the answering machine voice announced, meaning she was enjoying an idyll with Dominick. And Mariel was at a matinee concert with her new Milanese boyfriend.

A few months ago, Natalia was the only one of them with a boyfriend, someone to eat dinner with, sleep with, talk to when times got rough. Now her two best friends were occupied by their man friends, and Natalia was the one alone again. For a brief second, she contemplated calling Suzanna Ruttollo but changed her mind.

A seagull swooped low over the bay. A ferry sounded its horn as it pushed away from the dock and headed for one of the islands. Natalia would have liked to extend her walk, but a summons on her phone from Angelina had her rushing back to the station. A homicide call. Natalia arrived panting and slid into the passenger seat of their Alfa Romeo.

"Where?"

"Remember the gallery with the erotic sadomasochist photographs?"

"Of course. What's going on? Somebody offed the director?"

"No. We're not that lucky."

"So—what?"

"There's a body on the premises identified as Stefano Grappi."

"Grappi. Fuck. Not another one."

They arrived at the CAM gallery. Two municipal policemen stood guard outside. "You sure you want to go in?" one of them asked as Natalia and Angelina rushed up. "My partner here threw up."

Natalia nodded.

He saluted as he pulled open the heavy door.

Natalia strode ahead. The chill of the air conditioning felt intense after the sweltering street. Again, the sensation of a vast white space. A frozen landscape. A blur of violet flowers on a low, black table. A banner announced the show: SEX AND SENSIBILITY: OBJECTS OF TORTURE—AN HISTORIC SURVEY.

The gallery appeared empty, except for a knot of people at the far end of the room. As Natalia and Angelina made their way across the marble floor, they passed several artifacts: manacles rusted and attached to the wall. A guillotine with a newly polished blade. Some kind of wooden contraption Natalia recognized from history books—used to secure witches as recently as the nineteenth century in order for them to be displayed in the town squares; a treat for curiosity seekers before the so-called devil worshippers were burned at the stake.

Domenico Bertolli stood staring at the upright body of Stefano Grappi and tried to control his breathing. He seemed to be unaware of anyone else in the room. His face was sweaty. Two other policemen stood with their backs to the corpse. Angelina sat down on a long red bench, busying herself with notes, doing her best not to look up. Natalia didn't blame her. She could barely look herself.

Stefano Grappi, naked, squatted on a wooden platform. A stake had been driven up through him vertically.

Natalia came up beside the director.

"Mr. Bertolli?"

He didn't answer.

She touched his arm. "Mr. Bertolli?"

He turned his bleak face toward her.

"Officer Monte, remember? We need to speak with you. Did you find him here?"

"Yes." A whisper.

"Someone broke in?"

"The door was unlocked when I arrived."

"The alarm never went off?"

"No."

"Maybe you should sit down," Angelina suggested.

"No. I prefer to stand."

"Okay," Natalia said. "Can you tell me what it is, this device? Is it part of the exhibit?"

He nodded. "It's called a Judas Chair. Invented during the Inquisition."

"I take it the person's weight pushed down on the . . . the tip of the stake," Natalia said.

"Usually into the anus and then deeper as the prisoner descended. Or into the vagina in the case of . . . excuse me. If you don't have any more questions . . ."

"Not at the moment. We'll be in touch later," Natalia said. "Thank you."

Colonel Fabio dropped the crime scene photos back on his desk. "You know the perpetrator of this crime?"

"Ernesto Scavullo," Natalia answered, standing in front of his desk next to her partner.

"This is intolerable. Truly unspeakable." He tapped the pictures. "Explain this to me. Why?"

"It's Scavullo clearing the deck, sir, eliminating those

with firsthand knowledge of what he's done. Chief among them, Stefano Grappi."

"So it wasn't Garducci conspiring with Ernesto Scavullo?"

"No, sir. It was Stefano all along."

"Fooled us."

"Yes, sir. He had us fooled. So unlikely. Such a gentle-seeming man. But he was passionately in love with Vincente when he found out Lattaruzzo was planning to leave him—and for Garducci of all people. Vincente had cheated on him with countless men during their time together. When he found out about Garducci, Signor Grappi snapped."

Fabio pinched his lower lip. "Whereupon he set out to avenge himself on Vincente."

"Exactly," Angelina said.

"And Bagnatti got swept up in the bargain," Natalia continued. "Stefano conspired with Ernesto Scavullo to do in Bagnatti and Vincente Lattaruzzo both, each for their own reasons. He had discovered the story of the *contessa*'s father's betrayal at the hands of Vincente Lattaruzzo's forebearer and put it to work."

Fabio nodded.

Natalia went on. "Stefano sought out Scavullo and told him Bagnatti was preparing a gossip piece about a gay don. He got Scavullo to do his dirty work."

"But what I don't understand," Fabio said, "whatever possessed Bagnatti to write such a story outing Ernesto? He must have known Scavullo would react badly."

"They'd been sleeping together off and on for a long while—Bagnatti and Scavullo," Natalia said. "I think he may have lost his appeal and been shown the door in less than a gracious manner. Ernesto Scavullo hadn't known the story behind his father's detention by the Germans and how the *contessa*'s father extricated the young Gianni

Scavullo. When he found out, he must have realized how he could use it—make it appear to be the reason for killing Lattaruzzo."

"When Bagnatti's gossip piece was his real worry," the colonel muttered as he wrote something on a pad on his desk.

"Exactly." Natalia closed her eyes.

"God," Angelina said. "One man set this whole thing in motion."

Their boss crumpled the piece of paper and tossed it into the trash basket. "You may be interested to learn that *La Mattina* has named us the European capital of violent crimes against gays. Had you heard?"

"Yes, sir," Angelina answered.

"Maybe now we can turn that around, assuming we can prove what you've just reported. Can we?" He leaned forward.

"Not a word," Natalia said. "Scavullo did too good a job of controlling and planting evidence. What do you want us to do?"

The colonel stood. "I want you to change to black fatigues, load extra magazines and break out your field-grade weapons. Report to the incident room in forty minutes. This has gone on far too long."

In their jury-rigged locker room, they changed into their field uniforms and fatigue shirts with red piping at the collar and their rank insignia over their left breast pockets, CARABINIERE in bold print over the right.

They put on their wine-red berets with their shiny Carabinieri badges and checked their AR-70 assault rifles.

They stepped into the hall, joining dozens of officers similarly attired and armed, and converged in the incident room, its walls taken up with boards holding information and evidence accruing in various ongoing cases, each with a map.

Colonel Fabio stood in front of a board that outlined Ernesto Scavullo's organization, with the don on top, captains below, lieutenants in the second and third tiers.

"Marshal Cervino will circulate to collect your cell phones," Fabio instructed. "There are to be no outgoing calls from this station until we return from the mission in a few hours' time. All outside lines have been redirected through the reception desk. Why? Because in thirty minutes we will be rolling up the top three tiers of the Scavullo organization, starting with the lower echelons"—he tapped the board behind him—"and ending with Ernesto Scavullo himself."

An excited murmur rippled through the room.

"One of our units has accumulated evidence over the past eleven months documenting the Scavullo outfit's illicit trade in heroin, methamphetamine, their illegal gambling operations, tax evasion, racketeering and the like. You'll be going out in teams, each assigned a particular suspect. Any questions so far?"

There were none.

"Good. Each team's target was randomly drawn, with one exception. Captain Monte and Corporal Cavatelli will bring in Ernesto Scavullo as soon as his bodyguards and staff have been stripped."

The blood drained from Natalia's face. Would Ernesto Scavullo take this raid as betrayal—her failure—and make charges connecting Pino's weapon to Tina Gracci's death and the impropriety of Natalia's investigating it? If he even accepted arrest. He could easily resist, requiring force to take him down. Or he could take them down first.

Angelina looked at her with concern. It's okay, Natalia mouthed, and tried to convince herself it would be.

"Question, sir," Cervino said. "Do you think it wise for our two female officers to attempt arresting Scavullo? He may respond badly to that."

"Let's hope," Fabio said.

Laughter erupted.

"It ends here," Fabio said. "I want their cartel bled."

Eighteen minutes later the teams dispersed, each in pursuit of a different Scavullo *capo*. Angelina and Natalia held back, giving the others a head start before they would attempt to execute the warrant on Ernesto Scavullo.

The gate was open, the street blocked by fellow Carabinieri. No guards were left on duty. Presumably they'd been carted off.

"Our turn," Natalia said as they drove through. "Pull up to the front door."

They got out of the car, rifle barrels pointed down but stocks braced against their shoulders. They went through the front door, past a black marble cheetah, a brilliant replica of the cat from the Museo Archeologico right down to its eerie red eyes. Or had Scavullo extorted the original?

"Isn't that music?" Natalia said. "Sounds like it's coming from the back."

No maids scurried forth, no gardeners trimmed the hedges or watered the vast flower beds and lawn. The azure pool matched the sky. A colorful parrot eyed them quizzically from its perch standing under an umbrella shading a table and empty chairs. A paperback lay face down on a lounger. The music grew louder: opera. Verdi. An aria about love and yearning.

A pair of gold sandals lay abandoned under a glass table. Two glasses. The ice melted.

It was a vintage recording of wonderful quality playing on a state of the art sound system using exposed vacuum tubes in a design almost as old as the recording.

Angelina picked up an abandoned glass. "Rum." She pointed to the pink cabana on the far side of the pool. Rifles raised, they made their approach. The white louvered door was closed but not locked, and they slipped inside.

The air smelled of scented candle. A rack filled with weights occupied one wall; facing it, a floor-to-ceiling mirror on the wall opposite.

A pair of swinging saloon doors led into another room. White walls and again mirrors. The vanilla scent was stronger. Dozens of white fluffy towels lay stacked nearby, and a black silk robe draped across a stool next to an antique gramophone.

Ernesto Scavullo lay face down on the massage table, seemingly oblivious to what was transpiring around him. Or maybe just waiting for what he must have known was coming. A sheet draped his buttocks and legs. An intravenous line ran from the suspended saline and nutrient bags to his wrist. His world was being taken apart, and he was having a treatment.

"Cover me," she said to Angelina as she walked to the table.

Liquid dripped from the translucent bags into Ernesto's veins. He looked relaxed, peaceful, ingesting vitamins and electrolytes as he hydrated.

"Ernesto. Ernesto Scavullo. You're under arrest and must . . ."

One eye was open, the top of it clouded. Pupils fixed.

"Bastard didn't deserve an easy death," Angelina said. "Someone should have sliced his balls, gouged out his eyes."

Natalia reported their discovery on her transceiver and slung her weapon onto her shoulder. She and Angelina taped the perimeters of Scavullo's cabana and designated it a crime scene. A bird sang on. The partners collected and labeled evidence. Francesca would perform the official autopsy, but in the meantime Natalia put on her gloves and studied the victim. Even dead, Ernesto Scavullo gave her the creeps.

They fulfilled the basic crime scene investigation. Natalia was glad to get away from there. Returning to their lockers, they couldn't face the paperwork and signed out. The city smelled like baked stone. Sweet jasmine perfumed the air, competing with the smell of *mandarinis*, the tiny oranges vendors hawked on street corners. In front of a newsstand, a trim white van delivered the afternoon paper, and the local priest in long white vestments bought the first copy of the late edition of *Il Mattino*. They bid each other goodbye and went their separate ways.

Natalia approached the Forcella district. A family of tourists posed in front of the Santa Annunziata Church as a few worshipers exited after late Mass. Across the street, a bookseller lifted the plastic cover protecting his books and rearranged the titles.

On a landing one step up from the street, mad Carmella, boom box at full volume, launched into her daily performance, breasts escaping the skimpy tank top as she danced. Tourists stopped to gape. The Neapolitans passed without looking.

In the plaza, an old man, bent with age, reached into a

wrinkled paper bag and tossed out crumbs of bread. Natalia approached.

"May I sit?"

A cloud of birds rose in a swirl and hurtled off.

He nodded.

"That old Victrola," she said. "My grandparents had one just like it."

Pappa Gianni smiled, remembering. "He was fascinated with that machine as a kid. Four years old and he knew how to crank it up."

A young American girl in a sequined headscarf crossed the square.

"So many foreigners," he said. "It didn't used to be like this."

He scattered a handful of breadcrumbs. "Would you believe this is what I missed most in prison? I used to come here with Ernesto in his stroller. There were hundreds of birds. They would eat from my hand." He pointed to a bird. "My favorite looked just like that one."

"What happened?" she said.

"There's a code we live by. It's how I was raised. How Ernesto was brought up. But something happened with my son. Maybe if I hadn't encouraged him to be so tough early on. Maybe if I hadn't been away for so long." He sighed.

"I knew Renata since she was a girl. We lived on the same block. She was going to school to learn typing and book-keeping. One day she passed by, and we saw each other, like for the first time. She'd grown beautiful with me hardly noticing. We had one child. One."

He sat back.

"The first years in the can, he did everything asked of him. These last years he hardly came and accepted no orders when he did. Which might have been all right, given my age. But the way he carried on, bragging, blogging, parading his whores in public. The level of violence he employed. Killing for no reason. Maiming . . ."

He reached down into a ragged shoulder bag under the bench and brought out something wrapped in a plastic shopping bag. Up close his hands appeared arthritic, covered with deep brown age spots.

"Antonella suggested this should by rights be returned."

Natalia felt the bag. An automatic pistol.

He shook the remaining crumbs onto the black stone and stuffed the paper bag into his jacket pocket. A few more birds neared. When he stood, they retreated and rose in a grey mass, circling the plaza and finally settling in a large chestnut tree.

Natalia watched him make his way slowly across the uneven cobblestones, passing a bench with a weathered junkie slumped across it like a chaise, trying to roll a cigarette.

As far as the city and the Carabinieri were concerned, the investigation was at an end and another crime lord removed. They had only to wait to see what others would surface to replace him or take his territory.

August holidays in a week. Natalia didn't fancy a vacation, but Fabio ordered her to take some time off.

She and Angelina spent the balance of an afternoon tidying up their desks. Angelina and Giuletta were on their way to a stone cottage that had been in Giuletta's family for forever.

"It's great," Angelina said. "Wake up to the birds. Take a walk at night. Moon and stars."

"Sounds wonderful," Natalia said.

"It is. I can't wait. You feel like getting out of this

hellhole, give me a call . . . really. I'm not saying it to be polite. Giuletta's idea. Before I forget," she opened a drawer. "*Marmellata. Prugna.* Plum jam. My mother sent us a case, said to be sure my nice boss got one. You like?"

"I love. That's very generous. Tell her thank you. And Giuletta, too. For the invitation."

"Seriously, what are you going to do? Hang around here? Play footsies with Cervino?"

Natalia laughed. "Mariel and I are planning a trip to the Farnese."

"Sounds like something Giuletta would suggest. So that takes care of twenty-five minutes you won't get back. You gonna stay in a nice hotel at least?"

"You know Mariel. Get out of here, Officer Cavatelli. That's an order."

Natalia put on her best black dress and head scarf and slipped on black pumps. Black pocket book under her arm, she set off for the Duomo.

The caretaker's man had dragged a chair to the edge of the courtyard to escape his sweltering room, with its one skinny window that looked onto the street. She watched herself grow larger in the mirror propped just outside his door. With this invention, normally he could drink his coffee and read his newspaper without having to leave the kitchen table and still keep track of the people coming and going.

But today he sat outside, avoiding the trapped heat indoors.

So much for security, she thought, as she passed him, his eyes closed and his breathing heavy. A mild breeze ruffled the leaves of the potted plant beside him.

Passing a narrow doorway at the end of the street, the

thrum of a small press reached her, announcements piling up inside: births, baptisms, communions, weddings, deaths.

Raffi was posted as usual, facing the steps of the cathedral, telephoto lens snapped in place to record the Camorra mourners for his employers. Natalia nodded to him from the top step and entered the vestibule behind Suzanna, who wore a black veil, black suit and stilettos. She was arm in arm with her father-in-law and mother-in-law. Natalia slipped in among Scavullo uncles and their families as the whole group drifted slowly forward to the nave. The casket on the altar lay draped in a sea of white gardenias.

Gianni's favorite cousin escorted a teenager in a dark suit and tie, patent leather shoes and immaculate white shirt. Reaching the front pews, Suzanna turned and took charge of the boy, letting him precede her to sit next to Gianni Scavullo and Renata. Natalia reminded herself to check on the male who had accompanied Suzanna to Rome from London.

There were no professional mourners among the assembled, only professional killers. Nor did Suzanna wail and collapse on the burnished coffin of her estranged husband. Dotted throughout the assembly, lone women sat like shadows, Camorra widows all, attired in black head scarves, shoes, long-sleeved dresses, the odd white handkerchief visible at points in the gloom.

A *monsignor* officiated. Natalia recognized him from photographs taken at other Camorra funerals. Natalia was sure she'd never seen so many Camorra in one place, yet the funeral party only occupied the very front of the giant cathedral. The rest of it was given over to the daily business of confession, repentance, prayer and the lighting of white votive candles in small glass chalices that painted one

corner red in their reflected light, candles that commemo-
rated the dead.

Papa Gianni's reputation reminded Natalia a bit of Don
Cuoca. Would the old man lead a rehabilitated Scavullo
clan? Unlike the churchmen, the *camorristi* showed no leni-
ency and exempted no one. When Don Cuoca, the last of
the great dons, became a nuisance, he was taken off for a
sumptuous feast in Vincenzo a Mare. There, on the low cliff
outside the city, he enjoyed his favorite clams and a cool sea
breeze. Those assembled toasted and praised him all evening long, hugged him and kissed his cheeks, with tears
running down their own. Then led him away to be stabbed
but once by an expert with a mattress maker's needle.

Regardless, Papa Gianni's murderous son lay in his glass
bier—nails manicured, features made up and dressed in a
suit of impeccable taste, totally worthy of being worn into
eternity. His son would be buried like the Camorra prince
he was to have been. The world would pause and then con-
tinue, turning more easily in his absence.

Natalia rang the bell and heard the click of Lola's heels
approach but no barking.

"Where's Princess?" she said as the friends embraced.

"Taking a nap."

Lola's hair sported russet threads. Her white satin blouse
revealed the edges of a black lace bra and some cleavage.
Natalia wondered how she could breathe in her tight white
jeans.

"My baby needs her rest before her salon appointment,"
Lola said.

"You're kidding, right?"

"Upkeep, *cara mia.* She has a weekly appointment. You
could take a page from her book. Are you coming in?"

Natalia entered and surveyed the new potted plants ringing the room. "The Birds of Paradise are gorgeous."

"Suzanna treated me to a session with her decorator."

"Suzanna Ruttollo? Who would have guessed you'd be friends one day?"

"Yeah. Well, childhood rivalries aside, we are. So what's going on with Sergeant Loriano?"

"Pino turned in his papers and his weapon. Looks like he's going to be a civilian—at least in this life."

"That's interesting. You back with lover boy yet?"

"No. Pino's staying in Caserta."

"What's in Caserta?"

"A *zendo* looking for an acolyte."

"He's gonna be a monk now?

"Who knows?"

"He was young," Lola said.

"Only a year or two younger than me."

"Young in the head, I meant."

"Yeah, maybe."

"So what are you gonna do?"

"About him? Don't know. I'm not giving up my commission and relocating to Caserta. Maybe we'll try it long distance for a while. Maybe not. What would I do if I wasn't a Carabiniere?"

"You could work for us."

"Be serious."

"There's plenty of legit stuff to run."

"I don't think so."

"You are the noble captain. Sister Benedicta would be proud."

"You know the weird thing?" Natalia said. "He would have been better off with the girl."

"Tina?"

"Yeah."

"You're kidding, right?"

"No. She would have put him first. Loved him madly. Given him babies by the bushel. He likes babies."

"He is a baby," Lola exclaimed. Arms thrown open, she exclaimed, "Hey! Here's my baby now!" Micu clicked over to them. "How's Mama's treasure?" Lola picked up the dog and kissed it. "There's going to be a rumor going around tomorrow."

"I don't want to hear it."

"You'll want to hear this part."

"What?"

"Papa Gianni. He's stepping down."

"Really?"

"You saw him. The man is old, bent over."

"The gossip was that he had restored order in the clan."

"Yeah, so what. The day-to-day stuff is too much for him. He named someone else to actually run the operation."

"A trusted *capo*?"

"Family."

"Suzanna Scavullo," Natalia said.

"Yeah. This whole thing has been in the works for a while, I'm guessing. It's been two years since he first got in touch with her."

"So that's what brought her back. That and maybe introducing Gianni to his grandson when he got out of prison."

"How . . . ?" Lola checked her nails. "You're too smart for your own good."

"She never aborted the baby, didn't lose it."

"No. Nobody's supposed to know, though I suppose it was pretty obvious at the funeral that the kid was related."

"I would say so, yeah. Where is he, back in England?"

"The kid's in school in Rome."

"Wow. She's a cool one. What about her businesses in London? Frankfurt?"

"She'll multitask, I guess. More likely they'll fold them into the overall operation."

"And Suzanna is gonna run Ernesto's old crew? They're gonna take orders from a woman?"

"They're gone, Nat. The old crew. Nowhere to be found."

"Shit. Not Paolo, too."

"Yeah. We'll be long gone before they find their bones. Gianni brought back the old guys. People he trusts." Lola pulled on an emerald drop earring. "The other rumor isn't so pretty either, but I feel like I gotta tell you."

"What is it?"

"Tina didn't kill herself."

"Who are they saying did it?"

"Nobody's sure. The baby's father maybe. Maybe one of the cousins. Doesn't matter. The girl was a problem to the family, had been for a long time, what with falling for a Carabiniere and refusing jobs and all. She wanted out. Talked openly about stuff she shouldn't. Criticized. People warned her. She wouldn't shut her mouth."

"Poor kid just wanted a life."

"Yeah, well. You don't leave the family so easy. I could see the writing on the wall, Nat. It was gonna end bad for her one way or another. Then the poor fool gets pregnant and comes home. Why she took Pino's weapon . . . she might as well have shot herself. It was like the thing with Ernesto. It couldn't go on. Mama tucked her daughter in that morning and went to Mass. When she came home, it was over."

"I wish we could have done something."

"Listen! Come to the doggie parlor? It'll take your mind

off it. Dominick won't be home till later. We can have some girl time."

"No, I have to go. Thanks anyway."

"You sure? You look kind of shaky."

"I'm fine."

"Oh. Tough lady. Listen, call me—anytime. Okay?"

"Will do, honey."

"*Ciao*, Captain."

"*Ciao, bella.*"

"Love you."

"And you."

Natalia took the stairs slowly, pausing on the landings. Lola would make her move soon and rise even further. If she linked up with Suzanna, in a year or two she'd be the equal of any *capo* or don or *madrina* in Naples.

As Natalia adjusted to the blaring brightness of the street, a woman shifted her pillow on the window ledge and rested her ample chin on her arms in time to get Natalia firmly in her sights.

A falling sensation dropped through Natalia into the pit of her stomach. The clock had begun. It was just a matter of time before she'd have to decide whether she could live up to the oath she'd sworn. If Lola asked or needed her to look the other way, what would she do? For the first time in her career, she'd done something dishonest. She hadn't lived up to the code. If the situation presented itself in the future, would she do it again?

She stopped for coffee in the *piazzetta* across from Santa Maria la Nuova. A nun stood in the cool of the vestibule. Below, a cluster of young women milled about as they waited to pick up their children left in the nuns' care. Just then, the bells chimed noon, and several tiny creatures made for freedom.

For a moment, Natalia imagined what it would feel like to scoop one of them into her arms. The way her life was going, it seemed unlikely she ever would.

She was sorry Lola had told her the rumor about Tina and the child she carried being murdered. Cruelty knew no bounds. There were some mysteries she wished would remain shrouded and unsolved and far from her thoughts. She flashed on the other baby mystery that kept churning in her. Who fathered the baby Antonella Cavazza had lost? She turned the question over in her mind, willing herself not to dwell on Gianni and Antonella, star-crossed lovers but for the war.

Pino believed you would live multiple lives multiple times. She'd become convinced of the opposite. That you had the life you were born with, and that was it. You didn't get a second chance at the wheel.

She paid her bill and crossed the plaza. Even the pigeons had taken refuge from the heat. They cooed from the dark bell tower as she disappeared into the narrow alleys of Naples.

Acknowledgments

With gratitude to Juris Jurjevics for his brilliance, and help, and much thanks to Mark Doten and the staff at Soho.

JUN - 2014